THE SENATOR MUST DIE

Books by Edward I. Koch

Murder At City Hall
Murder On Broadway
Murder On 34th Street
The Senator Must Die

Published by Kensington Books

THE SENATOR MUST DIE

EDWARD I. KOCH

and Wendy Corsi Staub

Concept created by Herbert Resnicow

KENSINGTON BOOKS
http://www.kensingtonbooks.com

KENSINGTON BOOKS are published by

Kensington Publishing Corp.
850 Third Avenue
New York, NY 10022

Library of Congress Card Catalog Number: 98-065138
ISBN 1-57566-325-2

First Printing: October, 1998
10 9 8 7 6 5 4 3 2 1

Printed in the United States of America

ONE

Sure, being surrounded by bodyguards twenty-four hours a day has its drawbacks. But when you're a high-profile political figure and the target of regular threats, you don't have a say in the matter. Wherever you go, your security team goes. Period. Their job is to protect you from any lunatic who might see fit to cause you harm.

Here in New York City, we have our share of lunatics. Some ignorant outsiders might have you believe that we have more *than our share. Don't listen to them.*

Anyway, in all these years as mayor, I've never been faced with a single, serious assassination attempt. Until one chilly October night . . .

"Mr. Mayor . . ."

"Mr. Mayor . . ."

"Mr. Mayor . . ."

"Yes, Jake." I nodded and pointed at a familiar middle-aged face in the throng of reporters gathered beyond my podium.

"Is your decision to back Senator Hubbard's further investigation into the Holocaust victims' Swiss bank accounts influenced by your own Jewish background?"

"My decision stems from a responsibility to the people of this city, and a segment of the population is made up of Jews with Eastern European roots. Myself included."

"What do you have to say about rumors that you stand to profit personally from this endeavor?" another voice promptly asked.

"Ridiculous!" I retorted.

"Then you're saying that you have nothing to gain by backing the committee?"

"If you're asking whether I expect to feel spiritually rewarded in knowing that I have helped to see that justice has been served to the Holocaust survivors and their families, the answer is yes. I most certainly do have something to gain."

"What if the Senator's committee uncovers considerable funds that belonged to your ancestors?" an annoying voice persisted. "Would you collect the money?"

"Would *you*?" I shot back. "Anyway, you'll have to ask my parents about that, as they are the obvious heirs to any ancestral money. And I'm afraid they don't appear to be available for comment, do they?" I pretended to scan the crowd.

No, Joyce and Lou Koch were most certainly not among the hordes of press crammed into the drab makeshift press room on the twenty-third floor of this Wall Street building.

I happened to know that at that very moment, my parents were most likely poking into the shared closet in the master bedroom of their small apartment a few dozen blocks north of here, packing their suitcases in preparation for their annual seasonal relocation to their Boca Raton condo.

My mother would be reminding my father to bring his good suit, and he would be saying, "What, I need a good suit to sit by the cabana with Irving and Murray and play pinochle all day?"

Meanwhile, he would be urging her to pack a few more sweaters, and when she protested that there wasn't room in her bags, he would say, "Then I don't want to hear you complain that you're freezing every time we go to the early bird special at Beef on the Reef. You know how high they keep their air-conditioning."

And my mother would lift her chin stubbornly and give a shrug. "So I'll freeze."

"So freeze."

After "helping" my parents pack for last year's trip, I vowed never to get involved again. This year, I had a perfect excuse, thanks to today's lengthy meetings and the press conference, which had dragged on interminably.

"Mr. Mayor . . ."

"Mr. Mayor . . ."

"Mr. Mayor . . ."

"Yes, Karen," I said somewhat wearily, pointing at another familiar face.

"Is it true that you once said, regarding the Holocaust, and I quote, 'If there was anything I could do to engage in retribution, I was going to do it'?"

"That's true," I confirmed. "As you may know, I was with our military in Bavaria after the war, where I worked to remove Nazis who held public office. And later—several decades later—I visited a concentration camp. The experience was indescribable—and I speak not just as a Jew. I defy any of you to visit Dachau or Auschwitz and come away dry-eyed and unmoved."

"Are those experiences, then, motivating you to back Senator Hubbard's committee?"

"As mayor, I'm motivated to do what is right for the people of this city. And I'm convinced that the people of New York stand behind me in wanting to see some measure of justice for Holocaust survivors and the descendants of its victims."

"Mr. Mayor . . ."

"Mr. Mayor . . ."

"Mr. Mayor . . ."

The chorus of echoes kicked into high gear, and I answered a few more questions—some pertinent, others preposterous. Predictably, the topic shifted to the latest Koch controversy—my support of a proposal to build a nuclear power facility in the Bronx.

Finally, I turned over the podium to Sen. Anson Hubbard. My old friend was greeted by rousing applause, a very good sign. He had been slipping in the polls and his chances of being reelected had looked rather dim until recently.

His work on behalf of Holocaust victims and survivors had changed everything. No longer did the press—and voters—seem to focus on his reputation for being outspoken and obstinate. Now he was widely touted as the humanitarian he has always been.

I'm no stranger to political image-manipulation, and I haven't always shared Anson's views in the past. But in this case, I believed that he deserved his newfound reputation, and it was about time. He had long used his power and visibility to make a difference, to see that the world wouldn't overlook these people who deserved to be heard.

Later, after everyone—the press, other committee members, and his aides—had left, Anson and I gathered our belongings from the conference room where we had spent the better part of the day. He patted me on the back.

"Thanks, Ed," he said in his distinctive baritone voice, which had grown somewhat hoarse under the recent strain of too many heartfelt speeches and too little sleep.

"For the Glugol Muggle recipe?" I was referring to the tried and true Koch family remedy for laryngitis, which I had shared with him moments before.

"That, too," he said with a chuckle. "I'll try it later, when I get home. But thank you, mainly, for your outspoken support of my committee. Too many people think I'm wasting my time and the taxpayers' money, dredging this thing up after half a century. Or that I'm hoping to discover some long-lost Hubbard family fortune," he added ruefully.

I had to smirk at that. Anson Hubbard had more money than some third world countries, thanks to his marriage to the sole heiress to a vast pharmaceutical fortune. His father-in-law, Dr. Hans Jurgen, was the world-renowned Swiss scientist who, in 1950, had discovered the vaccine for Dobry's Syndrome, a deadly disease that was reaching epidemic status in Europe and had killed thousands of children.

Still, I teased him, "You mean, picking up some extra cash isn't the true motive behind your noble endeavor?"

A smile briefly lit his handsome face. "Not likely. Even if I needed extra cash, I wouldn't find it there. My ancestors were dirt-poor German Jews who fled to America without a penny long before World War Two began. Thank God. But millions of others weren't so lucky. And to have their financial assets virtually disappear in wartime Swiss banks—"

"I know. It's an outrage."

"So," he said with an earnest sigh, "it's up to us, to our committee, to uncover the truth. To see that the people involved get what is rightfully theirs."

"Mr. Mayor?"

I looked up to see that Carmine Bello, one of my deputy mayors, had poked his head into the doorway.

"Are you still planning to ride to the restaurant with the Senator?"

I glanced at Anson, who looked up from his open briefcase and nodded.

"Are you sure you wouldn't rather skip dinner and go right home to take care of that sore throat?" I asked him.

"I'm positive." He raked a hand through his shock of glossy black hair. "I need something to eat. And I'm anxious to try this chicken dish you've been raving about."

"You won't be disappointed," I assured him, then turned to Carmine. "Go on ahead with the others. We'll join you shortly."

"See you there," Carmine said cheerfully with a wave, and left.

My bodyguards hovered around Anson and me when we stepped onto the deserted elevator five minutes later. As we swooped the twenty-three stories to the lobby, two of them, Ambrose Kaloyeropoulos and Mohammed Johnson, chattered about the Yankees' chances of making it into the upcoming World Series.

"I don't know about that. My money's on the Orioles," commented the senator, whom I knew was a devoted baseball fan, as the elevator came to a stop.

My third bodyguard, a newcomer named Bill Kinsella, whose twinkling Irish eyes and quick grin had made me like him immediately, spoke up promptly. "So is my money, Senator. Baltimore's going all the way."

"Better watch how you talk in front of the boss," Ambrose told him with a grin as the doors slid open. "Where's your loyalty to the Big Apple, Kinsella?"

Bill blushed redder than his hair and looked at me. "I love everything about New York City, Mr. Mayor," he said hastily. "And the Yankees are a great baseball team. But I grew up in Maryland, so I guess I can't help pulling for the Orioles."

I raised my hands palms-outward and shook my head good-naturedly. "Far be it from me to meddle with a sports fan's allegiance."

The five of us stepped into the lobby, which was deserted except for a uniformed security guard stationed by the vast glass doors. Through them, at the curb, I could see a black limousine waiting, and behind it, an escort car containing two more of my bodyguards.

It was late, past nine o'clock. I was looking forward to the upcoming meal at my favorite Chinese restaurant, and later, returning to Gracie Mansion for a good night's sleep. It had been an exhausting day.

The guard greeted us and unlocked the doors so that we could step out onto the sidewalk. Wall Street was virtually deserted at this hour, in stark contrast to the bustle that had greeted us when we had arrived earlier, in the heart of the workday.

Our footsteps seemed to echo along the concrete as we walked toward the waiting cars.

"It's getting chilly out," Anson commented, pulling his navy Burberry trenchcoat closed at the collar.

"It's supposed to get down into the upper thirties tonight," I told him, remembering the weather forecast I had heard this morning on the way to City Hall. I paused in front of the open car door and glanced up at the sky, wondering if the rain showers that had been promised were going to materialize.

Above the towering skyscrapers, the sky was dark and overcast, and the evening air was still. Almost eerily still . . .

The calm before the storm.

No sooner did that thought cross my mind than my ears picked up the sound of a car engine starting nearby.

An innocuous noise, really. One a veteran New Yorker would expect to hear often in the streets of this enormous city.

Yet the sound startled me a bit.

Perhaps because I had just noted that the evening was unusually quiet, and was listening more keenly than usual.

Or perhaps because there is little traffic in lower Manhattan after business hours, so that the roar of a single engine coming to life tends to stand out.

And perhaps because, on some level, I had a premonition that something was about to happen.

Something terrible.

A split second later, I heard the peal of tires in the street and glanced up to see a small, dark-colored car pull away from the curb a few hundred feet away. It barrelled in our direction.

"Get down!" Mohammed hollered, shoving me into the car, where I sprawled across the seat face downward, momentarily stunned.

Outside, I heard the telltale sharp staccato of multiple gunshots.

And then, swiftly, the sound of the passing car faded, and in the distance, I heard the tires squeal around a corner.

"Are you all right, Mr. Mayor?" Ambrose's voice bellowed.

"I'm fine."

"He's all right. He's all right," he repeated urgently. "Check the Senator, Kinsella. Kinsella!"

Hearing a commotion and urgent voices outside the car, I wasted no time in scrambling upright and peering onto the sidewalk.

The first thing I saw was three figures huddled over a fourth that was lying prone on the ground.

And then I noticed the blood that had spattered all of them, pooling on the sidewalk and spilling over the edge of the curb into the gutter.

Someone had been shot.

I glanced at the three who worked over him and took a quick inventory.

Ambrose.

Mohammed.

The Senator.

So it was Kinsella who had been hit. The freckle-faced new guy, who only moments before had been bantering about the World Series.

Now, as Mohammed shouted to the driver to call 911 and Ambrose and the Senator began CPR, Kinsella lay on the sidewalk making terrible strangled moaning sounds as the blood—and the life—drained out of him.

TWO

"Mr. Mayor?"

I looked up from the Styrofoam cup of cold coffee in my hand and saw a doctor in a white coat over turquoise scrubs coming toward me. I promptly set the coffee on the low table beside my vinyl-cushioned chair and stood up, saying a brief prayer that the news would be good.

But, judging from the grim look on his face, it wasn't going to be.

"I'm Dr. Bhikkhu," he said, coming to a halt where I was standing and glancing briefly at my bodyguards, who had hastily risen from their seats beside mine. Both Ambrose and Mohammed were ashen-faced, still so shaken from what had happened that they were in no condition to be working. But they weren't on duty. Another team of bodyguards—their number beefed up to ten—was keeping watch over me now, posted in various spots here in the hospital waiting room and up and down the corridor.

Meanwhile, Ambrose and Mohammed were, like me, sitting here at 4:30 A.M. because they were concerned about their fallen comrade. Kinsella was in rough shape—that much we knew. He had been revived at the scene, only to fade again. As he was rushed away in a waiting ambulance, two medical technicians knelt over him, pumping his chest in an effort to bring him back again.

"I've been tending to Mr. Kinsella," Dr. Bhikkhu told us now, speaking in a low, calm voice that should have been soothing. But the somber expression on his dark, kindly face was unsettling.

"How is he?" I asked, prepared for the worst.

The physician shook his head. "I'm terribly sorry to report that he didn't make it through the surgery, Mr. Mayor."

"I see." Years of being in the public eye have taught me how to control my emotions, particularly in difficult circumstances such as these. I cleared my throat and swallowed hard, then thanked the doctor for his efforts on behalf of my bodyguard. So did Mohammed and Ambrose, both of whom were visibly shaken by the tragic news.

"Mr. Kinsella's wife is down the hall," Dr. Bhikkhu told me, after briefly describing the nature of the injuries that had taken his life, and what, precisely, had been done in the attempt to save him. "She's alone here. If you want to—"

"Of course," I said, picking up my trench coat and following him to the door, with Mohammed, Ambrose, and my security team on my heels.

I hadn't realized Kinsella was married. He had seemed like little more than a kid.

Now, Dr. Bhikkhu informed me that he and his wife, Candy, lived in Queens and had a four-month-old daughter. My gut twisted at that news.

It was horrific enough that a promising young man had been murdered. That tragedy was compounded by the realization that a young woman was left a widow and a little girl would grow up without a father.

"She's here alone," the doctor told me in a low voice, as we stopped in the hallway outside a small cubicle. I could hear sobbing coming from inside the room. "Her mother lives with them, but she had to stay behind with the baby."

I nodded and took a deep breath, steeling myself for the ordeal. Unfortunately, I've been through it before—far too often. Every time a police officer or fireman is struck down in the line of duty, I find myself facing their loved ones, struggling to comfort them in the worst hours of their lives. It's all a very necessary part of my job as mayor.

I entered the room and saw a woman hunched over in a chair,

her face buried in her hands. Her shoulders heaved as she sobbed, and when she lifted her head, I saw that she appeared to be scarcely out of her teens. Her eyes were swollen, her freckled cheeks tear-streaked, and her expression desolate. There was a flicker of recognition in her gaze, and she said, in a tremulous tone, "Oh, Mayor . . . Billy's gone. He didn't make it."

I went to her and put a comforting arm around her, holding her while she cried and murmuring to her. Finally, she pulled herself together, looking at me and asking in a voice that split my heart, "Who would do this to him? He was such a good man . . . he had everything to live for."

"Your husband died a hero, Mrs. Kinsella," I told her, knowing that knowledge might not take the edge off her raw pain now, but that it would possibly bring her solace sometime in the future. "He was killed in the line of duty, protecting me in the way that he was trained to do."

I was fully prepared for her to sling resentment or bitterness my way; under the circumstances, I almost expected it.

But to my surprise, she managed a faint smile and said, "That would have made Billy proud. He was so honored to be assigned to your bodyguard detail, Mayor."

"And I was honored to know him, Mrs. Kinsella."

I sat with her for at least an hour, letting her talk about and cry over her husband because she needed an ear, and there was no one else to be there for her. She told me about her widowed mother being home with the baby, and her husband's family being so far away.

"In Maryland, isn't it?" I asked, and she smiled and nodded.

"How did you know that?"

"Your husband was discussing the Orioles earlier this evening with Senator Hubbard," I told her.

"Senator Hubbard? The one who's launched that investigation into the Holocaust victims' missing assets?"

"Yes, that's right. Did you see our press conference on television yesterday afternoon?"

"No, but I keep reading about him lately, and hearing about him on the news. It seems like everywhere you turn, there's a story about what he's doing."

I nodded, realizing that Anson's efforts at publicity were paying off.

She sighed heavily and wiped at her eyes. "I need to call Billy's family in Maryland," she said, her voice trembling.

"Would you like me to ask the doctor to do it for you?" I asked sympathetically, wanting to spare her the heart-wrenching anguish.

She took a deep breath and let it out shakily. "No," she said bravely. "They should hear it from me. Will you wait here until I get back?"

I didn't hesitate to tell her that I would, even though the night was giving way to morning and Helen Garcia, my Deputy Mayor, was waiting for me back at Gracie Mansion.

While Mrs. Kinsella was gone, I placed a quick call to my friend Charley Deacon, the detective who had interviewed me here at the hospital shortly after I arrived. I asked him if they had come up with any leads yet.

"Not yet, Mr. Mayor, but it sure helped that you gave us that partial license plate number. We're working on that now."

"Good. Let me know if you come up with anything," I told him. "I wish I'd seen the whole thing."

"It's a miracle that you saw anything at all, under the circumstances."

In the confusion back at the shooting scene, I'd had the presence of mind to make sure I had a glimpse of the car as it sped away. I'd given Charley the make and model, and the first few numbers of the plate. I knew that might not be enough to catch whoever was responsible for the attack, but it was worth a try.

Mrs. Kinsella returned to the waiting room, looking ashen. "Billy's poor mother is hysterical," she reported. "She has a heart condition. I'm so worried about her. Oh, Mayor . . . tell me this is a nightmare. Tell me I'm going to wake up."

I helped her into a chair, then asked gently if there was somebody that she could call to meet her here at the hospital and take her home.

"You shouldn't go alone," I told her.

But she shook her head and said, "There's no one, really. Billy and I do have some friends in the neighborhood, but I wouldn't wake any of them at this hour. They have little children. Oh—"

She was sobbing again, and I patted her shoulder as she told me she had just thought about her daughter, Madeline. "She's so little, Mayor," she told me pitifully. "She'll never remember Billy. She'll never remember her father. And he loved her so much . . . It isn't fair . . . It just isn't fair."

"No," I agreed grimly. "It isn't fair."

And I vowed, then and there, to find the person who had robbed this sweet woman and her baby of a loving husband and father. I would find him, and I would see that he was prosecuted to the fullest extent of the law.

It wouldn't be the first time I had made such a vow. I've been known to track down a criminal or two recently. But this time, I was even more determined than ever before. This time, a cold-blooded killer had struck too close for comfort.

I sent Mohammed and Ambrose, who seemed grateful for a way to help, home with Mrs. Kinsella in a limousine, and they promised to stay with her as long as she needed them. Meanwhile, I headed uptown to Gracie Mansion to change my clothes and prepare a statement for the inevitable press briefing in a few hours at City Hall.

"Eddie? Is that you?"

That voice. It couldn't be . . .

But it was.

The voice belonged to my mother, and it was reverberating through the first floor of Gracie Mansion.

I closed the front door behind me and turned to see Joyce Koch hurling herself at me with all the speed her elderly legs could muster. She was clad in a pink flannel nightgown and white sneakers, and her face was deadly pale. Right on her heels was my father, wearing a pajama top and a pair of wool trousers, bellowing that it was about time I got back, and did I know what hour it was?

Directly behind the two of them was my Deputy Mayor, Helen, who had been with me earlier at the hospital and probably wished she'd stayed instead of dealing with these two.

"Where have you been?" Pop demanded.

"Why didn't you call?" Mom wanted to know.

"How's Kinsella?" Helen asked anxiously.

I turned to her and asked her to please wait in my study; I would be right in.

After she had left the room—looking grateful to get away from Mom and Pop, I might add—I turned to my parents and, mustering all my patience, asked, "What are you two doing here?"

"What are we doing here? Lou, did you hear that? Eddie wants to know what we're doing here," my mother said.

"What do you think we're doing here?" my father asked. "There we were, with all our packing finished, sitting down to watch the eleven o'clock news before bed, when we saw a special bulletin that somebody had tried to slaughter our son down on Wall Street."

"Slaughter—don't use that word, Lou," my mother admonished with a shudder. "It's such an ugly word."

"Well, that's what somebody tried to do to Eddie, Joyce."

"Eddie," my mother wailed, clutching my face with her hands on my cheeks and squeezing painfully. "Thank God you're all right. Thank God. I told your father I wouldn't believe it until I saw you with my own eyes, even though your friend Helen—"

"She's my Deputy Mayor," I interjected.

"—Told us that you were fine and you were at the hospital. 'If he's fine,' I said, 'then why isn't he here? Why is he at the hospital?' And she told us you were with that young bodyguard who was shot."

"She wouldn't even tell us which hospital," my father put in. "She told us just to wait here, and that you would be home soon."

Thank you, Helen, I thought. I've spoken about my parents enough to my Deputy Mayor so that she sensed I wouldn't want them showing up at the hospital. I shuddered at the thought of them barging into the waiting room, demanding to see their son, even as I had to admit, they had every right to be upset by the evening's events.

"We've been waiting for hours, Eddie," my mother pointed out. "Where have you been? What took you so long?"

"How's the kid?" Pop added.

"I'm afraid he didn't make it," I said briefly, taking off my trench coat and hanging it in the closet.

"He *died*? Oh, Eddie." Mom shook her head sadly. "That's so awful. They showed a picture of him on television. He looked like such a nice boy."

"Did they catch the rat who did this?" Pop asked, his nostrils flaring with fury.

"Not yet."

"But, Eddie," Mom said, her eyes wide behind her bifocals. "Whoever it was, was after you. Your bodyguard was hit by accident. You were the one they wanted to shoot."

"Mom—"

"You'll have to go into hiding," Pop announced, throwing up his hands with the air of someone who has made up his mind.

"We'll go with you," Mom said. "We're already packed—although I just realized, our clothes are more suitable for Boca Raton than—where is it that a mayor goes when he goes into hiding, Eddie?"

I sighed inwardly. "A mayor doesn't—"

"A Safe House," my father interrupted. "He goes to a Safe House, Joyce. Same as anyone else."

"Where would the Safe House be? Here in New York?"

"Not here in New York, Joyce. A killer wants to look for the mayor of New York, where's he going to look? In New York. You've got to be one step ahead. You've got to find some place out of touch, but not too far away—"

"Like Saratoga Springs?" Mom asked. "Remember how I loved Saratoga Springs, Lou? We haven't been there since '79, when we went for the races in August with Hy and Myrna Schafer. That was before Hy got the gangrene and lost—"

"Listen, Mom," I said impatiently, "I'm sorry to interrupt, but I have to go meet with Helen. Now that the two of you know I'm all right, why don't you head back home and get some sleep? You have to rest before your flight to Florida."

"Head back home?" my mother echoed incredulously. "Flight to Florida? A mother should leave her son when his life is on the line? No. I'm not leaving your side in your time of need, Eddie. Not after what happened tonight."

"*Last* night," Pop corrected with a yawn, checking his watch. "Eddie, we're not going anywhere tonight. In fact, your new housekeeper—what's her name? Rita?"

"Frieda."

"Frieda settled us into a guest room right down the hall from you. That way, we can keep an eye on things before we all move to the Safe House."

"Pop," I said, struggling to control my temper, "there isn't going to be—we're not moving to a Safe House."

"No Safe House?" My mother looked alarmed. "Then how are you supposed to hide from the assassin, Eddie?"

"The Mayor of New York City," I said succinctly, "doesn't go into hiding. From anyone. For any reason."

"But Eddie, someone tried to shoot you!"

I had my own theory about that particular angle, although I had yet to actually voice it to anyone. And I certainly wasn't going to start with my mother.

"And that maniac is still on the loose," Pop boomed. "You'd be a fool not to get out of town until they catch him."

"How would it look if the mayor ran scared, Pop? What kind of message would that send to the people of this city?"

"What kind of message are you sending by staying put?" Pop wanted to know. "You might as well go around with a big red and white bull's-eye target on your rear end. 'Here I am, Mr. Assassin . . . come and get me.' Don't be a fool, Eddie."

I rubbed my eyes, which were burning with exhaustion, and sighed. "Listen, I have to go meet with Helen right now. You two get some rest. We'll talk in the morning."

"It *is* morning," Mom said, reaching out and patting my cheek, peering into my face. "You're the one who needs rest, Eddie. You've got dark circles. Tell that nice Helen you'll talk to her later."

"I can't, Mom. There are things that need to be done."

"Well, you don't have to do everything around here."

"Sure I do, Mom." I kissed her on the cheek and headed into the other room, calling over my shoulder, "I'm the mayor, remember?"

Anson was waiting at my office when I arrived shortly after seven-thirty.

I had already spoken to him briefly from home about an hour ago, updating him on the situation.

He was as troubled as I was over the Kinsella kid's death, and asked if we could meet for coffee before my press conference. Knowing I'd be pressed for time this morning, I suggested City Hall.

Besides, I make better coffee than any of those Euro-style cafes that have been popping up all over the city. My good friend Sybil Baker dragged me to one of those places not long ago, insisting that I order a double skim half-decaf something-or-other. It was okay, but even if I *could* pronounce it, I wouldn't go around drinking it every day, the way Sybil does. I'm happy sticking with my own brew.

My recipe?

It's very simple. A can of Martinson's coffee, and cold water. No foam or syrup or artificial flavorings like they use at those trendy cafes. You don't need all those fancy trimmings when the coffee itself tastes as good as mine does.

Anson looked as though he'd gotten about as much sleep as I had: Zero. He was freshly shaven and impeccably dressed in a dark Armani suit, but his voice was even more hoarse than it had been last night, and he was clearly worn down.

With our steaming mugs of *full*-caf coffee in hand, we settled into chairs—him in a comfortable wingback, me in my favorite low-slung black leather armchair beneath the watchful gaze of Mayor La Guardia, whose portrait hangs in a spot of honor on my office wall.

"Any idea who's behind this assassination attempt, Ed?" Anson asked me. He's never been one to beat around the bush—a quality I happen to possess myself, and greatly admire in others.

"Nope," I said, still not ready to spill to anyone—not even Anson—the theory that had been bouncing around my head over the past few hours. It was too soon.

"Have you received any threats lately?"

The police had asked me the same question last night, when they were interviewing me at the hospital shortly after the shooting. I told Anson what I had told them.

Which was, "Nothing more than the usual."

Let's face it, when you're the mayor of a huge, volatile city like New York, you're going to get your share of threats. That's why I have bodyguards.

Some threats, I take seriously.

Some, I don't.

My security detail takes all of them seriously, but then, that's their job.

My job is to be the best mayor I can be, and not get sidetracked by a lot of worry over something I can't control.

"What about the nuke deal?" Anson wanted to know.

There was no need for him to elaborate on his question. I knew he was referring to my support for the proposal to build a nuclear power facility in the Bronx, a position that had been met with considerable controversy, to say the least.

"You think some environmental activist might have gotten so worked up over the issue that he took a shot at me?" I asked Anson.

"You never know." He cleared his scratchy throat.

"No, you never do," I agreed thoughtfully.

I supposed that scenario was entirely possible—particularly when you considered the tenacity of the No Nukes protestors who had been demonstrating outside City Hall for weeks now. Had one of them carried things too far?

"Look, Ed," Anson said, popping a lemon lozenge into his mouth, "I'm worried about you. You don't have to come to that committee meeting tomorrow night at the Grand Hyatt. There's going to be a lot of press, and you might want to keep as low a profile as you can over the next few days."

"You sound like my mother, Anson."

"From the look on your face, I take it that isn't a compliment."

I smirked. "Listen, don't worry about me. My security people are making sure I don't take any unnecessary chances. They've already canceled my appearance at a street fair uptown this afternoon."

And believe me, I hadn't been pleased about that turn of events. I was looking forward to eating a greasy hunk of cinnamon-sugar-covered fried dough from my favorite concession stand. I'm supposed to be sticking to a low-fat, low-cholesterol eating plan, but it wasn't my doctor who vetoed this particular appearance.

This time, it was Jim Milligan, my security chief, who put his foot down, and not because he was concerned about my diet. According to him, there simply wasn't time to take the extra precautions that would be necessary for my protection in such a crowd, in light of what had happened last night. Jim promised that he would see to it that I was able to resume my scheduled activities as soon as possible, but not before new safety measures had been put in place.

"Ed, are you sure you can make it to the meeting?" Anson asked. "Because I can have Bonnie e-mail you the notes afterward if you'd rather bow out."

I knew he was referring to Bonnie Tyson, his longtime aide. She had often served as a liaison between the Senator and me when he was in Washington. Until recently, we hadn't met face-to-face, but in our telephone conversations and computer correspondence, I had found her to be entirely efficient and responsible.

"I'll be there, Anson," I promised. "As long as nobody on my security team has a problem with it. This committee is important to me."

"To all of us. All right, Ed. I appreciate it. I just wanted to let you know that there's no pressure. You must be rattled by what happened last night. I know I am." He drained his coffee cup and set it on the table between our chairs. "I should be getting to my office. I've got a conference call with the White House in an hour."

"Please give the President my regards."

"I will. We're fortunate that he's been consistently supportive of this committee. In fact, I think it's remarkable that we've met with relatively little dissent on most fronts, now that we've gained momentum."

"Aside from the Association of Swiss Banks," I pointed out.

"You're right about that. Still, according to them, they have cooperated by publishing those lists of dormant accounts dating back to the war years."

"And there are still countless survivors whose relatives' names don't appear on those lists, but who were known to have Swiss accounts during the war," I pointed out.

"Exactly."

"We have to find out what happened to those records, Anson . . . and why they haven't shown up yet. And we can't accept anything less than full cooperation from the Association as we investigate."

"No, we can't. Still, their reaction isn't surprising. They're claiming that we're portraying them as criminals simply because we *are* investigating them. Obviously, they have little to gain by our prying into their records, Ed."

"But what is it, exactly, that they have to lose?" I mused.

Another question weighed more heavily on my mind as he left my office.

And if the Association did have something to hide, how far would they go to stop Hubbard's committee?

The morning's headlines were predictably dire and sensational, particularly those of the tabloids.

KOCH PLOT BOTCHED! read one.

MAYOR NEARLY MEETS HIS MAKER! trumpeted another.

And the *Daily Register,* for which my good friend Sybil Baker is a veteran gossip columnist, cheerfully queried, WHO WANTS ED DEAD?

It was a strange morning, spent in my office, plowing through the usual blizzard of paperwork and trying not to relive the gruesome events of the night before. But I kept hearing the ominous crackle of gunfire, and seeing Bill Kinsella's bright red blood spilling all over the gray sidewalk. I kept remembering his wife's agonized sobs, and the fact that a little girl had lost her daddy.

As I had told the throng of reporters who showed up for my press briefing, I had no idea who was behind this, but I had every confidence that the cold-blooded killer would be caught and brought to justice.

What I didn't mention publicly was that I personally intended to help the detectives with the case.

Nor did I say that I happened to have a growing hunch that *I* hadn't been the assassin's intended target.

Certainly, there was nothing concrete for me to base my theory on. No overt evidence I could use to convince the authorities to shift the focus of their investigation.

But whenever I relived the shooting and saw myself about to get into the waiting car, I couldn't help believing that the sniper should have had a clear shot at me. I was in front of the Senator and right out in the open in the seconds before Mohammed shoved me down into the car.

Meanwhile, Kinsella was bringing up the rear, walking several feet behind me, next to Anson Hubbard.

Either the gunman was a lousy shot, or he hadn't been aiming at me.

He had been aiming at Kinsella, or at Hubbard.

And since the fresh-faced security guard didn't have an enemy in the world, according to his wife, the most likely target was Hubbard.

Hubbard, who only an hour before the shooting had appeared on television to discuss the plans and goals of his newly formed committee.

What if someone had reason to stop the investigation?

It was common knowledge, as I had pointed out earlier to the Senator, that the Association of Swiss Banks wasn't exactly encouraging Hubbard to pry into their World War Two-era records, although they hadn't come right out and issued a statement of opposition, either.

I didn't want to believe that some faction of an internationally respected financial organization could have triggered last night's shooting, but the idea wasn't entirely farfetched. Not if someone involved had something to hide.

Of course, I could have been entirely off base in assuming that the shooting was related to yesterday's announcement.

There were other issues the Senator had been involved with lately, besides the Holocaust investigation committee. But none had been nearly as high profile or potentially volatile. In fact, his humanitarian efforts had been well received in the press for several months now. He had recently appeared at the Special Olympics and had helped to bring the issue of road rage into the public arena, following the shooting death of a young mother by an irate driver on the West Side Highway.

Who could argue with any of that?

And it wasn't as though his personal life was subject to scandal. He seemed to have a loving relationship with his wife, Gisele, whom I'd met on several occasions. The two of them were often portrayed in the media as the perfect power couple, and Anson often spoke of her with affection. Ever time I had seen them together, they were attentive to each other and came across as very content.

They had no children, but Anson had recently mentioned to me that he loved David Berkman like a son. The handsome, affable Manhattan attorney was from a working-class family, and had met the Senator years ago, while he was a college student working as a summer intern in his office. Anson was so impressed with Berkman's initiative and intelligence that he took him under his wing, paying for his education and making him a part of his family. Berkman often accompanied Gisele to charity functions when Anson was busy in Washington.

I had met him not long ago, and instantly liked him. He was an instrumental and vocal part of Hubbard's investigation committee, providing legal counsel for the planned proceedings. Watching him and Anson together, I had been struck by the easy banter and open affection between them.

Other than Gisele and David, I could think of no other prominent person in Anson's personal world. There had never been a hint of scandal. As far as I—and the rest of the world—knew, he led an exemplary lifestyle, both private and public.

So who would want to kill him?

And why?

Perhaps I *was* entirely off base, I told myself as I sat at my desk and glanced again at the morning's dark headlines.

Perhaps I really had been the intended target for the deadly bullet.

The idea was unsettling, yet hardly preposterous.

And yet . . .

And yet, I just wasn't convinced.

Experience has taught me that when I feel this strongly about something, I usually turn out to be right.

I felt that somebody wanted Anson Hubbard dead.

If that was the case, I needed to warn him. I should have done so in the first place, but something had made me hold back. I realized now that I had been reluctant to trust anyone, even him, with my private theory.

But the more I thought about the Senator, the more I realized that I could rely on him to keep my speculation to himself.

Yes, Anson Hubbard deserved my trust . . .

And he didn't deserve to die.

But if my gut instincts were on target, as they usually were, the assassin wasn't going to give up easily.

THREE

"Ed. You're alive."

"You sound surprised, Sybil," I said into the telephone receiver, huffing a little as I trotted along on my treadmill in the small state-of-the-art gym I'd had installed next door to my office, in what had once been an oversized supply closet.

Ironically, skipping the street fair—with its tempting fattening treats—had allowed me extra time for exercise this afternoon. I figured it would help perk me up after my sleepless night. I still had a long day ahead with several meetings scheduled, along with a late dinner with the Schools Chancellor. It would be nearly midnight before I got back to Gracie Mansion.

There would be no time to meet again today with Anson Hubbard, although I had spoken to him briefly on the telephone. I told him I wanted to discuss something important, and in person. His schedule was as jammed as mine, and we realized that our next opportunity to talk would be before tomorrow night's gathering at the Grand Hyatt.

"I'm not surprised you're alive, Ed; I'm relieved," Sybil said. "I've been worried sick about you ever since I heard the news."

I adjusted the treadmill to a slower pace and asked her, "How's Australia?"

"Rainy."

"Did you get a chance to scuba dive at the Great Barrier Reef?"

"Yesterday, finally," she said over the long-distance crackling on the line. "It was spectacular. But I've had enough of being Down Under. If I hear one more 'G'day, mate' or see one more blob of vegamite . . ."

"What you need is a nice New York bagel with chive cream cheese and nova lox," I told her.

"Or a big round mushroom knish and a thick tongue sandwich from the Merkin Deli. Promise you'll meet me there for lunch as soon as I get back."

"I promise."

If my security chief will let me, I added silently. Milligan had been jumpy all day, trying to talk me out of several upcoming appearances that I considered extremely low risk.

"When *are* you coming back?" I asked Sybil.

"Soon. I'm boarding a plane home in an hour."

Sybil is quite the world traveler, thanks, in part, to her husband Claude's job with the U.N., and thanks in part to her own insatiable thirst for adventure and fitness. A former Rockette, she's around my age, although she'd never admit to it. And while I pride myself on staying in shape, Sybil makes me look like somebody's frail maiden aunt.

Last month, she took up skydiving, and next summer, she's going to attempt to climb Mount Everest—again. Her last try would probably have been successful had she not been called back to New York from the base camp to cover a breaking scandal involving a major Hollywood director and a call girl ring. When you're a gossip columnist for New York's number one tabloid, it's hard to get a moment's peace, even on Mount Everest.

"So, Ed," she asked in her getting-back-to-business voice. "What happened? Who tried to blow your head off?"

"I have no idea," I told her honestly.

And even though I was almost convinced that I wasn't the intended victim, I couldn't help wincing slightly at her graphic choice of words.

"Was it that nasty No-Nukes bunch who have been camping out in front of City Hall lately?"

"That's the latest theory," I told her.

As the day had progressed, I had become aware that both the media and the detectives were focusing on that particular scenario.

"Well, who else would want you dead?"

"There was a time when I might have answered, 'Who wouldn't?' to that question, Sybil. But as you know, lately, I've been ruffling fewer feathers than usual."

"Don't bet on it. Didn't you once say, 'I don't get ulcers—I give them'?"

"Did I say that? How clever of me." I chuckled as I stepped off the treadmill and reached for a towel.

"You sound pretty chipper for someone whose life is in grave danger, Ed."

"What am I supposed to do? Go into hiding?" I asked, thinking of my parents and their Safe House plan.

"Nah. That's not your style, Ed. Why don't you make like Sherlock Holmes and get busy with a private investigation of your own? I'm sure you can figure out who's behind this assassination scheme. In fact, ten to one you'll have nabbed the suspect by the time my plane touches down at JFK tomorrow."

"I'm good, Sybil, but that's pushing it," I told her.

"Who figured out who was behind those Santa murders last Christmas?" she asked. "Who solved the death of that Broadway actor last year—what was his name?"

"Conor Matthews," I supplied, then added modestly, "And you're right. I did play a role in both of those cases, but—"

"A *role*? You solved them, Ed. And no professional detective is more competent than you are. Can I report in my column that you're working on this case?"

"No, you can't report that, Sybil," I said, exasperated.

Sometimes, I was almost able to forget she was a reporter.

Almost.

"Well, is it true?"

"I'm very busy, Sybil. I have a city to run. That's my primary concern at the moment. I'll leave the detective work to the detectives."

"I don't believe you."

I shrugged and said, "That's your choice, Sybil. Have a safe flight home."

"I will. Don't forget . . . we're going to do lunch."

"I won't forget. A knish and a tongue sandwich," I promised before hanging up.

My mouth watered at the very idea of lunch at the famed Merkin Deli.

Not that I was eager to face Sybil's probing questions about the case, and my involvement in the investigation. She likes to play up the Mayor-as-Detective angle in her column whenever possible.

Which doesn't exactly thrill the NYPD.

Don't get me wrong. I think that our detectives are among the finest and most competent in the world, and I don't blame them for bristling whenever somebody suggests that they can't function without the help of an amateur . . .

Namely, yours truly.

But the truth is, I've been blessed with unusually sharp powers of deduction, and when the city of New York—or any New Yorker—is in jeopardy, I feel compelled to use those skills if I can possibly be of any help.

Sometimes I can't.

And sometimes I can.

Only time would tell whether I would be able to shed any light on this particular case.

I met with Charley Deacon and Jim Milligan before leaving for my late dinner with the Schools Chancellor, the location of which had been moved from the Park Avalon bistro to a smaller, more intimate French restaurant a few blocks away. Jim had insisted on the change, pointing out that the Park Avalon was huge and invariably crowded, which would ostensibly make things harder for my beefed-up security team.

I couldn't help feeling a little disgruntled as I sat in my office with Charley and Jim, both of whom wore grim expressions. I had been looking forward to the chopped salad with feta cheese, roasted peppers, tomatoes, cucumbers, and fresh basil at the Park Avalon.

"How are you doing, Mr. Mayor?" Charley asked me, concern etched on his dark, handsome features.

"As well as can be expected. I'm feeling terrible about Bill Kinsella."

"We all are," he replied.

And Jim, who had hired Kinsella himself, nodded sadly.

"Any news on the license plate number, Charley?" I asked, tapping my fingertips impatiently on the desk top.

"Based on the partial numbers you gave us, we've narrowed it down somewhat. But we're still working on an ID."

I nodded.

"But," Charley went on, "we have gotten several calls from people claiming to be responsible for the attack."

At that, I raised an eyebrow. "Several phone calls?" I echoed.

Jim nodded and said, "You know how these things go, Mr. Mayor. Every nutcase with a vendetta against you or the city comes crawling out of the woodwork when something like this happens. We've heard from an underground Islamic terrorist group, the psychotic son of that woman whose cane was accidentally run over by your limo last spring, and a wino from Brooklyn who doesn't remember his own name but says he's your number one enemy."

"Terrific." I steepled my fingers and glanced at Charley. "I don't suppose there's anything to any of these claims?"

"Nothing," he said, "not that we're taking them lightly. We've checked out all of these so-called suspects, and so far, they seem like harmless pranks. We're still focusing our attention on the antinuke demonstrators who have been opposed to your stance on the Bronx nuclear facility project. You've received threats from various protestors in recent weeks, and we're looking very closing at them now."

"Aside from that," I said, "do you have any other theories?"

"You're the mayor of one of the world's biggest cities, Mr. Mayor. Plenty of people have reason to want you dead," Jim reminded me.

"But what if . . ." I paused, took a deep breath, and let it spill out. "What if I wasn't the intended victim?"

Both Charley and Jim frowned.

"Who else would it have been?" Jim asked.

"You mean the Senator?" asked Charley. "Sure, we've considered it. But you're the more likely target, Mr. Mayor. We're focusing this case on you. Nobody has come forward to claim responsibility for trying to kill the Senator."

"You just admitted those people were all nutcases."

"As mayor of New York, you draw a lot of attention from nutcases. Not all of them are harmless. The Senator isn't nearly as high profile," Jim said.

"We're not ruling anything out, Mr. Mayor," Charley told me. "But for now, we're going to assume that your life is in danger. You have to be careful."

"I'm always careful. I may not like being told what to do and where to eat"—I glanced pointedly at Jim—"But I'm no fool. I'm not taking any chances. And neither should Anson Hubbard."

"That's up to him," Jim said. "But where you're concerned, I've drawn up some new safety measures we need to go over, Mr. Mayor. It won't take up much of your time . . ."

"Good," I said, "because I'm already running late for my dinner."

I listened grimly as he ran down the list of additional precautions that would be taken for my protection from now until further notice. And as I did, I couldn't help wondering if hiding at a Safe House—even with my parents—wouldn't have been easier, after all.

"Eddie!"

"Mom?" I stopped short in the foyer of Gracie Mansion for the second night in a row, startled to see my mother standing there, having dashed in from the next room to greet me. "What are you doing here?"

"I made you some matzo balls," she said briskly, "and I organized your sock drawer. How was your dinner with the Schools Chancellor?"

"How did you know where I was?"

"I watch the evening news. My son, his business is right out there for everyone to know. That's not a good idea when there's a crazed killer on the loose, Eddie. You should try to keep things to yourself."

"You never answered my question . . . what are you doing here, Mom?"

"I'm keeping an eye on things. Making sure you're all right."

"You're *what*? But . . . you're supposed to be on your way to Florida with Pop—aren't you?"

"Your father is snoring in front of the television set in the other room. I told him he wouldn't be able to stay awake through the ball game. I wanted to switch it and watch my 'Dateline' program, but he wouldn't let me. Every time I reached for the remote, he woke up and told me he was watching the Yankees."

"But why are you two here?" I asked, still confused.

"Didn't anyone tell you? We've moved in," my mother said triumphantly. "We're in the guest room right down the hall from you. Of course, it's only temporary. Just until they find out who tried to hurt you. We want to be near you, Eddie. I couldn't rest knowing you were trying to cope with this alone."

Don't get me wrong—my mother is sweet, and I love her. She is a good, loyal, caring mother. She really is.

But it was all I could do not to demand that she and Pop get on the next plane to Boca, where they belonged. The last thing I needed was to have them underfoot at Gracie Mansion, organizing sock drawers and snoring and God only knew what else.

I said, very carefully, so as not to hurt her feelings, "I'm sorry, but you really can't stay here, Mom."

"Why not? There's plenty of room."

I could hardly argue with that.

"And your staff seems happy to have us around, Eddie. They've been so helpful—except for that chef of yours."

"Lucien?" I sighed. I could just imagine how the temperamental Frenchman had reacted to Mom poking around in "his" kitchen, mixing up a batch of matzo ball soup.

"He doesn't believe in sharing, does he, Eddie? I told him that the kitchen was plenty big enough for both of us, but I could tell he didn't want me there. He kept giving me dirty looks. You really should talk to him about his attitude when you have a chance."

"When I have a chance," I conceded wearily, because it was easier than disputing her opinion about Lucien.

"You look tired, Eddie."

"I am, Mom. I'm going to bed."

"They said on the eleven o'clock news that they still aren't making any progress on catching the person who shot at you yesterday. Maybe you should lend those detectives a hand, Eddie. You always were good at solving mysteries."

"I'm sure they're doing fine on their own, Mom," I told her. The last thing I needed was for her to know that I had every intention of looking into the case. She and Pop might decide they wanted to get involved with that, too.

"Listen, Mom," I said, before heading up the stairs, "do me a favor, will you? Don't tell anyone you're staying here with me."

"Anyone who?"

Uh oh.

"Anyone, anyone," I told her. "You haven't let anyone know, have you?"

"Just Rita."

"Who's Rita? Oh, you mean Frieda. The housekeeper."

"That's right," she said. "And Lucien. And the rest of the household staff. And of course, your security people—they always let me and your father right through when we come to the gate. They're so nice, Eddie. But I haven't told anyone else . . ."

"Are you sure?"

"Except Blanche across the hall. She's watering our plants and taking in our mail while we're here."

"Blanche, whose nephew is a reporter for that tabloid television program?" I asked with a sinking feeling.

"'Inside Scoop.' Yes, she's the one," Mom confirmed, looking pleased that I had correctly identified her friend. "Eddie, you really should get right to bed. You look exhausted."

"I am," I said glumly, and headed upstairs, wondering how long it would take before the entire world knew that my parents were staying at Gracie Mansion.

The next day was as uneventful as a day could be when you're the mayor of New York and there's a supposed assassination attempt hanging over your head. The papers were full of speculation and hearsay. As far as I knew, nothing concrete had been discovered yet. My morning was spent in a budget meeting with my financial advisors, and the afternoon holed up in my office with paperwork.

I was on my way out to the Grand Hyatt, where I would be meeting Anson Hubbard, when my secretary, Maria Perez, informed me that Charley Deacon was on the line for me.

"Charley . . . anything new?" I asked, snatching up the telephone and setting my briefcase on the desk again.

"That car came from a rental place out by Kennedy airport," he told me. "I'm on my way over there now to talk to the manager."

"Did you get the name of the person who rented it?"

"Not yet. But don't expect too much, Mr. Mayor. You and I both know that whoever it was probably used an alias and fake identification."

"I know. Still, you might be able to come up with something based on the rental forms."

"I might. I'll keep you posted. How about you? Are you hanging in there?"

"I'm fine, Charley. Just going about my business. I'm on my way out right now to a meeting uptown."

"Watch your back, Mr. Mayor."

"I always do, Charley."

I arrived at the Grand Hyatt fifteen minutes late. Traffic heading uptown had been unusually heavy, thanks to rush hour and tonight's Yankee playoff game in the Bronx. Finally, we reached Forty-Second Street and the familiar glass canopied entrance to the hotel, which is directly next door to a main entrance to Grand Central Station. The sidewalk was crowded with harried commuters, along with a knot of reporters who were clearly expecting me. The press had been encamped outside of City Hall all day, too.

Of course, being in my position, I'm used to being the object of media attention. But this was a bit different. Today, amidst the usual questions and comments, there was an undercurrent of tension. I couldn't help feeling as though they were waiting for a masked gunman to leap out of the shadows and take another shot at me.

When I got upstairs, Anson was waiting in the private suite where we'd arranged to meet. He looked a little less exhausted than he had the morning before, and his voice was almost back to normal.

I insisted that my bodyguards remain outside the door while we talked, something that didn't sit well with them. In fact, Lou Sabatino, who has been a part of my security team for years, insisted on calling Jim Milligan to clear it with him.

"Go ahead," I told him. "And while you do that, I'll be having a private meeting in here with Anson. We don't have any time to waste."

"But Mr. Mayor," Lou protested nervously, "we're not supposed to let you out of our sight."

"I'll be right in this room. What could possibly happen to me in here? There's only one door, and no windows, and you already swept the place to make sure nobody's hiding in the closet or under the table."

"I don't know . . ." Lou eyed Anson warily.

"Hey, don't look at me. I swear I don't have a reason to harm the mayor," Anson said teasingly, throwing up his hands in mock innocence.

Lou didn't crack a smile.

"Listen, Lou," I said, "I appreciate your efforts on my behalf. In fact, I've never felt more loved in my life. But I need to have a private discussion, and I have a right to do that. I promise I'll call you if I need you. We won't be long."

With that, I closed the door in his face.

"Sometimes," I told Anson, "you have to take charge."

"I can't say I blame you," he said, settling into a straight-backed chair beside the conference table. "My wife has been incredibly jumpy ever since the shooting."

"At least she's not camped outside the door," I pointed out.

"No, thank God. Actually, she's at our place up in Bedford. I thought the country air might relax her a bit. I'm meeting her there later. Thought it would be good for me to get out of the city for a few days, before my trip overseas."

"When are you leaving for Zurich?" I asked him.

"In the middle of next week."

Something in his tone made me ask, "Aren't you looking forward to it?"

He hesitated. "Not necessarily."

"But I thought you were anxious to get this investigation underway."

"Oh I am, Ed. It's just that I have this growing feeling that it's not going to be an easy road."

"Because of the Association of Swiss Banks?"

"Partly."

"What else is it, Anson?"

"It's just . . . I had a call from Seth Mandel today. Ever heard of him?"

"The name sounds vaguely familiar," I told him. "Who is he?"

"The spokesperson for an organization of Swiss Jews."

I nodded. "I know who you mean now. They're a rather militant organization, aren't they?"

"Very. And they're against what we're doing."

I frowned. "Ridiculous! Why would they be against something that will ultimately benefit all Jews?"

"According to Seth, some of my remarks on behalf of the cause have infuriated certain people in Switzerland. As a result, over the past few days, some Swiss Jews have been the victims of anti-Semitism, some of it relatively violent."

I shook my head. "That's a shame. But it doesn't mean we should stop the investigation, Anson."

"It does according to Mandel. He claims that the more I stir things up over there, the more trouble I'll cause for 'his people.' He predicted bloodshed, Ed."

"Was he threatening *you*?"

"No, nothing like that," Anson told me. "I just got the feeling that I won't be welcomed with open arms once I get over there. Not by most Swiss Jews, and certainly not by the banking officials."

I nodded thoughtfully.

"Mandel has requested that the investigation be turned over to him and his group. He says that as a non-Jew, I can't be expected to handle things properly."

"That's ridiculous!" I said again.

"That's what I told him, in so many words. But he told me I could expect to hear from him again."

"Sounds somewhat ominous."

"Maybe. Anyway, Ed," Anson said, straightening in his chair

and looking at me expectantly. "What was it that you wanted to talk to me about?"

"I don't want to alarm you, Anson. But the more I think about the assassination attempt, the more I have to wonder—" I paused, realizing there was no delicate way to put this. "I'm wondering whether *you* were the one who was supposed to be targeted."

Anson was silent, clearly pondering that—and hardly looking surprised.

"It's not something I haven't considered," he said at last.

"So you think it's possible, then?"

"Not just possible. Likely, Ed."

The expression on his face made me ask, "Have you received any threats lately, Anson?"

"No. But . . ." He cleared his throat. "As I said before, Ed, it's becoming more and more apparent that certain people aren't very happy with my investigation."

"It's hard to believe that someone would want to kill you over a cause that so obviously would bring justice to thousands of people. You don't think Seth Mandel and his group could be behind this, do you?"

"As I said, he didn't make a direct threat," Anson told me. "But he isn't on my side. And his group is militant. I don't know what they're capable of, Ed."

"Well, I might be wrong. The assassin's bullet might have been meant for me, just as everyone has assumed. I just think that you should watch yourself, Anson. Beef up your security. Maybe hire a few more bodyguards."

"I know . . . I'd just hate to do that . . ."

"Why?"

"It doesn't look good, Ed. After all I've gone through to get this committee underway, I'd hate to give the impression that I'm feeling vulnerable to any kind of terrorism. And besides, Gisele . . . well, she's a nervous person as it is. Always has been. If she actually thought my life was in danger . . ."

"Wouldn't it be better for her to know that you're taking precautions against further violence?" I asked impatiently. "You already had a close call the other night, Anson—regardless of who the gunman meant to hit. A man was killed. Clearly, the wrong man. That means someone is still out to get you or me."

"I realize that."

There was a knock on the door.

"Who is it?" I called, distracted.

The door opened a crack and Lou Sabatino peeked in. "I spoke to Jim, Mr. Mayor. He reiterated that I'm not to let you out of my sight. I'm sorry, but those were his strict orders. I'll have to come in and keep an eye on things."

"That's all right, Lou. We're just about done anyway," I said, noticing that Anson was checking his watch anxiously. It was time to head for the meeting.

As my bodyguard stepped over the threshold and stood right over my chair, I resigned myself to the fact that what with my extra-cautious security team, the press, and my parents encamped back at Gracie Mansion, I was going to have very little privacy until this case was solved.

The meeting ran until nearly midnight, and although it was fascinating, I found myself anxious to get back to Gracie Mansion, parents or no. I needed a good night's sleep to make up for the past few restless nights.

I was one of the first on my feet when the meeting adjourned, but realized there was no way I was going to make the quick getaway I'd intended. I found myself surrounded by people who wanted to express their alarm over the shooting, sympathy over Kinsella's death, and worry for my safety.

I made all the right responses, murmuring my thanks for their concern and saying over and over that no, I had no idea who was behind the murder, and as far as I knew, the police hadn't named any suspects. Thankfully, nobody asked whether I was personally involved in the investigation.

I finally reached the door, where the Senator was huddled in conversation with Bonnie Tyson and David Berkman.

Bonnie, a mousy-haired, bespectacled woman, appeared to be mostly listening and nodding. She's one of those people whose approximate age is a mystery. She could have been anywhere between thirty and fifty.

Meanwhile, I was aware that David Berkman was in his mid-thirties, the kind of man who always seemed relaxed and the picture of health. He had a full head of dark hair and there wasn't a fleck of gray in his neatly trimmed beard. He wore a well-cut, black custom-made suit and stood with his hands in his trouser pockets, earnestly engaged in conversation with Anson.

I nodded in their direction and started to leave the room, but Anson motioned me to join them.

As soon as I went over, he said in a low voice, "I've been telling Bonnie and David what you think about the shooting, Ed—that I was the one the gunman meant to kill, and not you."

Dismayed that he hadn't kept my theory to himself, I said only, "There's no way of knowing for sure."

"No, but it makes sense in light of recent developments in our investigation into the Holocaust victims' funds," Berkman commented.

"Meaning?"

"Meaning, Seth Mandel and his organization shouldn't be taken lightly," Berkman said with a shrug. "And they're not the only ones opposed to our committee. There are a couple of neo-Nazi groups that we should watch."

"Anybody in particular?" I asked.

He shrugged. "It's hard to tell."

"I told Anson to go to the authorities with the information about Mandel's group," Bonnie commented, her gray eyes solemn.

"And I reminded Bonnie that no specific threat was made," Anson told me. "Unless I have something concrete to report, I think it's inappropriate to go around pointing the finger at anyone."

"You're talking about murder," Berkman agreed. "False accusations could only alienate and further antagonize someone like Mandel. And right now, we can't afford for that to happen if it isn't absolutely necessary. It was a long, hard road getting the funding and support for our endeavor. We've got to keep a positive spin on this investigation now that things are finally underway."

"I agree with you there," I said. "But I'm concerned about Anson's safety. I strongly suggest reevaluating his security."

"That makes sense . . ." Berkman agreed.

I perceived a "but" coming on.

Anson himself provided it.

"But as I pointed out earlier, my wife is a nervous wreck already, Ed. I've got my usual security measures in place. What am I supposed to do? Install armed guards and dogs at our house in Bedford? Gisele will be a basket case."

Berkman was nodding. "She's so worried as it is, poor thing. We don't want to upset her any more than is absolutely necessary."

I was a little taken aback that Berkman shared Anson's almost coddling attitude toward his wife. The woman must be far more fragile than I ever realized.

Still, in my opinion, that wasn't a good reason not to beef up Anson's security. And judging by the expression on Bonnie's face, I wasn't the only one who thought so.

It's one thing to want to spare your loved ones unnecessary worry, but quite another to take foolish chances in order to do so. I told Anson just that, and he looked distressed.

"Believe me, I'm not taking chances, Ed. I'm just not ready to alarm my wife or anyone else until I know that I was the one targeted in the assassination attempt."

So there it was. Far be it from me to tell a man of Anson's station and intelligence what to do.

"I understand what you're saying," I told him, straightening my tie and glancing again toward the door. "And now, if you'll excuse me—"

"Before you go, Ed, can I interest you in coming up to dinner on Saturday night?" Anson asked, catching my arm as Bonnie and David drifted away.

"Saturday night?"

"Gisele and I are having a small get-together. Both Bonnie and David will be there, along with a few other friends. I thought it might be nice if you joined us. I realize it's short notice, and chances are that you've already got plans, but—are you busy?"

Actually, I wasn't. I'd been scheduled to have dinner with the French Ambassador, but his office had called just this afternoon to cancel because he'd been called back to Paris. Which left me free . . .

But hardly eager to venture up to northern Westchester County for dinner.

It's not that I didn't want to socialize with Anson and his wife, and despite what people say, I certainly have nothing against the suburbs. If people want to live up in the woods with the racoons and bugs, miles away from a decent bagel with lox, forced to shop in strip malls and see movies in multiplexes with tiny screens and uncomfortable seats, that's fine with me. I'll take the city any day.

And after such a hectic, emotionally draining week, I was really looking forward to the unexpected treat of relaxing at home on Saturday night. It's rare that I get any night to myself, let alone a weekend one. I figured I could rent the recent Woody Allen release I had somehow missed in the theater, order in some Chinese . . .

And curl up in the den with my adoring parents, both of whom were living with me for the time being.

I had forgotten all about that.

My mother would insist on making me some of her noodle kugel or matzo brie instead of ordering takeout, and Pop's taste in movies runs to old war films; he says he doesn't "get" Woody Allen.

"Actually, I am free on Saturday night," I told Anson abruptly, making up my mind. "I'd be glad to come to dinner."

"Good. Gisele will be pleased. But, Ed, please don't say anything in front of her about your suspicions. I don't want to—"

"Worry her. I understand," I said abruptly. "I won't say anything, Anson."

As I rode uptown surrounded by wary-eyed bodyguards, accompanied by two extra escort cars, I couldn't help but be reminded that the general consensus was that Yours Truly had been the killer's target.

If so, I couldn't afford to let my guard down, and I vowed that I wouldn't. It was hard to imagine somebody getting to me with the added security, but I wasn't brazen enough to think it impossible.

The very idea made the skin prickle on the back of my neck, and I lay awake long after I had settled my weary self into my bed at Gracie Mansion that night.

FOUR

"Ask Eddie then, Joyce, and see what he thinks."

"I should bother my son for something so minor? He's the mayor of New York City, not a makeup consultant."

"So, he's your son. He knows your face. Just ask him. I hear him coming now."

"Ask me what?" I stepped into the dining room reluctantly, realizing it was too late to escape to City Hall without joining my parents for breakfast now that they'd heard my footsteps approaching. I had intended to gobble down my usual grapefruit and take my coffee on the go, since I had an early meeting with my Parks Commissioner.

"Your mother has a problem," Pop informed me. He was sitting at one end of the vast table, a newspaper spread before him and a cup of coffee in his hand.

"I don't have a problem," she retorted, seated across from him and spreading a glob of thick, dark jam onto a slice of buttered whole-grain toast.

"You don't have a problem? Then why all the kvetching? I've heard nothing since last night except—"

"Do you think I use too much eyebrow pencil, Eddie?" my mother asked, waving my father into silence and turning to me as

I took my usual place at the end of the table. She tilted her face up, as though inviting me to inspect it.

"Too much . . . ?" I pretended to look closely at her brows and ponder the question. "To tell you the truth, I never thought about it."

"Well, look at my face. Does it look like too much?"

"No," I said, having not the slightest idea how much eyebrow pencil was too much.

"See? I told you," Pop said, looking pleased with my response. "Now let's drop the subject. The only reason Thelma said that to you was that she was jealous because you were on television and she wasn't."

"I don't know. Thelma used to be a Ziegfeld girl, Lou. She knows all about makeup and I don't think—"

"You were on television?" I interrupted with a sinking feeling. "When was this?"

"Last night. Didn't you see us?" Mom dipped back into the jar of blackberry jam.

"No, I didn't. What were you doing on television?"

"That nice reporter from 'Inside Scoop'—"

"Blanche's nephew," Pop inserted.

"—Did a segment about us staying here with you, keeping an eye on things."

"Of course he did." I shoved away the half grapefruit that had just been set in front of me, having lost my appetite. I had yet to read this morning's headlines or be briefed by my staff, but now I had a good idea what to expect.

It was going to be a long day.

"Eat your grapefruit, Eddie," Mom said. "You need your vitamin C. Cold and flu season is right around the corner."

"Mr. Mayor?" An aide poked her head into the room. "You have a telephone call from Charley Deacon."

Pop's ears perked right up. "Charley Deacon? Isn't he one of the detectives working on the shooting, Eddie?"

"I think so," I said vaguely, pushing my chair back and striding into the next room, where I snatched up the telephone receiver and said, "Charley? What's going on?"

"We've got a name, Mayor."

"From the car rental place?"

"That's right. Only we've determined that it's most likely an alias. The ID he provided couldn't be traced, the Manhattan address and phone number he gave were fake, and we've come up with nothing on the name he used."

"Which is . . . ?"

"Zedekiah Gold."

"*Zedekiah*?" I echoed, frowning at the unusual name. I scribbled it on a piece of paper as he spelled it for me.

"Not quite your typical alias, is it, Charley?"

"Hardly," he agreed, sounding grim. "I'm assuming, from your reaction, that it means nothing to you?"

"Nothing at all. Did the clerk who handled the rental paperwork remember anything about him?"

"Not a whole lot. And that's not surprising. The car rental places out by JFK are among the busiest in the city. There are hundreds of people in and out every day. This guy managed to blend into the crowd."

"Even with a name like Zedekiah."

"Exactly. We're checking with other employees of the rental place, though, as well as other customers who were there at the time that he was. Hopefully, we'll turn up someone who remembers something."

I glanced at my watch. "Listen, Charley, I've got to head downtown now. Keep me posted, will you?"

"Sure thing, Mayor."

A voice behind me made me jump as I hung up. I turned to see Pop standing in the doorway.

"Zedekiah? Who's Zedekiah?" he asked, obviously having overheard at least the tail end of my conversation with Charley.

I responded to his question with a weary one of my own. "What are you doing in here, Pop?"

He lowered his voice. "I just came to say that your mother's concerned you're angry with her for telling Blanche where we were going. Will you go in there and tell her you're not angry, Eddie, so she won't brood all day?"

I sighed. "Pop, I've got to get going. I'm going to be late."

"You haven't even eaten your breakfast yet."

"That's all right. All I ever have is grapefruit and coffee anyway."

"You know what your mother would say about that, Eddie."

"I do know, Pop, but I'm a grown man—and a Mayor. I don't necessarily need nutritional advice from my mother, even if she is under my roof."

"I know, I know." He threw up his hands in a but-what-are-you-gonna-do gesture and shook his head, then changed the subject. "So. Zedekiah. I had a cousin Zedekiah. You don't remember him. He died right after you were born—or maybe right before."

"You're right, I don't remember," I said hurriedly, striding into the hallway for my coat with my father right on my heels, undaunted.

"He was a real S.O.B., my cousin," he went on. "Ran a successful jewelry business, but a real crook. Never struck a square deal. Never bothered with his poor mother, my aunt Dolly—wouldn't even give her a cent when she was evicted from her apartment. Divorced his wife and abandoned his children when they were still in diapers."

"Mmm hmm." I stuck my arms into my coat sleeves and picked up my briefcase.

"Then one day—he wasn't even forty yet, I don't think—he was walking along Orchard Street during a thunderstorm, and *Bam!* He was struck by lightning. Didn't I ever tell you that story, Eddie?"

"Yes, but I thought it was Uncle Hy who was struck by lightning," I said briskly. "Listen, Pop—"

"Uncle Hy? No, no, he was the one who sat up in his casket right before they closed it and shocked the hell out of everyone. Good thing they didn't embalm people in those days. Uncle Hy lived a good twenty more years after that. No, it was Cousin Zedekiah who was killed by a bolt of lightning. My mother always said it was God's Justice because he was such a mean, miserable person. God's Justice. That's what Zedekiah means in Hebrew."

"Mmm hmm. That's interesting." I headed for the door, where my security guards waited. "I'll see you later, Pop. Tell Mom I said goodbye."

"Be careful, Eddie."

"I'm always careful, Pop," I said, stepping out into the bright October sunshine flanked by Ambrose, Mohammed, and the others.

Mayor's Mommy: Leave My Eddie Alone!

Scowling, I tossed aside the morning edition of the *Daily Register* with its glaring black headline and reached for the phone to call my Press Secretary. Something needed to be done about the embarrassing situation, although I wasn't sure anything would help at this point.

Before I could pick up the receiver, the intercom buzzed.

"Yes, Maria?"

My secretary's disembodied voice announced, "Senator Hubbard is on the line for you, Mr. Mayor. He says it's important."

"Thank you, Maria." I picked up the receiver. "Anson? Is everything all right?"

"No, Ed. We've been contacted by a source at a bank in Zurich that certain documents pertinent to our investigation have been or are being shredded."

"What kind of documents?"

"The source claims that they dated back to the 1940s and contained details about the bank's dealings with Germany during the war."

This was, I knew, in direct defiance to the Swiss government's recently passed regulation that any relevant paperwork from that era be handed over to our committee to facilitate our investigation.

"Who is the source?" I asked Anson.

He hesitated only briefly. "Actually, it's a bank custodian who happened to see the stacks of documents inside the shredding room waiting to be destroyed. He's a descendent of Holocaust survivors, and is sympathetic to our cause. He's risking his job and his reputation by coming to us with this information."

"Does he have any proof of his claims?"

"He secretly confiscated several of the documents and has promised to turn them over to me. David is negotiating that scenario with him now."

"What does this mean specifically, then, Anson?"

"It means that certain Swiss banking officials have something to hide, just as we've suspected all along. They're attempting to conceal records that might lead us directly to the bank accounts and gold that were confiscated by the Nazis with the help of supposedly neutral Swiss officials."

I nodded thoughtfully, something he had said jumping out at me. I couldn't believe I hadn't realized it before.

"There's my other line, Ed," Anson said as I heard a faint tone in the background. "I'll get back to you a little later. Will you be in the office all day?"

"I have a lunch date uptown, but I should be back afterward," I told him. "Thanks for the update, Anson. And Anson?"

"Yes?"

"I'm more certain than ever that you were the target of that assassination attempt."

"What makes you say that?"

"I'll explain later. Just . . . be careful."

"I will, Ed."

After hanging up, I quickly buzzed Maria and asked her to get Charley Deacon on the line for me. "Tell him it's important," I said.

She buzzed me back a few moments later. "He's unavailable at the moment, Mr. Mayor. I asked that he return your call as soon as possible."

"Thank you."

"Would you like me to confirm your reservation for lunch at Le Cirque 2000?"

I was meeting with Monica Hoffman, my Chairman of City Planning, who also happens to be a dear friend. I told Maria to go ahead and confirm the reservation, and to hold all calls for the next hour except Charley Deacon's. I had a mountain of paperwork to wade through.

But before I got down to business, I sat for a few moments, thrumming my fingertips on the polished surface of my prized desk that had once belonged to Fiorello La Guardia.

Anson had mentioned gold—the gold that the Nazis had confiscated from wealthy Jews, millions of dollars worth of gold—everything from wedding rings to Passover goblets to fillings from the teeth of Holocaust victims. I knew that much of the gold seized from Holocaust victims had been quickly disposed of through other countries. But about a hundred and forty million dollars worth of gold remains unaccounted for to this day, and Anson's theory—which he hasn't hesitated to voice publicly—is that it is stashed in Swiss vaults.

Zedekiah Gold.

What had Pop said this morning?

Zedekiah means God's Justice in Hebrew.

Zedekiah Gold.

Was it a coincidence?

Or a coded message by whoever had chosen that particular alias?

If the latter was true, it would clearly link the killer to the investigation committee—and to Anson Hubbard as the intended victim.

But the name Zedekiah was Hebrew. That seemed to rule out the killer being Swiss or a Neo-Nazi, pointing instead to someone of Jewish background.

Why would any Jew be against Anson's work?

Seth Mandel and his group came to mind, along with their allegations that the Senator's outspoken comments had resulted in anti-Semitic sentiments in Switzerland. Were they behind this?

Or was it somebody else, somebody with a reason to want to put a stop to the investigation?

I had no way of knowing.

But my instincts told me we hadn't heard the last from Zedekiah Gold, whoever he was.

Monica was waiting when I arrived fifteen minutes late at Le Cirque 2000, having been detained by a last-minute phone call from Charley Deacon. I had told him my theory about the gunman's alias being connected to the Senator's committee, and though he'd promised to look into it, I could tell he sounded dubious.

He said they had located a woman who had been in line at the car rental place that day directly behind the man calling himself Zedekiah Gold. She had given them a good description, and mentioned that she had picked up a piece of paper she thought he'd dropped when he hurried away from the counter. She called after him, but he either hadn't heard her, or had ignored her. She had glanced at it and saw that it was a receipt from a video rental place in Manhattan, so she tossed it into the garbage.

Still, she had come up with the name of the video store, and detectives were checking into it. She was also working with a police artist to come up with a sketch of the suspect.

Charley also said they were tracking down leads involving a cluster of radical antinuclear protestors who had been bragging that they were responsible for trying to assassinate me.

There might have been something to it, but my gut feeling was still that this was all tied to the Swiss bank investigation, and I secretly vowed to see what else I could find out.

Meanwhile, Monica and I had official business to discuss, and we did so over a bottle of Pellegrino and a curried tuna tartare appetizer followed by a first course of delicate foie gras ravioli in a savory consomme.

Monica, a gourmet chef in her own right, has always been partial to fine dining, and lunch with her is invariably a welcome reprieve from the pressures of a typical day at City Hall. On days that I lunch with Monica, I never schedule dinner meetings. I know I won't be hungry again until morning.

The restaurant was typically crowded, and has been ever since it reopened a few years ago in this new location in the Palace hotel. We were seated at a relatively private table in view of the bar, with its space-age, oversized geometric furnishings and vivid electric blue and red sculptures overhead that contrasted interestingly with the classic painted murals and elaborate antique wood moldings.

Several times, we were interrupted by acquaintances who stopped by to tell me how sorry they were about my bodyguard's death, and to ask whether the police had named any suspects yet. I kept my replies brief and vague, and was thankful that at least nobody mentioned the fact that my parents had moved temporarily into Gracie Mansion. By now the entire city must have known about that.

By the time our entrees arrived—rack of lamb for Monica, pheasant with chanterelles for me—our business discussion was completed and conversation turned, predictably, back to the shooting. Monica asked me point blank if it was true that I was conducting an investigation into the case.

I shrugged. "I'm certainly cooperating with the authorities," I told her. "And I've given them any pertinent information I can think of."

"Rumor has it that they depend on your extraordinary sleuthing powers these days, Ed." Monica narrowed her blue eyes at me and added, "You have to admit, without your help, the police might not have solved quite a few high-profile cases."

"True, but I'm no professional detective," I said modestly.

To change the subject, I asked about her husband, Sheldon, who had recently endured a triple bypass. She told me he was doing well, but having a difficult time adjusting to the dietary restrictions his doctor had set.

"That's why I suggested that we come here for lunch. I wanted some rich, delicious food to tide me over, because at home it's been nothing but lean poultry and steamed vegetables these days." Monica, who is rail-thin and looks decades younger than her sixty-some years, popped a large chunk of lamb into her mouth. "I couldn't even make my brisket for our Rosh Hashanah dinner this year, Ed. And you know how I love to keep those traditions alive."

"I know, I know." I'd had the privilege of being a guest at many a holiday celebration at the Hoffman household.

"It's so important to preserve our heritage. I keep telling my kids to give me some grandchildren so that our family feasts will be livelier, but so far, nobody's cooperating. I want to be one of those traditional grandmothers who's a great cook, a bit eccentric, and regales the little ones with tales of the old country."

"You can't possibly have many stories of the old country, Monica," I pointed out. "Weren't you ten years old when you came to America?"

"Thirteen," she corrected. "And you know, Ed, now that I think about it, the stories I could tell, no child should have to hear."

I nodded sympathetically, seeing a shadow in her expression. I was familiar with her past. Monica had been born in Austria and spent several years in a concentration camp during the war. She'd lost her parents, grandparents, and older siblings in the gas chambers—everyone except an aunt who later brought her to America and raised her.

"I was glad to see that you're supporting Senator Hubbard's committee, Ed," she said quietly. "You know, I didn't just lose my family in the Holocaust, although that was the most devastating part about it. But I also lost what would have been a good-sized inheritance. My father was a wealthy merchant, and he saw what was happening in Europe long before the Nazis came for us. He had stashed money in a Swiss bank, like so many others were doing, and he told us that if anything happened to him, we would be provided for. All we had to do was get the money after the war."

"But that didn't happen," I guessed, setting down my fork and pushing my plate back, unable to eat another bite. I was fascinated by Monica's story.

"No, that didn't happen. After the war, I finally set out to find out what had happened to my father's money, with my aunt's help." Her gaze shifted to the ornate mural up near the ceiling, and there was a bitter note in her voice when she said, "I found that everything Papa had left had vanished without a trace. We were told that we would have to provide proof of the account."

"And you had no proof."

"Nothing other than my father's word, which I wholeheartedly believed then, and do to this day. Do you know that when I had no other information about the account, the bank demanded a death certificate for my father?"

"I've heard of that happening," I told her.

"You know, I don't know exactly how much is at stake. I do know that we lived very well back in the years before the war, Ed. We had a large house and servants, and we traveled quite extensively. I don't doubt that my father had stashed away a considerable amount of money, and my aunt agreed. She said he also had a stockpile of heirloom jewelry—watches, rings, that sort of thing, most of it gold—and all of it vanished as well."

The waiter appeared to whisk away our plates then, and ask if we wanted dessert. I declined, but Monica ordered the famed Le Cirque chocolate stove.

When the waiter had left again, she leaned forward and confided, "I never can pass up a treat. Maybe that's partly because of all those years when I had nothing. There were so many times over the years when that money my father left would have come in handy . . . not that I didn't make it through anyway."

"Of course you did," I told her. "But you should have what is rightfully yours, Monica. And so should the thousands of others whose family fortunes vanished into the Swiss banks over fifty years ago."

"That's why I'm so pleased with what you and Anson and the others are doing, Ed. If I ever do have grandchildren, they'll know that justice was served, and they'll benefit from my father's years of hard work as he built up his business. He was so proud of what he'd earned . . . and they took it all away."

"I hope that the committee's efforts will be able to restore at least some of it, Monica," I said grimly.

As we lingered over dessert, we discussed other, more cheerful topics. Yet there was an undercurrent of sadness and loss, and when we parted ways in the courtyard of the Palace Hotel outside the restaurant, I promised Monica that I would do everything in my power to make sure that the investigation persevered.

"Thank you, Ed," she said, with tears in her eyes. "I can't believe that it still matters so much after all these years, but it really does. It's a matter of the truth being told. It's a matter of proving that not everything could be wiped out as easily as the Nazis wanted to believe."

As my car headed back downtown to City Hall, I felt a renewed sense of responsibility and determination to do what I could for Anson's cause. Thousands of people were depending on our committee, and we couldn't let them down.

"Ed, I'm back in town, and just in the nick of time," Sybil's voice greeted me over my private line late that night, as I sat in my office wrapping up a revised budget report that had been giving me trouble all afternoon.

"Welcome back. Why in the nick of time?" I asked, pushing the pile of papers aside and settling back in my chair for a short chat. It had been one of those days—I hadn't come up for air since I'd returned from my lunch with Monica.

"All hell seems to have broken loose in my absence," Sybil noted.

"You always were inclined toward understatement," I said dryly.

"Oh, come on, Ed. First someone takes a shot at you. Now your parents have moved into Gracie Mansion. Don't get me wrong—they're very sweet—but you must be going out of your mind."

"Well, the press—of which you *are* a member, dear Sybil—isn't helping matters much," I told her. "Can't you have a word with whoever wrote today's horrible headline down at the *Register*?"

"I'll see what I can do," she said, sounding genuinely sympathetic for a change. "In the meantime, I had something else in mind to cheer you up."

"What would that be?"

"That lunch at the Merkin Deli. Tomorrow at three o'clock? I like to eat late on Saturdays."

"So do I, but I have to be at a dinner party up in Westchester by seven, so let's make it earlier. Although not too early." I had to attend Bill Kinsella's funeral out in Queens in the morning.

"Two, then," she said easily. "Who are you dining with tomorrow night? Anyone I know?"

"Yes, as a matter of fact. It's Anson Hubbard and his wife."

"That man is such a peach," Sybil said. "And he seems to be everybody's darling now that it's full speed ahead for his investigation. But Gisele . . ."

"What about her?"

"Mmm . . . never mind."

"What aren't you telling me?" I asked, sensing that Sybil was obviously sitting on a juicy tidbit of gossip. Normally, I don't particularly like to dish, particularly about people I know personally. But in this case I was curious about whatever it was, particularly in light of recent events.

"Just that the lovely and esteemed Gisele Hubbard isn't the most stable woman in the world, Ed. But then, you might already have known that."

"Actually, I didn't. I've only met her a few times, and then only briefly. What can you tell me about her?"

"I'll fill you in tomorrow over lunch. I'm late for a session with Enrique and he's hardly the patient type."

Enrique, I knew, was her personal trainer. He speaks very little English, works her like an Olympic coach, and has a terrible temper, but for some reason, Sybil just adores the man.

"Didn't you just get in from Australia?" I asked her.

"Yes . . . why?"

"Your energy never ceases to amaze me, Sybil. Most people would be ready to drop from exhaustion after flying halfway around the globe."

"All I did was sit there for hours on end, Ed. I need to get the kinks out of my muscles. I'm looking forward to a nice round of kick-boxing."

"Sounds very relaxing."

"I'll see you tomorrow at the Merkin."

"I'll be there," I promised.

"Alone?"

"Alone? What is that supposed to mean?"

"I thought maybe your parents would want to join us. I know how much your father loves the Merkin, having been a waiter there at one time."

"I'll be there alone, Sybil," I said curtly. "Pop can go to the Merkin any time. I thought you said you were coming to my rescue."

"And so I am," she said, and added a breezy, slightly smug little, "Ta ta, *Eddie*," before hanging up.

FIVE

David Berkman called me on Saturday morning just as I was sitting down to read the morning papers. Thankfully—at least, for me—the tabloid headlines trumpeted the latest divorce proceedings of a many-times-married rock star.

"David, what can I do for you?" I asked, sitting at my desk with the telephone receiver in one hand and a steaming cup of Martinson's in the other.

He apologized for bothering me so early and on a weekend, which made me chuckle. "I'm the Mayor of New York City," I reminded him. "I'm used to calls at all hours of the day, seven days a week. It goes with the territory."

"Well, Anson suggested that I call to update you on the paper shredding situation, Mr. Mayor," he said in his calm, professional way.

"Have there been any new developments?"

"We have received copies of the documents the janitor managed to confiscate, and they are clearly tied to the Holocaust victims. These particular reports detail transactions involving Swiss banks and the German government in the spring of 1940. Some seem to imply arrangements for the sale of confiscated goods and properties. We have contacted Georg Hadwin, the head of the Association of Swiss Banks, to discuss the matter."

"And . . . ?"

"And he's positively outraged. He denies any knowledge of document shredding. In fact, he accused Anson of manufacturing a scandal."

"Why would Anson want to do that?"

"According to Hadwin, because he's hoping to cast the Association in a negative light in order to boost public support for our cause."

"We already have public support."

"Not in Switzerland. Besides, the Banking Association and the Swiss government are particularly vulnerable to the press. They say they're being unfairly portrayed as Nazi sympathizers who willingly aided in stealing the assets of the Holocaust victims."

"Well, maybe they did. Is there any other evidence of the paper shredding?" I asked David. "Anyone else we can talk to, other than that custodian?"

"Nobody. The custodian has already been suspended by Hadwin and threatened with an investigation for violating bank secrecy laws. He's no longer willing to talk to us. We're lucky we've got the evidence he did manage to seize, but that's as far as it goes now."

"If the association is shredding documents we need for our investigation, they won't get away with it," I said grimly.

"I'd like to think they won't," David agreed, "but there isn't much we can do about it, Mr. Mayor."

"There's something I can do about it. I can get the city council to bar official deposits in Swiss banks until reparations are made to the Holocaust victims. Anson can speak with the governor, and he can warn the banks that they can lose their operating licenses in this state if they fail to cooperate with the investigation."

There was a moment of silence. Then David said, "Those are pretty drastic measures, Mr. Mayor."

"So is shredding official documents. The committee was supposed to be granted full access to pertinent documents. The Association is apparently backing out of their end of the bargain. We can't let that happen."

"No, but Georg Hadwin is a force to be reckoned with."

"And so am I," I retorted.

"But your public image isn't at stake. Anson will be up for reelection. He can't afford controversy or a scandal right now."

"No politician can ever afford that, David. Listen, we can talk more about this when we get together tonight."

"I doubt that," David said. "It's a dinner party. Gisele doesn't necessarily like to mix business with dinner conversation. It upsets her."

I frowned. Was there anything that didn't upset Anson's wife? I found myself eager to meet Sybil and get her take on the apparently delicate Mrs. Hubbard.

"After dinner, you and I and Anson might be able to find some private time in his study, though, Mr. Mayor," David went on. "This matter does need to be addressed."

"It certainly does. What does Anson intend to do in the meantime?"

"He has told Georg Hadwin that he won't tolerate any blatant lack of cooperation, and that we're going to investigate the paper shredding matter further. Unfortunately, there isn't much we can do without evidence or an ally within the Association."

"We'll see," I said, leaning back in my chair and rubbing my chin thoughtfully.

I didn't like the sound of things, particularly in light of what I was now convinced had been an attempt on Anson's life. The situation was growing more complicated—and maybe, I feared, more dangerous.

I've been to far more funerals than anyone should have to attend. Of course, they're always sad. But the most heart-wrenching, by far, are when the person has died tragically, violently—and heroically. Funerals for city police officers and firemen who were killed in the line of duty always get the biggest turnout.

Bill Kinsella's funeral was no exception.

The church, an old-fashioned brick structure on the fringes of Astoria, was jammed with mourners, and so were the sidewalks and streets surrounding it. The press was there to complicate matters, adding to the congestion, and of course, I was bombarded with questions the moment I stepped from my car, flanked by extra-heavy security.

"Mr. Mayor, is there a suspect in the murder?"

"Are you worried the killer is going to go after you again?"

"How involved are you in the investigation?"

I stopped and made a brief statement, skillfully managing to reveal nothing particularly relevant, yet to appease the hungry horde. I've always been good at dealing with the press, but there are times—like at a funeral—when their presence seems truly invasive.

Still, I knew they were just doing their jobs, and I wasn't in the mood for confrontation, so I played along and got past them as quickly as possible.

I was seated in the front of the church, not far from Bill Kinsella's widow. She was dressed in black and her pretty face looked positively ravaged. Throughout the service, she clung to a red-haired, freckle-faced woman, both of them weeping audibly. I assumed her to be his mother from Maryland. There were numerous Irish-looking siblings present, as well as Kinsella's father, who managed to give a moving eulogy before breaking down.

The funeral was truly painful, and I knew it would stay with me for a long time. Again, I vowed to find out who was responsible for Kinsella's death, and to make certain that they were brought to justice.

I promised as much to his widow and grieving parents after the mass, after first telling them how truly sorry I was about their loss. It had crossed my mind that in their anguish, they might want to pin the blame somewhere, and that it could be on me, since Kinsella had died while a member of my entourage. But his family couldn't have been more noble, and his mother told me—as his wife had—how honored and proud Bill had been to be employed as a part of my security team.

"Won't you join us for lunch after the burial, Mr. Mayor?" his father invited, clutching a well-used hanky in his trembling hand.

"I'm afraid I have another engagement," I told him. "But thank you for asking me."

"Thank you for being here, for honoring my boy," was his reply.

I nodded sadly and watched as the family moved away, heads

bowed and shoulders heaving with sobs as they followed the polished casket to the hearse.

I've been going to the Merkin Deli on West Fifty-Third Street for as long as I can remember. Pop was a waiter there years ago, before he met my mother, and when I was a little boy, he used to take me in for lunch.

I have vivid memories of sitting at "our" mottled gray plastic table with chrome edging, situated halfway back in the large dining space, where I could keep an eye on the man behind the high glass counter as he worked the enormous metal meat slicing machine. I remember being fascinated by the way he deftly glided the blade in a smooth, rhythmic motion so that paper-thin slices of cold cuts fell neatly onto the white butcher's paper.

Pop and I would order celery tonics and pastrami on seeded rye with mustard. Sometimes, we would have a big round potato knish or a cup of steaming mushroom-barley soup, but we always, *always* had the celery tonic and pastrami on rye, sandwiches as thick as they were wide. While we waited for our sandwiches, we would munch on cole slaw and pickles from the heaping glass bowls the waitress would place between us: real New York deli pickles, not the strangely dark green ones you can buy in a jar on a supermarket shelf today. The pickles at the Merkin Deli have always been fresh and crunchy and have a strong cucumber taste that you just don't find in a jar.

Though Pop usually proclaimed himself "full-to-bursting" at the end of the meal, I invariably would leave room for dessert, and still do. The rice pudding at the Merkin Deli is even better than the kind my Bubbe used to make, though no one would have dared to tell her. It's rich and creamy and mild, with just the right amount of cinnamon sprinkled on top.

I hadn't told Pop where I was going when I left Gracie Mansion just after one-thirty. If I had, he would have invited himself along, as he always does. He feels as though the Merkin is *his* territory, and brags that everyone greets him by name whenever he goes in. Of course, everyone greets me by name as well—but then, I'm the mayor, and that happens wherever I go. For Pop, who is a part of the Merkin's history, being recognized is an honor and a novelty. And I have to admit, I get a better table when I'm there with him than when I'm alone.

But today, I wanted to dine privately with Sybil, so that we could talk about Gisele Hubbard and anything else she might know about the Senator's private world. Any guilt I had about discussing it with a friend—who also happened to be a gossip columnist—could be dismissed because I was doing it for Anson's own good. I was convinced that somebody wanted him dead, and I had to find out who it was. That meant uncovering every possible lead.

Sybil was waiting at a small table amidst the lunchtime crowd that jammed the deli when I arrived. I was waylaid on my way to join her by a group of southern tourists who stopped me to sign autographs and pose for pictures.

"Did you enjoy your lunch?" I asked, noting that they were just about finished.

"You bet!" exclaimed the apparent matriarch of the bunch. "Y'all sure know how to make a sandwich up here in the Big Apple. But Mayor, if you ever get down to Biloxi, you'll have to stop by our place for some real southern cookin'—hush puppies, black eyed peas, cornbread—the works!"

I promised her that I would keep that in mind, and was rewarded with an address and telephone number scribbled on the back of a slightly mustard-stained paper napkin, which I tucked into my pocket before politely excusing myself.

"You're looking well rested, Sybil," I commented, slipping into the seat across from her. I noticed that her fine-featured face was deeply tanned, and her snappy blue green eyes were positively sparkling.

"I wish I could say the same for you. You look like you could use a vacation, Ed," she told me in her straightforward Sybil style.

I snorted at that. "I can't remember my last true vacation," I pointed out. I had been scheduled to spend a week in Barbados the previous December, but that had been indefinitely postponed due to a rash of department store Santa killings. Instead of basking on a tropical beach, I had found myself donning a red velour suit and whiskers to pinch hit for the Jolly One—it's a long story. But at least I wound up catching the murderer, and restoring the season's merriment to my favorite city.

"Well, Claude and I are going climbing in the Alps next month," Sybil told me. "So if you can possibly get away to join us . . ."

"You call climbing the Alps *relaxing*?" I retorted. "I'd get more rest staying put and dealing with a transit strike."

"Is that going to happen?" Sybil asked, a telltale gleam in her eye that told me she sensed a tidbit of gossip and wouldn't hesitate to report it to the rest of the world if I spilled the beans.

"Not if I can help it. I'm meeting with the union leaders first thing Monday, and I'm sure everything can be worked out, so don't you dare go—"

"Mr. Mayor!"

I looked up to see Sol, the white-haired, wizened owner of the Merkin, standing over our table.

"Long time no see," he said, clapping me on the back.

"I've been on a low-cholesterol, low-fat diet, Sol," I said regretfully. "I didn't want to tempt myself."

"Ah, a little pastrami never hurt anybody," he replied with the confidence of one who was well into his ninth robust decade of life. "How's your father doing? I saw that he decided not to leave for Florida this week after what happened to you. He's been living with you at the Mansion, eh?"

"For the time being," I said, ignoring the smirk on Sybil's face.

"You be careful, Mr. Mayor. Listen to your father and mother. Don't go taking any chances. We can't afford to lose the best mayor this city has ever had."

"No, we wouldn't want that," I agreed wryly.

After presenting us with pickles and slaw and taking our order—a Reuben and a mushroom knish for Sybil; pastrami on rye and cup of split pea soup for me—Sol retreated behind the counter, and I got down to business.

"Tell me," I addressed Sybil, who was munching happily on a fist-sized half-sour, "about Gisele Hubbard."

"What do you want to know?"

"You said she was unstable. In what way?"

"The woman is a basket case, that's all."

"I find that hard to believe, Sybil. I've known Gisele and Anson for years, and they always appear to be the perfect political couple. He dotes on her—"

"Of course he does. The man is crazy about her. Why else would he have stayed with her for so many years? She didn't give him the children he so badly wanted—I don't know if she was incapable of bearing them, or if he knew she could never handle the responsibility. But still he's stayed with her, looking for all the world like a happily married man."

"Are you saying that he isn't?" I spooned some cole slaw into one of the small bowls the waitress presented and picked up my fork.

"No, that isn't what I'm saying at all. I think that Anson Hubbard *is* very happily married. But that doesn't mean his wife isn't a nut job."

"I see." I bit into a pickle and paused to crunch and swallow, then asked the ever-eloquent Sybil to define "nut job."

"It isn't common knowledge, but I've heard that she had a nervous breakdown in the early days of her marriage to Anson. It was right after her mother committed suicide."

I raised my eyebrows at that.

"Back up a little, Sybil . . . Her mother committed suicide?"

She nodded. "You did know, Ed, that Gisele's father, Dr. Hans Jurgen, was a Swiss scientist?"

"I knew that. He discovered the vaccine for Dobry's Syndrome."

"And amassed a vast fortune as a result. That's right. But Gisele's mother, Margot, had a history of mental instability—and violence, even. In fact, she was rumored to have once tried to kill the doctor."

"Her husband?"

"That's right. Everything was kept hush-hush, because the Jurgen family was very high profile and as image-conscious as they come. Ultimately, the marriage between Hans and Margot survived, and of course they were incredibly wealthy. But she never was quite right, and finally hung herself from the rafters of the barn on their estate in France."

"Causing her daughter to have a nervous breakdown."

"That's what I heard."

"From whom?"

Sybil fluttered her eyelashes at me. "I never reveal a source, Ed. You know that."

I decided not to press her, as it might not be important at this point. Instead, I asked, "So it wasn't common knowledge?"

"The official cause of death, reported in the press, was heart failure. Not a word was ever published about the fact that Margo committed suicide."

"Why hasn't anybody realized until now that Anson's wife isn't the unblemished society matron she appears to be?"

"Oh, some people have whispered about it for years," Sybil told me. "But Anson is fiercely protective of her—and his own reputation. He's a politician, after all. Besides, Gisele handles herself very well in public. She thrives on attention—always has. Her father doted on her. She was Hans and Margot's only child, and she had everything a little girl could want."

"Except a sane mother."

"That's exactly right. I'm assuming her father tried to make up for his wife's shortcomings by spoiling Gisele and treating her as his little darling. And, of course, he's a hero in Europe. He saved the lives of thousands of children when he wiped out Dobry's Syndrome. He and his family were practically regarded as royalty, particularly in Switzerland. Gisele has always been used to the spotlight, and she knows how to hide her little foibles and behave in public."

"She must. She's certainly had me fooled—not that I ever paid much attention to her in the past."

"But now . . ." Sybil prompted.

"Now, I'm curious. After all, I'm heavily involved in the Senator's investigation committee—"

"And in the murder case," Sybil cut in. "You want to find out who tried to kill him, and you're looking into every facet of his existence."

"Very shrewd of you to make that assumption," I told her, looking her in the eye. "But I never said that."

"You didn't have to, Ed. Don't worry. I respect our friendship.

I won't go reporting that you're sleuthing around on this latest case. But I am going to assume that we'll abide by our usual deal."

"Which is?"

"I get an exclusive when the case is solved."

"We'll see," I said in a noncommittal tone, as the waitress appeared with our mile-high sandwiches.

We spent the rest of the lunch chatting about food, mutual acquaintances, and Sybil's deep-sea diving adventures on the Great Barrier Reef. She told one amusing story after another, and I found myself laughing harder than I had in a long time.

Still, what she'd told me about Gisele was in the back of my mind during the entire meal, and I was anxious to dine with the Senator and his wife that evening to see their interaction for myself.

Bedford Village is a quaint, woodsy spot in the northern reaches of affluent Westchester county, where many of New York City's most powerful and elite residents have weekend homes. The narrow country lanes, bordered by breathtaking foliage, are dotted with rock walls, horse stables, and sprawling estates, and as you drive along, it's not unusual to have to swerve to miss deer or other creatures that venture from amidst the trees.

My driver, who is, of course, adept at maneuvering Manhattan's narrow, congested streets, seemed slightly out of his element here, particularly as he guided the sedan over the rutted, winding dirt road leading through dense woods to the Hubbard home.

"Where *is* this place, Mr. Mayor?" Ambrose asked nervously at one point, when it felt as though we were miles from civilization.

"Straight ahead, according to the directions I have," I told him. "I'm sure we'll get there soon."

But as we plodded on, I was struck with incredulity that anyone would choose to live way out here. I thought of my own beloved apartment on Washington Place in the heart of Greenwich Village, and of Gracie Mansion conveniently perched on the bustling Upper East Side. Anything I could ever want was within blocks of both places. Here, you had to drive for what seemed like hours just to get to the supermarket and dry cleaner's.

To each his own, I suppose.

Finally, it came into view—a three-story stone mansion set in the middle of a vast clearing. There were chimneys, windows, and porches galore; it was a grand and imposing sort of house that one might expect from a man as wealthy and refined as the Senator.

The whole place was lit up, and there were three other cars parked in the circular driveway out front. I checked my watch to make sure we weren't terribly late. I had gotten tied up on the phone with my Commissioner of Housing shortly before we left, and traffic on the Hutchinson Parkway had been backed up due to a fender bender.

The door was answered by a serious-faced butler complete with a British accent, and we were led through a two-story, marble-floored entrance hall to a long, narrow drawing room that seemed to run along one whole side of the house. There, my bodyguards surreptitiously took up posts in various spots as Anson and Gisele rose to greet me.

"Ed, it's good to see you," the Senator said, shaking my hand.

"We're so glad you could join us," Gisele added graciously.

I had forgotten what a startlingly lovely woman she is, with her blond hair piled high on her head and her dainty features expertly enhanced with makeup. She has porcelain skin and a petite frame that, along with her wispy-soft voice, have always made her seem almost childlike. Tonight I wondered whether that aura seemed enhanced because of what I knew about her supposed emotional fragility. She wore a tasteful, pale pink full-skirted frock with pearls at her throat and ears, looking every inch the poised society hostess, though her handshake was somewhat trembly. She excused herself to go check with the caterer in the kitchen, leaving Anson to offer me a drink and introduce me to the other guests.

David Berkman was there, polished and professional as ever despite his weekend-casual clothing: neatly creased khakis, loafers, and a navy Ralph Lauren pullover. He sat on a low green couch, sipping a martini and chatting with his date, a pleasant, outgoing young woman he introduced as Rachel.

Bonnie Tyson stood with a glass of white wine by the enormous stone fireplace with its roaring blaze at the hearth. She seemed deep in conversation with an elderly couple, but all three smiled and paused to shake my hand when Anson escorted me over. The strangers were Tom and Mary Beth Mason, old friends of his.

They claimed to be big fans of mine and said they never missed my weekly radio chat.

"And when it comes to movie reviews, we always take your word for it, Mr. Mayor," Mary Beth told me. "Were you ever right about that last Spielberg picture!"

"Listen, I tell it like it is," I said with a shrug.

"Is it true that you're working on another murder mystery?" Tom wanted to know.

"Yes, we read in today's paper that you were investigating the shooting of your bodyguard," his wife added.

"I'm very busy with city business," I told them, "but of course I'm helping the authorities in every possible way, hoping to find out who killed Bill Kinsella."

"Are there any suspects yet, Mr. Mayor?"

"Not that I know of," I replied to Tom Mason. "But I'm confident that the police will track down the gunman."

"I imagine you won't rest easily until he's behind bars," Mary Beth commented.

"And neither will Anson," Bonnie spoke up. "Nobody's sure whether the shooter was aiming for him or for the mayor. But after what happened this afternoon—"

"What happened this afternoon?" I asked, looking at Anson, who shifted his weight, looking slightly uncomfortable.

"Nothing, really. I was driving on the Saw Mill River Parkway over in Bedford Hills and an irate driver tried to get the best of me. I think I cut him off as I entered."

"You said he tried to force your car off the road," Bonnie told him, her face filled with concern. She turned to me. "The Senator thinks that if it was a deliberate attack against him, it might be related to his recent stance against Road Rage—you know, somebody trying to prove something. But I pointed out that you never know. What if it was more than that? What if somebody really does want him dead?"

Anson cleared his throat loudly as Gisele swept back into the room, and hurriedly changed the subject. "Would anyone like another drink before dinner?" he asked.

"Actually," Gisele said, "we're about ready to sit down, if you would like to come into the dining room."

As she and Anson led the way through a set of French doors to the large room adjoining this one, I glanced over at Bonnie. Her mouth was set grimly, and unless I was mistaken, she had shot a look of irritation at Gisele when she had interrupted the conversation.

I found myself wondering whether the two women got along, and realized they couldn't possibly have much in common. Bonnie was a cerebral, no-nonsense type. She wore her dark hair pulled straight back from a plain face that was rarely enhanced by makeup; her clothes were, if not necessarily frumpy, then merely functional. She was the plain Jane in contrast to Gisele's Euro-glamour. Yet, she hardly seemed intimidated by Anson's wife. Rather, I got the sense that she might find Gisele slightly vapid.

I focused my attention on our hostess, who was pointing out the eighteenth-century painting hanging on the far wall of the dining room.

"A gift from Anson for our thirty-fifth anniversary," she said, linking her arm through her husband's. "He spoils me."

"And you deserve it," he replied, gazing down at her with an affectionate smile.

They looked for all the world like a pair of contented lovebirds. She reached up on her tiptoes to plant a kiss on his cheek, and I, feeling uncomfortably like a voyeur, turned my attention elsewhere.

The focal point of the grand room was a massive antique table that looked as though it could easily seat twenty. It was set with elegant gold and cream china, polished silver, and delicate crystal. Overhead was a grand chandelier that matched the flickering sconces protruding from the walls around the room. All of the floor-to-ceiling windows were framed by heavy burgundy and gold draperies in a pattern that complemented the vast oriental rug covering most of the hardwood floor.

It was a lovely room, just as the drawing room had been. But I noticed that there was little sense of the homey atmosphere you might expect in the dwelling of a couple that had been married as long as Anson and Gisele. I couldn't help remembering what Sybil had said about Anson resigning himself to the fact that he would never have children, and wondered whether that might have made a difference.

I found myself seated between David's girlfriend, Rachel, and Tom Mason for the meal. Gisele was directly across from me, but Anson was at the far end of the table, so there was no opportunity to watch them interact. However, I did notice that Anson and David, who were next to each other, seemed to have an easy comraderie. They joked and laughed and teased each other comfortably.

"Isn't it nice that they have each other?" Rachel commented at one point as we finished our soup course—a delicious harvest vegetable bisque laced with cream.

I followed her gaze and saw that David was chattering in an animated manner with Anson, who was listening to him with obvious adoration.

"It's very nice," I agreed.

"Anson is like the dad David never had," she went on.

"Did he lose his own father, then?"

"Oh, no. Not really. His dad raised him and everything, if that's what you mean. But David says he was never really there for him. He was always working—they were very poor, and they lived in a run-down part of Brooklyn. Anyway, when his father was there, he was always preoccupied. He had lost almost his whole family in the Holocaust, along with all their money. I understand David's grandparents were fairly well off in Europe before that."

"That's a shame."

"Yes, it is. That's why this investigation committee is so important to David."

"Did his family lose their money through the Swiss banks?"

"I don't think so. David says that he has nothing to gain personally by opening the investigation. He just wants to see justice served. But you never know. Maybe he'll be able to track down some of his grandparents' lost fortune. It sure would come in handy."

"Why is that?" I half-expected her to tell me that she and David were planning to marry and start a family soon.

Instead, she confided, "He's planning on running for Congress next year. Hasn't he told you?"

"No, he hasn't. But then, I don't know him very well."

So he had political aspirations. That was an interesting revelation, I thought, glancing at David Berkman.

"I think he'd make an excellent congressman, don't you? He's so intelligent and charming, and he really cares about people. Look at the way he's taken care of Anson and Gisele for all these years."

"In what way?"

"He's always visiting them, making sure they're happy and healthy. He reminds Anson to have his blood pressure checked every few months—Anson has high blood pressure, did you know that?—and he keeps an eye on their Manhattan townhouse when they're up here in Bedford . . . You know. The kind of stuff a son does for his parents."

"What about his real parents?"

"They still live in Brooklyn. He sees them. But he's closer to Anson and Gisele. David has seven brothers and sisters, and I think he feels that he gets lost in the crowd at home. Here, he's an only child. Anson and Gisele adore him. They consider him their son. They even named him as their only heir and executor of their estate when they updated their will a few months ago."

"No kidding," I mused, grateful for Rachel's effusive nature.

As the black-tuxedoed servers brought in the salad course, I found myself eying David Berkman and wondering if there was a chance he wasn't as devoted to the Hubbards as he seemed. It was hard to believe that the seemingly earnest young lawyer could be up to something so devious, but then, I had learned—in my political career and in my part-time detective work—that appearances can be deceiving.

After dinner, Anson suggested that we all adjourn to the front parlor for brandy and dessert. As we made our way along the broad corridor, he leaned toward me and said in a low voice, "I would like to see you in my study for a few moments, Ed, if you wouldn't mind slipping away."

"Not at all," I agreed, and we fell behind the rest of the group, who were oohing and aahing over the pastries Gisele was describing, which would be served for dessert.

Anson led the way up the winding staircase in the foyer to an airy second floor hallway lined with beautifully framed artwork and closed doors. Opening one close to the top of the stairs, he stepped over the threshold, and I followed, trailed as usual by Ambrose and the rest of my security team.

By now, I knew better than to request that they all remain in the hallway, but I did ask that only Ambrose come inside. He had been with me the longest, and I trusted him implicitly.

Anson's study was as oversized, impeccably furnished and tastefully decorated as the rest of the house. There were large floor-to-ceiling windows running the length of the room, and they were left bare, with no window treatments to mar what must have been a spectacular view of the countryside in daylight. On the other three walls, all of them dark-paneled, were framed humanitarian awards he'd received, as well as black and white photographs documenting his long career.

I stepped closer to a familiar one and saw Anson and myself, years younger and posing at Democratic headquarters shortly after I won my first mayoral election.

"Remember that night, Ed?" he asked, following my gaze.

"Of course. Seems like yesterday."

"Not to me. I feel old lately, Ed," Anson commented, sounding somewhat wistful. He sat heavily in a big leather chair beside the fireplace and leaned his head back. "Old, and tired. Last night, I realized that I've already lived longer than my father did. He dropped dead in what seemed like the prime of his life, and never really got to enjoy himself. I'm wondering if I should run for reelection after all."

"It's a big decision, Anson. Not something you can decide overnight."

"I don't intend to. But with everything that happened this week . . . Well, it just got me thinking."

I nodded, then said, after a few moments of silence, "David told me about Georg Hadwin—that he's denying any knowledge of the paper-shredding incident."

"I expected as much."

"We can put pressure on his Association, Anson. We can bar official deposits in Swiss banks. We can withhold their operating licenses in this state."

"I know we can."

"And we will, if they refuse to cooperate with our investigation," I said, sitting in the chair opposite his. "There's too much at stake. Too many people are counting on us to restore what is rightfully theirs."

Anson nodded, but I sensed that something had changed in his attitude toward the cause. He had been fiery and outspoken about it only a few days ago. Now, he almost seemed—if not passive, then, at the very least, distracted.

"What's the matter, Anson?" I asked.

"It's nothing, Ed. I just . . . I get the feeling you were right about that shooting. That they meant for me to take that bullet."

"What makes you say that?"

"Partly it's a feeling I've got, and it's been growing over the past few days. I can almost sense something dark hanging over me. When I was driving on the Saw Mill today and that other driver started acting crazy . . ."

"It was no random incident of road rage, was it, Anson?"

"I don't think so, Ed. But I didn't want to say anything to the others about it. I don't want Gisele to start worrying every time I get behind the wheel."

"Did you get a look at the other driver?"

"No. I tried, but we were going too fast, and it was all I could do just to stay in control and keep my car on the road."

I told him about Zedekiah Gold, and my theory about the name being a clue that whoever had killed Kinsella was against the work that the committee was doing.

"It isn't hard to make that assumption, particularly with the initial protests from Seth Mandel's group, and now this paper-shredding incident," Anson said. "Ed, I know there's opposition to our investigation, but I never imagined that it would become violent. I never thought a man would lose his life because of it."

I thought of Bill Kinsella, of his sobbing young wife and fatherless daughter, and sorrow welled up inside of me. It wasn't right. It wasn't fair.

Yet, we couldn't stop what we were doing, and I told Anson just that.

"Oh, I realize that," he said quickly. "I'm not suggesting that we stop. I just want to be cautious as we move ahead. My trip to Switzerland this week—I want to take some extra steps to smooth the way for the investigation."

"Such as?"

"I'm going to bring Gisele with me, for one thing."

"You are?" That surprised me. I couldn't imagine his motive.

He nodded. "They love her in Switzerland. I don't know if you realize that. Her father discovered a vaccine to cure a deadly childhood disease—"

"Dobry's Syndrome," I supplied.

"That's right. So you know. Anyway, Hans's work saved thousands and thousands of children's lives. He became a national hero, and Gisele, as his daughter, was, quite naturally, the focus of considerable attention as she was growing up. Her father was a great philanthropist after he became wealthy, and that made the Swiss people love the Jurgen family even more. To this day, their name is on countless hospitals and clinics and charitable funds. So, having Gisele with me can't hurt."

"No, it can't. It's a very good idea, in fact," I said honestly.

"You should have seen the way they treated us when we spent a week in Zurich a few Christmases ago. Everywhere we went, we were mobbed by the press, and people stopped her to tell her how grateful they were for her family's good work."

"But does she want to go along with you this time, especially on such short notice?" I asked Anson.

"I've already discussed it with her, and she said of course she'll go. She understands that there are certain obligations when you're a politician's wife. And anyway, she always enjoys returning to her homeland. I haven't told her the real reason behind my request for her to go—she doesn't know that I believe my life is in danger because of the investigation. And I don't want her to find out."

"Why not?"

He shrugged. "If you were married, Ed, you might understand how it is. My wife—she worries about me. About everything. I don't want to put unnecessary stress on her if I can help it."

"Well, what other precautions did you have in mind?" I asked Anson.

"I've scheduled a meeting with Seth Mandel. I figured that if we could talk face-to-face, I'd have a better chance of making him see that what I'm doing will benefit all Jewish people. And that as much as I regret the anti-Semitic incidents that have taken place in Switzerland as a result, I don't think that I should stop the investigation, or turn it over to his group. With the backing of our Senate Banking commission, we have more power and credibility to get things accomplished."

"Of course we do."

"And as for Georg Hadwin," Anson went on, "I'm planning to meet with him as well. He needs to be aware that we won't stand for paper shredding or any other questionable action by his association. If they have no intention of allowing us full and complete access to the necessary paperwork, we'll have no choice but to retaliate."

I nodded my approval. "I know the governor will back us on any efforts to do that, Anson. He believes as strongly in this cause as we do."

He steepled his fingers and looked pensive. For a few moments, he said nothing. Then he told me, "I'm going to take your advice, Ed, and hire some extra security for while I'm over there. Nothing elaborate. I just don't want to leave myself open to anything."

"And you shouldn't," I agreed. "Don't worry about it, Anson. Everything is going to work out."

But I didn't feel nearly as confident as I sounded. Nor did I like the shadowed expression in his eyes, and it haunted me long after I had returned to Gracie Mansion late that evening.

SIX

On Sunday, I reluctantly agreed to join my parents for brunch at their favorite diner, which happens to be in the heart of their East Thirties neighborhood. They live in a big prewar building just off Lexington Avenue, where they've had the same neighbors for years. And just about every Sunday that they're in town, they eat at the diner, where they invariably order the same thing—scrambled eggs with lox and onions for Pop, challah French toast for Mom.

"After we're done eating," Mom said as we walked into the place, with my bodyguards right behind us, "we'll stop by and check on our apartment. I want to make sure Blanche isn't stealing my Spiegel catalogues, and check on the philodendron. Hopefully, it hasn't shriveled away."

I seized the opportunity to say, "Mom, you must really miss being home."

"Nah," she said, with a shrug and a wave of her hand.

"You think our place is any treat compared to living in Gracie Mansion?" Pop piped up—so loudly that several diners seated near the door turned and looked.

Of course, we were instantly recognized, and the nudges and whispering began.

"Don't be surprised if we never want to leave, Eddie," Mom said, winking at me. "We're getting very comfortable there."

I wisely decided not to say anything more about the subject for the time being, realizing that several people were eavesdropping.

The place was jammed, but we were quickly seated in a booth and given menus by a waitress in a pale blue uniform who greeted me with a cheerful, "Hello there, Ed!"

"How'm I doing?" I returned pleasantly, and she gave me a grin and a prompt, double thumbs-up.

"Who was that?" Pop wanted to know when she had walked away.

"What do you mean who was that? It was the waitress," my mother told him, shaking her head and shooting me a look that said, *Isn't he dense sometimes*?

"I know *that*, Joyce. But I thought Eddie knew her, the way they were talking and carrying on."

Carrying on? I shook my head and buried it in my menu.

"Lou, when are you going to realize that everyone in the world knows who our son is?" my mother asked proudly.

"Not everyone in the *world*," I protested, looking up.

"Everyone in the country, then."

I couldn't argue with that. I happen to be mayor of the most prominent city in America; wherever I travel, people certainly do seem to know who I am.

"And it's a damn shame that somebody out there wants Eddie dead," my father said, effectively putting a damper on the conversation.

"Pop," I said wearily, "I'm in politics. This kind of thing goes with the territory."

"But how many mayors are assassinated? Not many."

"I wasn't assassinated," I pointed out.

"You almost were," Mom said with a shudder. "Eddie, don't play down the situation. You're in grave danger." She turned to my bodyguards, who were assembled in various watchful positions around our booth, and asked Mohammed, who was standing the closest, "Isn't he in grave danger?"

Mohammed looked taken aback, and flashed an apologetic look at me as he said, "I don't necessarily think there's anything to be alarmed about right here and now, Mrs. Koch, but we are taking precautions to keep the Mayor safe."

"And so are we," Pop piped up. "That's why we're staying with you these days, Eddie, instead of playing pinochle by the cabana in Boca."

"I don't play pinochle," my mother protested.

"Well, you should, Joyce. I've told you over and over that we can use another player. Irving is always dropping out because of his bursitis, and—"

"*Anyway,*" I said loudly, "it really isn't necessary for the two of you to stay on at Gracie Mansion with me. I'm hardly ever home, and there's really nothing you can do that my security people aren't already taking care of."

"Every extra pair of eyes and ears helps in a situation like this, Eddie," Pop said.

"Exactly," Mom agreed. "You never know when the culprit might be lurking behind the next closed door."

"I think you've both been watching too many 'Murder, She Wrote' reruns," I said with a sigh. "Besides, it doesn't look good for you to be living with me."

"Well, it's only temporary," Mom said, as Pop asked, frowning, "Why doesn't it look good?"

"City taxpayers might not like the idea of anyone . . ." I searched for a tactful way to put it, but opted, as usual, to be quite necessarily blunt, "*freeloading* on city property."

"Freeloading? Us?" Pop looked indignant.

"We've been no trouble to anyone. We even brought all our own food with us, Eddie," my mother said. "But that grouchy chef of yours acts as though we're putting him out by using up some of his precious refrigerator space. The other day I caught him sniffing a Tupperware container of my homemade gefilte fish, making a face. I invited him to try some, but do you think he would? 'Taste just a little,' I said. 'If you don't like it, it won't kill you.' You'd think he'd want to be a little adventurous. He's a chef, after all."

"And your mother made a big pot of chicken soup and some blintzes last night," Pop put in. "She fed everyone on the staff."

"I think Esperanza really liked my matzo balls," Mom added modestly. "She said they were the best she's ever had."

I was fairly certain they were the only matzo balls Esperanza had ever had, but I didn't want to burst Mom's bubble.

And anyway, we were getting way off track again.

"My point is," I began, "that the two of you really should—"

"Ready to order?" the waitress asked, popping up again.

And I let the subject drop, figuring it might just be a lost cause.

But again, I realized, the sooner the killer was caught, the better . . . for everyone involved.

After stopping at my parents' apartment to account for my mother's Spiegel catalogues and the well-being of her philodendron, I parted ways with them. They had decided to join some friends for a card game at the nearby Senior Center, which was hardly my idea of fun. I had played cards with them and their cronies before, and the sessions would invariably end with somebody accusing somebody else of cheating, or with a player dropping out because of some physical ailment or other.

"But what are you going to do, Eddie?" Mom asked worriedly as we emerged onto Lexington Avenue in front of their building.

"I think I'll go downtown and check on *my* apartment," I decided. "I haven't been there in awhile."

When I became mayor, I was more than happy to move into the official residence. Gracie Mansion is a charming and beautiful place, a home suited to the mayor of the world's most important city.

But I'm no fool. I've had my apartment in the Village for years. It's in a great location, very affordable, and all of my most prized possessions are kept there, including my two Barcelona chairs and the brass bed I bought ages ago at a farm auction for nine dollars—a real steal. I always sleep better in that bed than anywhere else in the world.

Just as I do my best thinking in my apartment, which is, after all, truly my home. I like to spend weekends there whenever I can, but lately, I had been too busy to pay more than an occasional visit.

As soon as I got there, I opened the doors to the terrace and let the fresh air blow through. It was a warm, gray autumn afternoon with rain in the forecast; perfect weather for classical music and strong coffee. I put a CD on, made myself a cup of Martinson's, and settled back on my leather couch to contemplate the events of the past few days.

There was no doubt in my mind that both Seth Mandel and Georg Hadwin—or at least, some of their cronies—were suspects in the case.

Seth Mandel, as a member of the Jewish organization, made more sense simply based on the Hebrew alias that was used by the driver of the car. The man himself was in Switzerland when the shooting had occurred—Charley had checked on that for me. But that didn't mean he hadn't sent a colleague here to do his dirty work. The fact that the car had been obtained at a Kennedy airport rental agency seemed to support that theory. Most international flights coming into the New York area land at JFK.

But then, anyone already in the city who wanted to get lost in a crowd while renting a car would be wise to choose an agency out at one of the airports. Those places are busier than the others, and it stands to reason that the staff wouldn't pay as much personal attention to the customers as they would in a less crowded agency, say in midtown.

I considered the woman standing behind the suspect in line, and the fact that she believed he had dropped a rental slip from a Manhattan video store. That would seem to rule out the fact that the man was from out of the country—though he could, of course, have been a hit man hired by a foreigner. On the other hand, there was always the chance that the woman had been mistaken; that he hadn't dropped the receipt after all.

So Seth Mandel would remain a viable suspect.

Then there was Georg Hadwin—who was also accounted for during the time the murder had taken place. If he had masterminded the assassination attempt, he, too, had most likely used a hired hit man. It was hard to believe that a respected international banking organization could possibly be behind a murder, but the Association of Swiss Banks was clearly opposed to our investigation, which ostensibly gave them a motive.

Speaking of motives, I mused, what about David Berkman?

The lawyer might have been beloved by both the Senator and Mrs. Hubbard, and he might have been a respected attorney among

Manhattan's most high-powered professionals, but that didn't mean he wasn't capable of murder. I would have been hard-pressed to come up with a motive before last night. But something his girlfriend Rachel had said had set off warning bells in my mind.

David Berkman was heir to Anson Hubbard's fortune.

And he was planning to run for office.

What if he had targeted the Senator for assassination? Getting Anson out of the way would vacate his seat in the Senate, in addition to making David Berkman a wealthy man. He would have the financial means to run a campaign, and could fuel it with the common knowledge that he was the late senator's protégé.

Of course, if something happened to Anson, Gisele would ostensibly inherit his fortune before David would. But if she was as emotionally fragile as Sybil had claimed, it wouldn't be hard for David to get her out of the picture. Who would question it if she supposedly took her own life after losing her beloved husband?

I felt slightly sick at the thought of the polished young lawyer executing such a dastardly scheme. I had instinctively liked David Berkman from the moment I first met him. Yet I'm nothing if not jaded. Liking him wasn't enough to convince me of his innocence.

And what about Gisele? The woman was the picture of refinement, a devoted wife and genteel hostess. Yet her past was reportedly riddled with tragedy, due to her mother's mental instability. Her mother had tried to kill her father, according to Sybil, and had taken her own life. If that was true—and I had no way of knowing whether it was—then Gisele might have been left with severe emotional scars. Perhaps she had even inherited her mother's mental illness.

I realized my theory was farfetched. Just because the woman was high-strung didn't mean she had tried to kill her husband.

But someone did, I reminded myself. *And you must look at every possibility*.

So, assuming Gisele was behind the attempted murder—what possible motive could she have had? Pure blood lust, if she really was dangerously mentally ill. Then again, the car had been rented by a man. How likely was it that a psychotic wife who wanted to kill her husband merely for the sake of killing him would hire an accomplice?

If she was behind it, and had an accomplice, then she must have a legitimate motive.

I knew it couldn't be money. She was wealthy in her own right, thanks to her father's trust. She would never have to worry, with or without Anson being alive.

What if she caught Anson cheating on her? I wondered, turning to the most obvious motive. But I quickly dismissed it, based only on my gut instinct. Anson wasn't the kind of man who would cheat, period. I had known him for years. He was my friend. I believed wholeheartedly in his integrity.

As for Gisele . . .

What if she fell in love with another man and wanted Anson out of the way? Another obvious point of reasoning, and one that I had no way of proving or disproving from where I sat now.

I resolved to spend the next few days finding out whatever I could about both Gisele Jurgen Hubbard and David Berkman. It wouldn't be easy—I had a lot of official business going on, what with the threatened transit strike. But I fully expected things to die down a bit later in the week, as long as I managed to diffuse the strike—and I had every intention of doing so now, as I had in the past.

If I found myself with free time, I would use it to investigate all four suspects on my list . . . and perhaps to come up with others.

The meeting with the transit union leaders on Monday lasted all day and well into the evening. Still, in the end, it couldn't have gone more smoothly. I had managed to avoid both a substantial wage hike and the threat of a strike, and had pushed for several improvements that I had wanted to see for quite some time now.

I was humming when I returned to City Hall late that night to wrap up some loose ends and meet with my deputy mayors. We discussed the agenda for the upcoming week. My schedule had been left fairly open in case of a strike. It looked like I might have some time to look into the Hubbard case after all.

When the meeting had adjourned, I grabbed an apple from the kitchenette that's off my office and settled down at my desk to review the day's messages and notes from Maria. There were several minor calamities that would need to be addressed in the morning, I saw, as I flipped through the sheaf of memos.

A scaffolding collapse at a municipal building that was being painted in the Bronx had resulted in no injuries, thank God, but a woman below had been splashed with white paint, ruining her leather coat, and was threatening to sue the city.

A high-powered city real estate developer—whom I personally found abrasive and tyrannical—had applied for, and been denied, a tax exemption to build a new waterfront office and condominium complex in Brooklyn. He had scheduled a press conference for tomorrow and was claiming that I had seen to it that his application was refused by my Commissioner of Housing because he had campaigned on behalf of my opponent in the last election.

A fifteen-year-old drug addict had been killed in a gang-related shooting on the Lower East Side, and his mother, an innocent bystander, had been critically wounded.

One of my favorite restaurants had been cited by the Board of Health for three different violations. The owner had called, wanting to know if there was anything I could do to "fix things" before she lost all kinds of business.

And—in a thankfully happy ending—a little boy who had been missing for several days from his home in Stuyvesant Town, and feared kidnaped, had turned up alive and well in Washington, D.C. It seemed he had run away, sneaking onto the Metroliner and leaving town because his parents wouldn't let him have a pet boa constrictor.

Finally, mixed in with a stack of other telephone messages I would need to return, there was one from David Berkman.

I glanced at the clock to see whether it was too late to call him back now. It was past ten o'clock. Being anxious to find out what he wanted, I decided that was a fairly reasonable hour and dialed the home number he had left.

He answered on the first ring. "David Berkman speaking."

"David, Ed Koch, returning your call."

"Mr. Mayor—it's good to hear from you. I just saw on Fox News that you've managed to save us all from the MTA's threats. Congratulations. Nobody expected such a positive outcome, and so quickly."

"That's what I'm here for," I replied. "What can I do for you, David?"

"I'm actually calling about Anson."

"Is he all right? Did something happen?"

"I talked to him a short time ago. He's fine. Actually, he's busy packing his bags for the trip to Switzerland this week. But frankly, Mr. Mayor, I'm worried about him."

"Why is that?"

"He told you on Saturday night what happened the other day when he was driving on the Saw Mill Parkway, didn't he?"

"He mentioned that somebody cut him off," I said, deliberately vague.

"Somebody tried to force him off the road, Mr. Mayor. That's what happened. And if you ask me, it was no random incident. It had nothing to do with road rage, even if that does happen to be one of his latest causes."

"What do you think happened, then?"

"I think it's obvious that somebody's out to get him, Mr. Mayor. And I think it has to do with the work he's doing on the committee. I don't want to be an alarmist, but I'm wondering . . . maybe he should postpone his trip to Switzerland."

A warning bell went off in my head. David Berkman had been a major player in the establishment of the Senator's committee; he had come across as wholeheartedly committed to the cause. Yet now he was suggesting that Anson back out of an instrumental step in the investigation. Why?

Was it because he was genuinely concerned about Anson's well-being?

Or did he have another, more sinister reason for wanting to throw a hitch in the committee's progress?

What if he wanted Anson dead, and not just because of the fortune he would inherit and the senate seat that would be vacated? What if he had a reason for wanting to stop the committee's investigation?

But what could that possibly be? Everything I knew about him pointed to his being a man who had every reason to back the investigation. He was Jewish and took pride in his heritage; his own parents were concentration camp survivors who had been left penniless by the Holocaust, according to Anson. He would seem to have every reason in the world to want to see justice prevail.

"Did you mention your feelings to Anson?" I asked him, careful not to let on that I suspected anything might be amiss.

"Not straight out. I hinted that he might want to reschedule—but he simply wouldn't hear of it. He said that he can't appear to be backing down now. He's worked too long and too hard to make this investigation happen. And I understand that, Mr. Mayor. Really, I do. We've all put our hearts and souls into this cause. It's just . . . I'm worried about him."

It sounded like there was genuine concern and affection in his voice. And yet, I couldn't be absolutely sure.

"I'm sure Anson is capable of taking the necessary precautions to ensure his personal safety," I responded. "He'll be traveling with reliable security—"

"Even the best security in the world can't prevent some things from happening, Mr. Mayor," Berkman interrupted. "You should know that. Look at what happened when you were surrounded by your own bodyguards."

"You have a point," I agreed. "There are no guarantees. But backing down and going into hiding isn't always the best course of action to be taken."

I remembered something then. When I had talked with Anson and David Berkman last week about the possibility of Anson's life being in danger, Berkman hadn't exactly encouraged Anson to beef up the security at his estate. In fact, he had seemed to agree with Anson that added security would unnecessarily upset Gisele.

Now I found myself wondering who had initially established that particular concern. Had it been Berkman who had pointed it out to the Senator, in an effort to dissuade him from increasing his protection?

"I'm assuming you aren't going to get in touch with Anson and back me up on this, then?" David Berkman said now, sounding resigned.

"Is that why you called me?"

"Pretty much. I know you and he are old friends. He respects your opinions, Mr. Mayor. He would listen to you."

"Doesn't he respect your opinions? Doesn't he listen to you?"

"To a certain extent. But my influence only goes so far."

Or does it? I wondered.

Aloud, I said, "I've cautioned him to watch his step. There's nothing more I can do, short of driving up to Bedford and making him a prisoner in that fortress of his."

He sighed. "I guess you're right. I'm just worried. And then there's Gisele . . ."

"What about her?"

"She's going along to Europe with him. He thinks it will be good for publicity. After all, Switzerland is her homeland. Her father is a hero there . . ."

"So I've heard."

"But she's very . . . delicate. She's going to be alarmed by the extra security—"

There it was again, I thought.

"—And by the protestors, if they're hostile and decide to make things uncomfortable for the Senator's entourage."

"Are you referring to Seth Mandel's group?"

"Possibly. But they aren't the only ones who aren't happy with our investigation, as you know. There are plenty of Swiss citizens who resent what they see as an accusation of their government teaming with Hitler to conspire against the Jews during the war. They won't take kindly to Anson's presence."

"David, when you're in politics, there are always going to be people who don't take kindly to your presence. Wherever I go, I tend to meet with protests of some sort or another. People are always griping. The vast majority of them aren't threatening."

"And what about the few who are?"

I paused. "When you really believe in something, then you take your chances," was the best answer I could come up with. "You take your chances, and you hope that somebody's looking out for you."

"Well, I just hope somebody's looking out for Anson. He's already had two close calls. What if the third time, he's not so lucky?"

"Let's hope for the best," I said, telling myself that just because Berkman sounded worried, it didn't mean he was on the up and up.

"If there's no way I can talk Anson out of going to Zurich, then I think I'm going to have to go with him," Berkman said abruptly.

Startled, I echoed, "Go with him?"

"I have to, Mr. Mayor. If he went over there without me and something happened to him, I could never forgive myself."

"But what are you going to be able to do that a team of security people can't?" I asked him, careful to keep my voice neutral.

"I don't know. Just . . . keep an eye on things. And if, God forbid, anything happened to Anson, I could be there for Gisele. You just don't know her, Mr. Mayor. Losing him would be devastating for her."

"That's understandable," I murmured, and added something along the lines of, *the Hubbards are very lucky to have such a caring friend.*

"Oh, I'm more than a friend, Mr. Mayor. I'm the son they never had. And I love them like parents. It's up to me to look out for them."

Either he was a real gem, and Anson and Gisele were indeed lucky to have him in their lives . . .

Or they had been dangerously deceived by a clever con artist.

I would definitely be leaving David Berkman on my mental list of suspects—at least, for the time being. And with that in mind I wasn't at all comfortable with the thought of his accompanying the Senator and Gisele to Europe.

The problem was, Anson trusted him. He *did* love him like a son. How would he react if I warned him that David might be up to something?

Would he believe me?

Probably not.

Would he resent the very notion that his life might be in jeopardy at the hand of his adored protégé?

Probably.

I made a mental note to learn everything I could about David Berkman's past, and as soon as possible.

SEVEN

Tuesday was filled with meetings, press briefings, and handling the hundreds of details that can invade what was supposed to be a relatively low-profile day in the life of the mayor of the world's most high-profile city.

To cap off the afternoon, I met with several federal officials regarding the proposed nuclear plant in the Bronx. The project was ultimately moving forward slowly but surely, though the meeting was fraught with setbacks and potential problems that needed to be tended to.

By the time evening rolled around, I was anxious to go back to Gracie Mansion, put my feet up, and relax for the first time all day.

Instead, I had to change into a tuxedo and head downtown to the premiere of a new movie that had been filmed last spring in New York. It was a quirky, relatively low-budget "indie" film. But the director, who must have been all of twenty-seven, had gotten considerable press at a recent film festival, mostly due to the fact that he was reportedly dating a blond Hollywood bombshell who wasn't yet legally separated from her action hero hubby.

The theater, a grand old movie palace on Fourteenth Street, was mobbed with reporters hoping to snap a picture of the director with his rumored flame. But he had wisely shown up with his middle-aged, bespectacled mother instead, which left the press scrambling for replacement dirt. Being one of the few celebrities in the low-key crowd—and having filmed a cameo role in the movie—I drew my share of attention when I stepped out of my car surrounded by my ever-vigilant bodyguards.

"How'm I doin'?" I greeted them, and was met with heartening cheers.

As I paused to answer questions about my role in the movie, I heard someone holler, "Koch is trying to kill us all!"

Startled, I glanced up to see a long-haired young man on the fringes of the crowd, waving a sign that read BAN NUKES—SAVE LIVES. There were a few other people with him, all holding poster-boards bearing similar messages.

"Don't let Koch turn the Bronx into another Chernobyl!" yelled another voice in the group as my bodyguards closed in around me, their tension palpable.

"Do you have any response to these obvious protests to your support of the Bronx nuclear facility, Mr. Mayor?" asked a female reporter, shoving a microphone into my face.

"Of course I have a response," I said calmly. "My response is, there's just no way anyone with a reasonable amount of intelligence can logically compare what happened years ago at Chernobyl—a crudely built, antiquated facility, might I add—to the proposed New York City facility, which will of course be carefully constructed in accordance with modern Western standards."

"What about the dangers associated with nuclear energy plants in general?" another reporter wanted to know.

"What about the dangers associated with fossil fuels?" I fired back. "Think about recent oil spills, and the havoc wreaked on the environment. Think about the perils of coal-mining—and the environmental hazards associated with coal. And what about the economic implications of our growing dependence on foreign oil? The truth is, none of us can afford to ignore the fact that modern, standardized nuclear power plants are safe, relatively inexpensive, and efficient. They are the future of this country, regardless of the protests of radical activists who haven't even taken the responsibility of gathering all of the facts before spouting off criticism and ridiculous accusations."

As I spoke, the protesters had begun an irritating, deafening

"No Nukes" chant, and attempted to wave their signs in front of the television cameras.

"Mr. Mayor," another reporter began, but my bodyguards hustled me inside the theater, and I didn't argue.

I had learned long ago that there's no reasoning with radicals.

Besides, why take chances?

By now, I was almost entirely convinced that Anson, and not I, had been the target of the assassin's bullet. But then again, you never know . . .

I fell into bed after midnight and drifted immediately into a deep, dreamless sleep.

A knock on my door awakened me a few hours later.

It was one of my aides, bringing dire news.

Anson Hubbard had been shot and was in critical condition at Northern Westchester Medical Center.

My car arrived at the hospital precisely as the sun was coming up, streaking the October sky with shades of rose and gold. I couldn't help recalling the last sunrise I had seen—an equally glorious sunrise, about a week ago, from the windows of the Manhattan hospital where Bill Kinsella had died in the wee hours of the morning. I could only pray that this ordeal wouldn't end as tragically.

I hurried along the quiet corridors to the trauma unit with my bodyguards at my side, all of them appropriately wary, yet somber, over this tragic turn of events. I had been briefed on Anson's condition just before leaving Gracie Mansion an hour earlier. He had taken a bullet in the chest, and his condition was still unstable. I didn't even know the details of the shooting yet—only that it had occurred on the grounds of the Bedford estate, and that the gunman had evaded capture.

I was shown to a small waiting area near the trauma unit where Anson lay fighting for his life. The first person I saw when I entered the room was Gisele Hubbard. Actually, I had heard her from down the hall. She was alternately wailing and shrieking, demanding that she be allowed to see her husband "before it's too late."

"Are you acquainted with Mrs. Hubbard, Mr. Mayor?" asked a nurse who had been trying to comfort her.

"Yes, I am."

"Is there anything you can do to calm her down until her son comes back?"

"I'll try," I promised, and approached Gisele as the nurse scurried over to answer a ringing telephone on the wall.

I was fully conscious of the reference to "her son," and assumed that David Berkman must be around here someplace. I wondered whether he had presented himself as Anson's son, or if the hospital personnel had simply made that assumption.

Gisele Hubbard sat doubled over in a vinyl chair, rocking back and forth and weeping audibly. I noticed that she wore a silk nightgown and matching robe, with a short black fur jacket tossed over that. I remembered that Anson had once mentioned that his wife, with her fine European sense of style, was partial to furs despite the raging controversy over the slaughter of animals for the sake of fashion. He had told me that he'd asked her not to wear the few she owned to public engagements, out of deference to his political career, and she had always willingly complied.

"You don't know what a sacrifice it is to a woman like my wife, Ed," Anson had chuckled affectionately. "But she's always willing to do whatever it takes to keep my political standing favorable."

I put a hand on Gisele's arm.

"David?" she asked, the name almost a moan as it spilled from her lips. She kept her head buried in her hands, still rocking back and forth slightly, her shoulders visibly trembling.

"No, Gisele. It's me," I said gently.

She jumped and glanced up, clearly startled. Her big blue eyes were tear-filled and rimmed with dark smears of makeup, and her blond hair was disheveled.

"Oh, Ed," she wailed, "Someone's killed him! Someone's killed my Anson."

Startled, I looked over at the nurse, who had just hung up the telephone receiver. She shook her head and hurried back over, saying, "Mrs. Hubbard, your husband hasn't been killed. He's badly wounded, but the doctors are doing everything they can. You have to remain hopeful that he'll pull through."

"I . . . I'll try," she wept, sounding desolate. "He's my whole world. I need him desperately. Oh, Anson . . ."

I put an arm around her and tried to tell myself that this could be an act. That she could have pulled the trigger herself.

But, hard as I tried to be open-minded, that scenario just wasn't very believable. The woman seemed utterly distraught, and I was certain that on the occasions I had seen them together, I had witnessed true affection between Anson and Gisele. Accepting his wife as a suspect in his attempted murder just didn't feel natural.

Still, I told myself that she wasn't off the suspect list until I had good reason to remove her. And until now, there had been no evidence that she *wasn't* the would-be killer.

"Can you tell me exactly what happened to Anson?" I asked the nurse in a low voice, as Gisele buried her head in her lap again.

"I'm afraid I have to get back into the operating room, Mr. Mayor," she said apologetically, as she moved toward the doorway. "But here comes his son now. I'm sure he can tell you what happened."

I glanced up to see David Berkman coming down the hall. His stride was purposeful; his head bent as though he was lost in thought—or prayer. In his hands, he carried two Styrofoam cups.

He didn't glance up until he reached the doorway. When he did, he saw me standing there, and said, "Mr. Mayor. I'm glad you're here. I thought that notifying you was the right thing to do. Anson would have wanted you to know right away."

"Thank you for calling me," I said, studying his face. He looked pale and there were dark circles rimming his eyes behind his glasses. He wore a rumpled dress shirt and suit pants with suspenders, and the knot of his striped tie rode low on his chest.

"How is Gisele?" he asked softly, his gaze flicking to the woman who sat slumped in the nearby seat.

"She's obviously very upset," I replied. "Can you tell me exactly what happened? I want to know everything."

"In a minute, if you don't mind, Mr. Mayor," he said, and crossed the room to Anson's wife.

I watched as he sat in the chair next to her, put an arm around her, and gave her one of the Styrofoam cups.

"Drink it," he urged when she tried to protest. "It's camomile tea, and I put honey in, just the way you like it. It'll help you relax."

"How can I relax when Anson is just lying there with his chest ripped open?" she asked plaintively, and convulsed into sobs again.

David consoled her, stroking her hair and murmuring in her ear in a voice too low for me to hear. Whatever he said must have had an effect, because gradually Gisele's tears subsided and she lifted the cup of tea obediently to her lips.

"Will you be all right for a few moments while I step outside to have a talk with the Mayor?" I heard him ask her when she had taken a couple of swallows of tea and seemingly calmed down considerably.

"Don't go far away," was her reply.

He promised he wouldn't, then stood, and signaled me to join him in the hall outside the waiting room. It wasn't as eerily quiet and deserted as it had been when I'd arrived a short time ago. Doctors, nurses, and medical technicians bustled up and down, carts rattled by, phones rang, and the intercom crackled with pages.

We stepped far enough away from the doorway so that what we said wouldn't be overheard by anyone in the waiting room, standing in a secluded corner by the elevator. Ambrose positioned himself nearby, keeping an eye on things.

"Tell me everything," I told David again, standing so that I faced the wall. The last thing I wanted right now was to be recognized by anyone. I needed to focus entirely on Anson and what had happened to him.

"He was in his study after dinner, at about nine o'clock, sitting at his desk, when someone shot him from outside," David said simply. "The bullet came through a window and hit him in the back."

I remembered Anson's study—how the many large windows had been left stark and bare, with no blinds or draperies to shield the room from prying eyes that might lurk outside. At the time, I hadn't given it much thought.

Now, I wondered how Anson could possibly have been foolish enough to leave himself open to anyone who wanted to shoot at him from the trees that bordered his large piece of property.

"And the gunman got away?" I asked David Berkman flatly.

"The gunman got away," he confirmed. "Gisele did get a look at him, though. When she heard the shot and the breaking glass, she was in the back parlor on the first floor. She looked out and saw a figure running across the property."

"How did she see someone running outside if she was inside the house with the light on?" I mused, more to myself than to David.

He seemed to bristle. "She said she had just gone into the parlor and was about to turn on the light when it happened. The room was dark."

"I see."

I noticed that he was watching me, wearing a suspicious expression.

"Why," he asked, somewhat coldly, "would you even question something like that?"

I shrugged. "Second nature," I said unapologetically. "I'm used to questioning everything. When you tell me that someone looked out the window at night and saw something, I tell myself it might not be possible, if the light from the room were reflecting on the glass."

"There was no light in the room," he said again.

"I see," I said again, and asked, "Was she able to describe the figure?"

He hesitated only briefly before getting the conversation back on track, though there was still a slight chill in his voice. "She said that he was dressed in black from head to toe, and seemed to have been concealed behind a stand of tall lilac shrubs that sit in the middle of the clearing at the back of the house."

"She said it was a 'he'?" I questioned.

"Actually, she wasn't sure. She said that it might have been a woman, but that she doubted it."

"And why is that?"

"She didn't specify," Berkman told me. "But when you know Gisele as well as I do, you don't have to ask. She's an old-fashioned woman, Mr. Mayor. She has old-fashioned ideals. My guess is that she doesn't believe a woman would be capable of such a violent act."

"But you and I know that isn't necessarily true," I pointed out.

David Berkman shrugged. "I suppose we do," he allowed.

"What did Gisele do after seeing the gunman running away?"

"She screamed for help. She was hysterical. All of the servants had left for the night, except the housekeeper, Carla, who lives in. She's been with the Hubbards for years. She had already gone to bed in her room, which is located at the front of the house, up on the third floor. She gets up before dawn every morning, and she goes to sleep by eight every night to compensate."

I nodded impatiently. "So Gisele roused Carla . . ."

"She finally roused Carla with her screams as she ran up to Anson's study and found him lying there. The bullet had pierced his lung." David paused and bit down on his lip, seeming to need a moment to collect himself.

I watched, wondering if his emotion was real. It certainly seemed to be.

"Carla called 9-1-1 immediately," he went on, his voice less forceful, "and the police and emergency medical technicians came as quickly as they could. But as you know, the Hubbards' home is somewhat remote—"

"Somewhat?" I couldn't help snorting. "It's in the middle of nowhere."

"Exactly," David said. "So it took some time before help arrived. Gisele was hysterical in the interim, according to Carla. And Carla—she doesn't speak much English, but from what I gathered, she tried to perform CPR on Anson. Poor Gisele—I know she has CPR training—Anson insisted that they both take it a few years back, as part of an awareness campaign he was organizing for the state. But anyway, she was too far gone to think clearly enough to help him. The doctor I spoke with earlier told me that Carla might very well have saved his life." He let out a shuddering sigh. "We should get back to the waiting room and see if there's any update on his condition . . ."

"We will, in a minute," I said hurriedly. "Just tell me . . . when did you find out what had happened?"

"Gisele called me while they were waiting for the ambulance. Luckily, I was at home, packing. I was supposed to go out with Rachel last night, but I had a headache and I had canceled."

"You were packing? So you were planning to go to Switzerland with the Hubbards, then?"

He nodded. "As I told you, I just couldn't let them go off alone."

I didn't bother to point out that Anson and Gisele were a grown man and woman, and that they would hardly be alone, given the expected entourage of aides and security.

Instead, I asked, "And Gisele called you before help arrived? I thought you said she was hysterical."

"She was," he said, a chill creeping into his voice again. "I could barely understand what she was saying, other than, 'please, David, please come . . . we need you.' She just kept shrieking that over and over again."

"When did you get here?"

"In less than an hour, miraculously. I live on Park Avenue South. I got right into my car after hanging up with Gisele and drove straight up here to the hospital. They had taken Anson into surgery and were still trying to stabilize him the last I knew. Look, Mr. Mayor, with all due respect . . . I don't know why you're asking me so many questions. I don't—"

"I'm asking you questions because I want to find out what happened to my friend," I cut in. "The more information you can provide about what happened, the more likely that we can find out who did this to him."

"You don't think Gisele could have . . . ?"

"No, I really don't," I said hastily—partly because it was *almost* the truth, and partly because I didn't want to scare him off. I figured, the more he talked, the better.

Besides, if he thought I considered Gisele a possible suspect, he would realize that I considered him one, too.

It wasn't that either of them seemed particularly guilty, or anything as strong as a concrete clue. But I wasn't yet prepared to close any doors.

Bonnie showed up at the hospital by mid-morning, looking shaken.

"How is he?" she asked, standing in the doorway of the small waiting room where David, Gisele, my bodyguards, and I sat in brooding silence.

"They've stabilized him, but he hasn't regained consciousness yet," David told her. "The doctor said he'll let us know if anything changes."

"But how does it look? Where was he shot?"

"In the chest."

"Oh, my God." She sank into a chair, looking paler than usual. "Is he going to pull through?"

After glancing quickly at Gisele, David told her, "He's a strong old guy. If anyone can pull through, he will."

Bonnie nodded, furtively wiping at her cheeks. I saw faint trails of tears glistening there, and realized how upset she was. But when she spoke again, her voice sounded calm and straightforward.

"Why didn't anyone call to tell me what had happened?"

I didn't miss the look Bonnie flashed at Gisele and then at David, her tear-filled gray eyes appearing almost accusatory behind her thick horn-rimmed glasses.

When no one answered her question, she said, "I found out on the morning news, which I happened to turn on as I was getting ready to leave for the airport. I just . . . I can't believe it. What happened, exactly?"

"What did they say about it on the news?" David asked, as Gisele sat beside him in silence, apparently lost in her own faraway thoughts. I kept out of the conversation, prefering to observe the intriguing undercurrents in the room.

"They said that he was shot by a sniper at his house in Bedford. And that the gunman managed to escape. That was about all."

"That's about all we know," David said. He quickly repeated the basic details of what he had told me, tactfully leaving out the part about Gisele having been too distraught to perform CPR on her stricken husband.

As he spoke, Gisele began trembling again, and whimpered slightly. I realized she had tuned back in to the conversation. David turned to her, patted her arm, and murmured something soothing into her ear.

Bonnie turned to me. "What about the trip to Switzerland, Mr. Mayor?"

I blinked. "What about it?"

"It meant so much to Anson. He had waited so long to get the investigation underway. Any kind of delay could result in more months of negotiations with the Swiss government and the Association of Swiss Banks."

"That's true. But with Anson injured, and who knows how gravely . . ."

"You're not suggesting that we still go, are you, Bonnie?" David asked, frowning. "Because that would be—"

"Exactly what Anson would want us to do," she cut in. "He has worked too hard for us to just drop everything. And if we don't go, we'll be letting whoever shot him realize that they've succeeded."

"*If* stopping the investigation was the motive behind the whole thing," David specified. "We don't know that it is."

"What else would it be?" Bonnie asked.

Gisele spoke, her voice warbling and her fingers fluttering in her lap. "Why else would Anson have been shot? He's such a good man, such a decent man . . . what else could he possibly have done to anger somebody to this extent? I *told* him this was going to happen . . ."

"You did?" I asked when she trailed off, staring into space. "What made you think he was in danger, Gisele?"

"I don't know, exactly. But when I realized how complicated this whole thing was going to be, I told him he shouldn't get involved. I just knew something awful was going to happen."

"But how did you know?" I pressed.

"Because I was once a Swiss citizen, Ed. I know how things work over there. I know how the Swiss banks value their code of secrecy—it's why their clients trust them. And I know how the Swiss government prides itself on its neutrality. When you ask to go over there and invade private bank files, accusing the government of working with the Nazis to cheat the Holocaust victims out of their assets . . . you're just asking for trouble. I tried to tell Anson that, but he didn't want to listen. He just told me that I worry too much. And now . . . look at him . . ." Her voice broke and she buried her face in her hands.

"Shhh . . . it's all right, Gisele," David said softly. "There was nothing you could have done to stop Anson from pursuing a cause he believed in."

"Don't talk about him that way!" she protested shrilly, shoving his hand from her back. "Don't talk about him in the past tense, as if he were already dead! Don't do that, David. Just don't!"

"I'm sorry, Gisele," he said hastily. "I didn't mean to do that. I just—"

"You think he's going to die, don't you?" She was on her feet, pacing the room, her voice high-pitched and unnatural. "You think he's already dead, and they're not telling us. Don't you? Isn't that what you think?"

"Gisele, calm down," David said, standing and going to her.

She wrenched herself from his grasp and raked a manicured hand through her already disheveled blond hair, so that she wound up looking like Einstein. She bellowed, "Leave me alone, David!"

She kicked a chair, knocking it against the wall with a clatter.

"Gisele," David said, grabbing the chair before it could topple to the floor. "Relax. Calm down . . ."

"No!" she screamed, grabbing a handful of magazines from the table and throwing them on the floor. Her eyes were glazed and their expression was reckless, her behavior reminiscent of my three-year-old niece Schuyler, when she was having one of her notorious toddler tantrums.

"Gisele, you really do need to calm down," Bonnie echoed David matter-of-factly.

"Don't *you* tell me what to do! How dare you?"

Bonnie shrugged. She didn't seem particularly thrown by the woman's near-hysteria. Nor did David, though he was clearly more concerned about her than Bonnie was, as he tried to take hold of her and soothe her, though she kept squirming away.

I realized that the two of them must have witnessed scenes like this before. Was this what Sybil had meant when she had called Gisele unstable?

I reminded myself that the woman had been through a terrible trauma, and that anyone would be capable of behaving this way under the circumstances. But then I thought of Candy Kinsella, with whom I had sat in a similar waiting room under similar circumstances just a week ago. She had been distraught, yes—but not out of control the way Gisele seemed to be.

Still . . .

Different people react to stress in different ways, I told myself. Giselle's behavior wasn't necessarily suspicious or even unusual.

She was sobbing now, letting out great heaves and moving blindly around the room like an agitated animal in a cage. She picked up her fur jacket, which had been tossed over a chair, and hurled it to the floor.

"What's this doing here?" she asked shrilly. "We can't have this! Anson hates fur! Take this out of here!"

"You wore it here, Gisele," David reminded her gently.

"I never wear fur!"

"You were in a hurry to get to the hospital. You weren't thinking clearly. You must have just grabbed it out of the closet."

"No! No, it isn't mine!"

"Gisele . . ."

"No!" She was frantic.

David managed to grab hold of her shoulders and held her steady. She squirmed, but he grasped her firmly until she stopped struggling.

"It's going to be all right," he told her softly.

"No, it isn't. What if I lose Anson, David? My husband . . . he's my whole world . . . my whole world . . ."

"Is everything all right in here?"

We all looked up at the doorway to see the nurse who had been in the room earlier. She was looking at Gisele, her face full of concern. Then she shifted her gaze to the toppled chair, and the pile of magazines scattered all over the floor and the fur jacket discarded in a heap in one corner.

"Mrs. Hubbard is just very worried about her husband," David said, as Gisele buried her face in his shoulder and moaned. "I'm sure you can understand . . ."

"Of course. But if you'd like, I can see about giving her something to help with the anxiety," the nurse suggested.

"No!" Gisele protested, her voice rising in pitch and volume with every word she uttered. "You can't drug me up. You can't! I won't let you!"

The nurse looked taken aback and said apologetically, "That isn't what I—"

"Get out of here!" Gisele commanded. "Just go. Why are you here? You're supposed to be taking care of my husband. Oh, Anson . . . Oh, Anson . . . don't die on me . . ."

Her voice had faded to a near whisper now, and I could see her trembling all over as she leaned into David.

"Is there any word on Anson's condition?" I asked the rattled nurse.

"I'm not sure, Mr. Mayor. But I'll go check and I'll come back if there's been any change," she offered, and swiftly left the room, obviously glad for a reason to escape.

I settled back in my chair and saw that David and Giselle were once again seated side by side. She was clutching his hand, and even from here, I could see her white knuckles.

Meanwhile, Bonnie sat quietly apart from them, a contemplative expression on her plain-Jane face.

I thought about what she had said—how the trip to Switzerland shouldn't be cancelled because of what had happened. I found myself wondering if she was right.

But if Anson didn't go . . .

Who would take his place?

"It should be you, Mr. Mayor."

I lifted my eyebrows at Bonnie, who sat across from me in the hospital cafeteria, half-heartedly nibbling on a tuna sandwich.

"Me?" I asked, as if I had never heard of such a preposterous idea.

Actually, though, it was something that had already crossed my mind. It wasn't that I was anxious to go jetting off to Switzerland on short notice to do a job that would be complicated at best, dangerous at worst.

However, Anson was someone I greatly respected, and so was the cause. I knew that whoever replaced him on the journey to Switzerland—*if* anyone replaced him—would have to be competent, close to the cause, and preferably high profile enough to be taken seriously.

I certainly fit the bill.

"You certainly fit the bill, Mr. Mayor."

What did I tell you?

Bonnie took a sip of her soda before adding, "I know you're busy. You must be *beyond* busy. And to drop everything and leave the country—"

"Something like that isn't easily done, Bonnie," I confirmed, and spooned some lukewarm vegetable soup from the paper bowl into my mouth.

"But is it impossible?" she wanted to know.

"Impossible?" I contemplated that. "Probably not."

My week wasn't as full as it might normally be, since I had deliberately left my schedule relatively free in case of the transit strike. But that had been successfully averted. There was a mountain of paperwork waiting in my office, as usual. But paperwork could be done on a plane. Lord knew there would be plenty of time on an international flight.

"I know Anson would want you to go in his place, Mr. Mayor," Bonnie said.

I didn't doubt that she was right. Still . . .

"You owe it to him. And to everyone who was counting on his committee to uncover the truth."

Something clicked in my brain. I thought of Anson, lying unconscious and critically wounded in his hospital bed upstairs.

I thought of the thousands of Jews who had seen disaster coming and had entrusted the Swiss banks with every penny they had in the world, only to see it all vanish somehow in the aftermath.

I thought of the nameless, faceless gunman who had twice tried to stop Anson from taking the trip and launching the investigation.

And I set down my plastic spoon and nodded.

"I'll go," I told Bonnie. "If I can possibly arrange it, I'll go."

She broke into a smile that made her surprisingly attractive. "Anson would be so pleased," she said softly. Then she burst out, "Oh, Mr. Mayor, do you think he's going to make it?"

I wanted to tell her that of course he would make it. But I don't like to lie if I can help it and it wasn't necessary to lie now.

"I don't know, Bonnie," I said somberly.

We both knew that Gisele and David were consulting with the

doctors even as we spoke. They had been summoned from the waiting room by a nurse whose expression revealed nothing.

Gisele had immediately convulsed into hysterical sobbing, convinced she was about to be told that her husband was dead. The nurse told her that wasn't the case, but would reveal nothing more.

So here Bonnie and I sat in the crowded cafeteria, eating mediocre food and making decisions that needed to be made.

"We'll have to fly out tomorrow," she told me, her professional decorum having been restored. "I can make the arrangements. You won't even have to miss anything. Anson didn't have any meetings scheduled until the end of the week. He wanted a day or so to settle in there. And of course you won't have to stay the entire week, as he had planned to. He and Giselle were going to tack on some time for sight-seeing after taking care of official business. You can be back in New York by early next week."

I nodded. "That would be fine . . . *if* I can arrange to get away, Bonnie. I'm going to do my best."

"Nobody would expect anything less from you, Mr. Mayor," she said with a smile.

"Eddie, is it true?"

"Are you really going to Switzerland in the morning?"

My parents, clad in their pajamas, robes, and slippers, pounced on me the moment I walked into Gracie Mansion that night. I was bone-weary from a long afternoon and evening of tying up loose ends and rearranging my schedule.

Luckily, that daunting chore hadn't been as complicated as I had thought it might be. It turned out that my deputy mayors would be able to step in and cover for me at various meetings and events, none of them of earth-shattering importance.

Meanwhile, I would be bringing piles of backed-up paperwork with me—paperwork that isn't easily attended to when I'm in my office, being interrupted all day. So in one way, the trip would allow me to accomplish more work than usual.

"Yes, it's true—I'm going to Switzerland," I told my parents, who followed me from the coat closet, where I hurriedly hung my rain-dampened trench coat, into my study, where I turned on the light and eyed the daunting pile of documents on my desk, awaiting my perusal and signature. These, too, would need to be packed up and brought along to be worked on during the long plane trip.

"And we had to hear about it on the ten o'clock news?" My mother shook her head. "Eddie, that's not right. A son should tell his mother when he's leaving the country. Shouldn't he, Lou?"

"This isn't a cover plan, is it?" Pop wanted to know.

"A cover plan?"

"You know what I mean." He winked at me. "You're not really planning to go into hiding instead of going to Europe, are you?"

"Pop—"

"Eh-eh-eh . . . Never mind," he cut me off, holding out a hand. "I don't need to know. It's safer for both of us if you don't tell me. You should keep your plan to yourself, the way they probably told you to."

I didn't bother to wonder who "they" were. Instead, I began sorting and loading the stacks of papers into my briefcase.

"Eddie, how is the Senator doing?" my mother asked worriedly. "The last thing we heard on the news, the poor man was still in critical condition."

"That was the last thing I heard, too," I told her. I had been in contact with the hospital just before leaving my office to come home.

Anson was still unconscious, but he was expected to pull through, thank God. There had been considerable damage from the bullet, so his prognosis wasn't yet clear and wouldn't be for quite some time.

"I'm so worried about you, Eddie," Mom fretted. "All this shooting . . . and now you're going to be taking Anson Hubbard's place on this trip to Switzerland. You have to be careful over there."

"Of course I'll be careful, Mom. I'm no fool. I won't be taking any chances. After all, eight million people are counting on me to come back safely and run their city."

I had said virtually the same thing to Jim, my security chief, this afternoon. He had been understandably reluctant to have me take the trip. My security would be at an all-time high, and I felt confident in my bodyguards' ability to keep me as safe as they possibly could.

Of course, in the back of my mind was the knowledge that someone—or maybe a group of someones—wanted to put a halt to the investigation, and had already resorted to violent measures to do just that.

They had effectively stopped Anson.

Would they now try to stop me?

"Make sure you pack a bullet-proof vest, Eddie," Pop advised.

"And some long underwear," Mom put in. "It's cold in Switzerland."

"You should bring a pistol for your own protection. Do you have a pistol, Eddie?" Pop asked.

Mom talked right over him. "And remember to bring some aspirin along. I always do when I'm travelling. Aspirin is good, in case you get a headache."

"I think I need some now," I muttered, snapping my briefcase closed.

"And I'm going to give you that little tape recorder I always take with me when I'm traveling," my mother went on. "It's a wonderful way to keep a travel diary."

"A travel diary? I'm going on business, Mom, and besides—"

"That doesn't mean you won't be seeing beautiful sights in Switzerland, Eddie. You should describe them into the tape recorder so you won't forget them. I know you. You won't carry a journal along and write down your impressions."

"A journal? Impressions? He's not going on a pleasure trip, Joyce!" my father announced. "He's involved in a dangerous situation. He's been shot at."

"I haven't—"

"I know he's been shot at. Do you think I want him to go?" Mom demanded, wringing her hands.

"Listen, I don't want you two to sit around worrying while I'm gone," I said reasonably. "Why don't you head down to Boca? Relaxing in the sun will probably do you some good."

"I should lie in the sun while my son is being shot at?" Mom shook her head resolutely. "Absolutely not, Eddie."

"We'll stay put in New York," Pop agreed. "We'll be waiting for you when you get back. But I think we'll go back home as long as you're not going to be around Gracie Mansion for a while."

Hallelujah, I thought.

Mom nodded vigorously in agreement with Pop. "We really should go home if you won't be needing us. I miss the flame on my gas stove. The flame here is just too unpredictable. I scorched the blintzes this morning."

"They were like charred black boomerangs," Pop told me.

Mom punched him in the arm. "Lou! How could you say such a thing?"

"You were the one who said it," he said, rubbing his arm.

"I said I scorched them. I didn't say they were charred black boomerangs. What a thing to say!"

"Good night," I said, giving Mom a kiss on her cheek. She barely noticed.

I shook Pop's hand. He didn't notice, either.

And I went upstairs to bed, leaving them arguing about the blintzes.

EIGHT

As traffic was light and the hour was early, I arrived at JFK airport the next morning with plenty of time to spare before my flight.

The press was waiting, of course.

"Mr. Mayor, are you afraid to make this trip?"

"Mr. Mayor, are you hoping, through this investigation, to recover lost gold belonging to your own family?"

"How will you react if you're attacked as Senator Hubbard has been?"

I was bombarded with these ridiculous questions and plenty of others the moment I stepped out of my car. Luckily, my bodyguards hustled me straight into the terminal, and I didn't have to waste my time trying to answer.

In the private lounge, I settled down with a mediocre cup of coffee and the morning papers to wait until it was time to board the flight. Bonnie hadn't arrived yet, although a few other members of Anson's entourage were milling around.

Byron Klein, the respected news journalist whom Anson had assigned to travel with the group and cover the proceedings, arrived shortly after I did. I've met him on numerous occasions and we've always gotten along well. In fact, I gave him an exclusive interview during my last reelection campaign, knowing he can always be trusted to report the facts in a straightforward, nonsensational way.

"It's good to see you here, sir," he said, making his way over to me. "Are you looking forward to the trip?"

"I always enjoy travelling," I said truthfully, since "looking forward to the trip" was, under the circumstances, stretching it a bit.

"Have you ever been to Switzerland?"

"A few times," I told him. "It's a beautiful place."

"I've never been there, and I'm afraid I don't know much about it. The Swiss make fine watches and fine chocolate," he said with a grin. "That's about the extent of my expertise on the country."

"There's considerably more to it than that," I said with a smile. "Although I can vouch for both the watches and the chocolate."

"Can I interview you briefly about your objectives for the trip, sir?"

I was about to oblige when I saw, out of the corner of my eye, a familiar figure sweeping into the lounge.

My jaw must have dropped, because Byron Klein said, "What? What is it?" and turned his head to follow my gaze.

"What's *she* doing here?" he asked.

I shook my head and watched as Gisele Hubbard, wearing a pair of dark glasses, stopped in front of a chair across the room, shrugged out of her long designer coat, and adjusted the jacket of the smart pink and black suit she was wearing. She took off the glasses, reached into her leather handbag, pulled out a compact, and snapped it open to check her lipstick. Frowning slightly and pursing her lips, she pulled out a small tube of lipstick and ran the stuff lightly over her already-perfectly-pink mouth.

That accomplished, she glanced up, spotted us, and waved. There was nothing jaunty or upbeat about the gesture. She looked weary as she made her way across the lounge, her shoulders slumped and her pace somewhat halting.

"Is she coming on the trip?" Byron asked me in a low voice.

"Apparently," was all I could think to reply before Gisele arrived a few feet away.

At this proximity, I could see that her eyes were red-rimmed and deeply trenched in dark shadows, as though she had done her share of crying and not sleeping during the past few days. The blusher on her cheeks seemed unnaturally bright against her pale skin, and there was an aura of sadness about her, even when she smiled faintly and greeted us.

"How is Anson, Giselle?" I asked before allowing myself to even think about anything else.

"He's stable."

"Has he come to?"

"No, he's still unconscious. There's no telling how long he'll be out. But the doctors say he'll make it," she said, her voice trembling slightly. "I sat with him most of the night. David is there now."

"That's good," I responded, for lack of anything else to say.

My mind was racing. What was she doing here? How could she be planning to proceed with this trip when her husband lay seriously injured in a hospital bed?

"You're probably wondering what I'm doing here," she said, as though she had read my thoughts.

"Obviously, you're going to fly to Switzerland as planned," Byron said.

She nodded. "Some people might think that I would be better off staying at Anson's bedside right now. They might think that's where I belong. But those people simply don't know me, and they don't know Anson. My husband would want me to stand in for him in his absence . . . don't you agree, Ed?"

"I'm sure he would," I said, not about to argue.

After all, maybe she was right. Who was I to judge?

"David has promised to stay by Anson's side night and day," she went on. "And the doctors assured me that there's very little I can do while he's unconscious. He might not wake up for days. But if anything changes, I will be contacted and I can fly right back to him."

Both Byron and I nodded. I wondered if she was trying to convince us, or herself, that she was doing the right thing.

"It's been so hard," she said softly, her mood shifting abruptly. "Seeing him lying there like that, just lying there . . ."

It occurred to me then that her motives might not be as noble as she wanted us to believe. After all, she was a fragile woman; a woman who was prone to anxiety and hysteria.

How difficult it would be for anyone—especially a woman like

Gisele Hubbard—to keep a vigil at the bedside of a critically injured spouse.

And how simple it would be for her to find an out, an escape—a way to avoid the long, sad hours spent just watching, and waiting.

Going to Switzerland would give her a reprieve, I realized. It was her homeland, a familiar, beloved place where she was reportedly adored by the masses. Perhaps she needed that distraction right now, at the darkest time in her life.

I might not behave the same way in her shoes, but I could understand where she was coming from, if that was actually her reasoning.

Then again, perhaps, I felt compelled to remind myself, she was making the trip for another reason. A darker, more complicated reason.

I looked into her blue eyes, wondering if the woman could possibly be capable of trying to kill a husband she professed to love—a husband who so obviously adored her. And for what possible reason?

She had been born in Switzerland; had spent a good part of her childhood there. What if she was secretly opposed to Anson's investigation because of her loyalty to her homeland? What if her resentment had built up until she exploded in violence against him?

It wasn't hard to believe that a woman as emotionally unstable as she seemed—and with her family history, if what Sybil had said was true—would be capable of erratic, even dangerous behavior.

What didn't make sense to me was that she had seemed truly distraught at the hospital yesterday. I got the sense that she really was frantic over Anson's condition—and that she genuinely loved him.

I could be wrong . . .

But when I'm listening to my gut instinct, I very rarely am.

Besides, I recalled Anson telling me, way back when he first proposed the investigation into the missing funds, that Gisele was fully backing him on it, the way she stood behind him in support of everything else involving his career. She had agreed that he needed a noble cause to boost his standings in the polls. And I remembered him joking that she was hoping they would have a good excuse to spend some extended time in Switzerland.

"Sometimes she gets homesick," he had said fondly. "And with my schedule, we don't have a lot of spare time to travel all the way to Europe very often."

"You must be looking forward to being in Switzerland again," I commented to her now, and she shrugged.

"It's always good to go there," she said, "but like this . . . leaving Anson behind . . . this isn't going to be an ideal visit. Far from it."

"Anson would be proud of you for carrying on, Gisele," Byron commented.

"And when he recovers, the two of you can plan a pleasure trip," I added, watching her carefully.

She brightened. "That would be wonderful. It's not that I mind going places on official business, but we very rarely get to take vacations. The last one was over a year ago, when we went on that Alaskan cruise. It wasn't my first choice for a destination, but David assured us we would love it, and he was right. He usually is."

Her comment triggered an arresting thought. I wondered whether David, who clearly wielded tremendous influence over the Hubbards, was the one who had talked her into making this trip to Zurich.

If he was behind the murder attempt, then his motives for sending Gisele to Switzerland could be twofold.

First, he could have an accomplice travelling to Switzerland or already in place there, ready to eliminate her as the other heir to Anson's fortune.

And—the realization chilled me to the bone—he had gotten her out of the way so that he could make sure Anson didn't survive his devastating chest wound.

What was it Gisele had said only minutes ago?

David has promised to stay by Anson's side night and day.

Suddenly, those words seemed ominous.

But there was little I could do. I could hardly tell Gisele that I considered David a possible suspect in the murder attempt. Knowing how she felt about him, she would undoubtedly be outraged, and might very well tip him off. Besides, she, too, was on my list of possible culprits. The last thing I wanted to do was alert her that I was conducting a private investigation.

I thought of my friend Anson, lying helpless in his hospital bed with the man he loved like a son keeping watch over him. I could only hope that David was innocent, and that his presence there was supportive, and not lethal. But there was no way of knowing for certain until the case was solved.

Even if David and Gisele were both innocent, there was still someone out there who had desperately tried to stop the investigation. Someone who was willing to kill in order to achieve that goal.

Now I was flying right into the thick of the storm, quite possibly putting my own life in danger. It wasn't a new realization, and I wasn't about to back down. That had never been my style. I firmly believed that the investigation needed to be launched in a no-nonsense way, no matter what daunting setbacks had transpired over the past week.

Still, I couldn't help wondering what, besides fine watches and fine chocolate, I would encounter on this journey to Switzerland.

"Ladies and gentlemen," came a voice over the public address system. "Flight 502 to Zurich will begin boarding in just a few moments."

"Here we go," Gisele said somewhat shakily, as she turned to me with a slight, nervous smile.

"Here we go," I echoed, feeling a surge of trepidation.

What was I getting myself into?

I couldn't help noticing, after we had boarded, that Gisele asked the flight attendant for a glass of water. When it came, she reached into her purse, removed a small orange plastic prescription bottle, and furtively popped a pill into her mouth, swallowing it with a large gulp of water.

Watching her out of the corner of my eye, I wondered idly what it was that she had taken, and why.

Bonnie Tyson showed up on the plane shortly before takeoff, slightly out of breath and looking a bit frazzled. As she settled into her assigned seat—which was right beside mine—she told me that she had gone to the hospital to visit Anson before leaving for the airport.

"That's considerably out of your way, isn't it?" I asked, impressed by her loyalty to the senator.

She shrugged. "Not so bad. I live in lower Westchester—in Larchmont."

"My sister lives in that area," I commented. "It's very nice."

I didn't add that it was far too suburban and out of the way for my taste.

"It *is* nice," Bonnie agreed. "I grew up there. But on my salary, I can't afford anything more than a tiny apartment. And if they raise my rent next year the way the landlord is threatening to do, I'll have to move someplace else."

"Or make Anson give you a big raise," I said, deliberately making the comforting assumption that the senator would be around to do that.

She shrugged. "I didn't get into this business for the money. It's just that it's not easy for a single woman to survive in this area at my income level."

"How was Anson?" I asked, not particularly comfortable with the subject of money—or a lack thereof.

"No change. He's still in a coma. David was with him—"

"Ladies and gentlemen," the flight attendant's voice cut into our conversation. "In preparation for takeoff, please make sure that your seatbelts are fastened tightly around your waist and that your tray tables and seats are in their upright position . . ."

Both Bonnie and I were silent for several moments as we listened to the airline's usual safety spiel.

Then, as the plane was taxiing out to the runway, she spoke again, although her eyes had a faraway expression and she seemed almost to be talking to herself.

"He looked so pale," she said, shaking her head. "So helpless. Not like Anson at all. He's always been so full of life . . ."

"I know," I murmured sympathetically.

"I held his hand and I told him to hang in there, to fight. I told him that a lot of people were counting on him to pull through this."

"It was good that you did that," I told her. "You never know what people are aware of when they're supposedly unconscious. He might have known you were there."

"Do you think so? I just couldn't stand the thought of going off to Europe without seeing him, just in case . . ." She trailed off.

But I knew the rest.

Just in case something happens to him while we're gone.

"David looked like hell, and he hadn't eaten anything in almost twenty-four hours," Bonnie went on then. "I felt sorry for him. I offered to stay at Anson's bedside while he went down to the cafeteria to get some coffee and a bagel. That's why I'm so late. I just didn't want Anson lying there alone for any amount of time if I could help it."

With that, she shot a glance across the aisle at Gisele, who sat in the window seat with an empty space next to her. Her head was tilted back and her eyes closed behind the dark glasses. It was impossible to tell whether she was asleep or merely resting.

I knew what Bonnie was thinking. It was clear by her expression and her tone that she didn't think Gisele should be making the trip under these circumstances.

"David said he promised Gisele he would stay with Anson and let her know if anything changes while she's gone," Bonnie commented, still sounding disapproving.

"That's what she told me," I said cautiously, not wanting to be perceived as taking sides. "She feels that she can be more useful making the trip on his behalf than she would be sitting in the hospital."

Bonnie's mouth tightened into a tight line, and she said, "Well, that's one way of looking at things."

"What's another way?" I couldn't resist asking.

"That she can't take the strain of being there," she replied in a low voice that couldn't be overheard. "She's not strong enough to go through the emotional trauma of seeing him like that. Leaving the country is the ideal escape for her."

Which was exactly the scenario I had already considered—not that I told Bonnie so now. I wasn't ready to trust anybody involved in this thing—not even the Senator's longtime aide, who had always struck me as completely loyal to Anson and his cause.

Now, though, as I watched Bonnie shoot another glance across the aisle at Gisele, I wondered if I had overlooked her as a possible suspect.

It seemed farfetched, to be certain . . .

But not entirely out of the question. I simply couldn't afford to rule anybody out until I had more information.

If Bonnie was the killer, I speculated as the plane careened down the runway, what possible motive could she have?

She could, of course, be opposed to the Swiss bank investigation . . . but on what grounds? She didn't have anything personal at stake, and she had certainly never given the slightest hint of being anything less than supportive of the cause in all the time we had worked to get it off the ground.

No, I suspected that if she was the culprit, her motives weren't political.

We were taking off now, the plane's nose lifting easily off the runway as we banked up into the bright blue October sky and out over the water.

Anyway, my thoughts proceeded, Bonnie had been with the Senator for many years, long before he had ever considered backing this particular investigation—far too long for her to be a deliberate plant.

But what if somebody opposed to the cause had gotten to her? What if somebody had taken advantage of her access to the Senator, and bribed her?

Hadn't she just mentioned financial difficulties? How desperate was she? How weak of character?

I had to admit that even though I didn't know her very well at all, the idea that Bonnie Tyson would deliberately harm the Senator—and strictly for money—seemed more than a little preposterous.

But what other possible motive could she have?

"What's the matter, Mr. Mayor?" she asked suddenly, and I realized I had been staring off into space, contemplating the situation.

I started and shook my head, telling her, "Nothing's the matter. Nothing at all."

"You looked troubled."

"I was just thinking about Anson," I told her. "Just wondering who could have done such a terrible thing to such a good man."

"I keep wondering the same thing myself," she said, shaking her head grimly. "But maybe we'll never know."

I nodded, then changed the subject, standing and pulling my bulging briefcase from the overhead bin. "I hope you won't mind if I settle in and get some work done," I said, sitting again and snapping it open to remove a stack of papers.

"Not at all. I usually sleep on planes anyway."

She leaned back and closed her eyes, her posture identical to that of Gisele, who appeared to have fallen asleep across the aisle.

I resolved to put my suspicions out of my head for the time being.

But as I opened the first document that would require my signature, I found myself thinking again of Anson in the hospital, with David at his side.

Are you in greater danger with him there? I silently asked my friend. *Or can you trust him the way you think you can? Can you trust anyone? Your wife? Your longtime aide?*

There was no way of knowing.

And I had an idea that the case would only grow more complicated once we arrived in Zurich.

The airport in Zurich was, predictably, crowded with members of the press. As our entourage made its way through the rather sterile and efficient terminal, we were dogged by photographers and questions—many of them addressed to me, and having to do with our committee's investigation.

None were particularly provocative, and I answered them willingly, fumbling for the right words a few times as I replied in whatever language the questions had been posed in. Luckily, most people in Swizterland speak German, a language I happen to understand and speak fairly well. However, the Allemanic Schwyzertutsch dialect makes the German language spoken in Swizterland somewhat difficult to comprehend at times, and I occasionally had to rely on an interpreter.

I couldn't help noticing that quite a few cameras were aimed solely in Gisele's direction, and that she, too, had the considerable focus of both the press and the Swiss citizens and other travellers along our route to the main terminal.

She had slept throughout most of the flight despite some severe turbulence at one point, leading me to believe that the pill she had swallowed before takeoff might very well have been a sedative. Nothing unusual about that, I told myself. Many people are nervous fliers. Besides, she had been through a terrible time these past few days.

Now, though, as we strode through the airport amidst the clamoring press, Gisele seemed fully alert; even perky. She smiled and waved and posed graciously for photos, her expression sobering only when she was asked about her husband's condition.

"He's doing as well as can be expected," she replied in flawless Schwyzertutsch, her voice trembling slightly and her expression concealed behind the dark glasses she still wore. "I appreciate your concern and ask for your prayers to ensure a quick and total recovery for my husband."

Several cars were waiting to transport us from the airport to our hotel overlooking the Limmat River, which runs through the city. I found myself riding alone with my team of bodyguards, all of whom seemed particularly tense and alert.

I, too, had felt an undercurrent of apprehension since I had stepped off the plane. It wasn't as though I had spotted a shady character slinking toward me in the terminal or been the target of shouted threats from the crowd. But I couldn't shake my uneasiness, or the sense that I wasn't entirely safe here.

We rode through the picturesque old city en route to the hotel, and I tried to shake the aura of foreboding as I took in the scenery. I hadn't been to Switzerland in years, but I was happy to see that Zurich's charm hadn't diminished. Once we got past the outlying district, with its industrial buildings and warehouses, we were in the more picturesque part of the city with its old world architecture. Through the windows of the car, I gazed at the clusters of church spires, the historic town squares, the quaint houses lining winding cobblestone lanes. There were beautiful bridges spanning the river, and quaint little nooks everywhere you looked, and small shops with painted wooden signs proclaiming chocolatiers and watchmakers.

"This place is pretty different from home, isn't it, sir?" Tony, one of my bodyguards, commented. "The air feels so pure here, and everything seems so much cleaner than in New York."

"Zurich is a remarkably clean city," I agreed. "It's also a heck of a lot smaller than New York." Litter happens to be one of my mayoral pet peeves, and I've done quite a bit to clean up the streets back home, if I do say so myself.

"Look at that view of the mountains," Ambrose added, craning his neck to look up at the rugged white peaks that formed a backdrop to the city. "Wow. What would it be like to wake up in a place like this every day?"

I shrugged and reminded him, "Travellers from all over the world come to New York and wonder the same thing. We've got it all right there. And notice that Zurich has no skyline to speak of."

Lou Sabatino grinned. "You can take the mayor out of New York . . ."

"But you can't take the New York out of the mayor," Ambrose concluded with a smile. "But don't worry. We wouldn't expect you to waver in your loyalty to the Big Apple, Mr. Mayor."

"Why would I? I've been all over the world, and as much as I can appreciate other places, I'm always glad to get back home to New York again."

This trip would be no exception—and this time, I reminded myself with perhaps forced optimism, there would be the added relief of having made it home in one piece after all the worry I had caused my security advisors—not to mention my parents.

Again I struggled against a twinge of anxiety, determined not to lose sight of the importance of my presence on this trip. Ultimately, though, I found myself unable to get past the notion that something sinister was lurking nearby.

Concern over my personal safety, however, wasn't why I had decided not to join Gisele and the others for dinner at Haus zum Ruden, a nearby restaurant. In fact, I was quite tempted by the notion of relaxing and dining on sumptuous local fare in a guild house dating back to the thirteenth century. But I had mayoral duties to address once I had settled into my room in the grand old riverfront hotel where our group was staying.

I spent nearly two hours on a telephone conference call with my deputy mayors, being briefed on various matters—none of them earth-shattering, yet all important enough to demand my attention and input. After I hung up, I tackled more paperwork as I dined on an unremarkable room service meal of weiner schnitzel and potatoes.

Though I kept busy, the troubling question of who had tried to kill Anson Hubbard was in the back of my mind all evening. Rather than feeling closer to a solution, I felt as though the case was growing more complex.

Sleep eluded me long after I had settled into the unfamiliar bed. I wanted to be refreshed for our early morning meeting with Georg Hadwin, but my travel alarm went off only an hour after I finally drifted off.

Its shrill peal shattered a vivid nightmare in which I was struggling to climb a snowy mountain peak as a disembodied hand clawed at my legs, determined to pull me back. In the dream, I kept turning my head and looking down, trying to see who the hand belonged to, but the face was completely shrouded in fog and mist.

NINE

I had time for a quick breakfast in the hotel dining room before leaving for the meeting, and ran into Bonnie as I was waiting to be seated. She was dressed in a conservative navy suit, her hair pulled into a tight knot at the back of her head.

"Good morning, Mr. Mayor," she greeted me politely. "We missed you at dinner last night."

"I'm sorry I couldn't be there, but I had business to take care of."

"I'm sure it must be hard for somebody like you to drop everything and leave town for any amount of time," she said. "But I know Anson would be glad that you were able to come in his place."

"Have you heard anything about his condition?"

"Gisele spoke to David last night, before and during dinner. In fact, she called him several times, poor guy—and it was the wee hours of the morning there."

"Did something change? Is Anson all right?"

"The same. But she's very nervous about being so far away from him. If you ask me . . ." She leaned closer to me and put a hand alongside her mouth. "She's feeling guilty for leaving him. I don't think she thought it through before she decided to go ahead with the trip."

"Well, Anson was right—she certainly seems to be an asset to our cause," I pointed out. "The Swiss people love her."

"I can't argue with that. You should have seen the way we were treated at the restaurant last night. The staff bent over backward to take care of our table, and people kept sending over bottles of wine and champagne, and stopping to chat with her. Apparently, she's the national celebrity—thanks to her father."

"Is the doctor still alive?"

"No, he died of cancer years ago, not long after her mother."

"What happened to her mother?" I asked casually.

Bonnie hesitated. "She had some kind of accident, I think."

Something told me she wasn't telling the whole truth. I thought about what Sybil had said about Margot committing suicide, and how it had always been kept hush-hush. I considered asking Bonnie point-blank about the rumor, but the restaurant hostess interrupted our conversation just then to ask me politely, in heavily accented English, "How many in your party, Mr. Koch?"

Amused and mildly surprised that I had been recognized, I glanced at Bonnie. "Would you care to join me?"

She seemed uncertain. "Oh, Mr. Mayor, you don't have to—"

"No, it's fine," I assured her.

The hostess showed us to our table.

"Thank you for inviting me to join you," Bonnie said when we had been seated. "I'm used to eating alone, but it gets lonely sometimes."

There was a hollow, somewhat wistful note in her voice that told me she might not be entirely happy being a single woman. I remembered that she hadn't brought a date to the Hubbards' dinner party last Saturday night, as David had. I wondered whether she was involved with anyone, but I wouldn't dare to ask such a personal question.

A waitress promptly appeared. I ordered my customary cup of coffee and a cup of fruit. Bonnie decided on the continental breakfast, which in Zurich is a substantial spread including rolls and jam, cheese, cold cuts, fruit, muesli, and a steaming mug of hot chocolate.

As we ate, we discussed various aspects of Switzerland—this

was Bonnie's first visit to the country—and the upcoming meeting with Georg Hadwin.

"I keep imagining that he's going to throw a wrench into our investigation somehow," Bonnie told me. "I mean, I don't know every detail about the motives of this investigation, but I do know that Anson feared Hadwin was going to stop us from accessing the official documents that we need to see."

"Legally, we have a right to full access," I pointed out.

"But that doesn't mean we're going to get it."

"No, of course it doesn't." I thought of the paper-shredding incident. If what that custodian had said was true, the Association of Swiss Banks had something to hide, and they were taking extreme measures to do so. But did that have anything to do with the attempted murder of Anson Hubbard?

"Maybe we should ask Gisele to come to the meeting and win over Georg Hadwin," Bonnie said lightly, spooning some muesli into her mouth. "Then again, even *she* might not be able to charm him into seeing things our way."

"I have a feeling it's going to take more than charm," I replied, sipping the last of my coffee and checking my watch. "And if you're almost done, we really should be on our way. The Swiss are sticklers for punctuality, and we need to get off on the right foot."

But I had a feeling *that* was going to take more than punctuality.

And as usual, I was right.

The meeting took place at the headquarters for the Association of Swiss Banks. It was located in the heart of Zurich, and the towering, cosmopolitan chrome and glass structure seemed a world away from the charming cobblestone streets of Old Town.

The press was waiting outside, and I paused to answer several very basic questions, most of them phrased in English.

"Do you expect the investigation to go smoothly, Herr Koch?"

"Yes, I do—with the cooperation of the Association of Swiss Banks in allowing us access to pertinent documents."

"So you don't expect the Association to stand in your way?"

"Why would they want to do that?" I returned.

"Is it true that this investigation implies a cover-up?"

"The investigation implies only that millions of dollars in assets have been lost or misplaced along the way, and that it's time those funds were located and returned to their rightful owners or their heirs."

"But how would you explain the fact that Switzerland managed to escape a Nazi invasion during the war?"

"I'm a politician, not a historian," I responded snappily. "How would *you* explain it?"

"Were you the victim of any death threats because of your involvement with this cause, Herr Koch?" another voice asked.

"Absolutely not," I said, and threw up my hands to call a halt to the impromptu press conference. "Now if you'll excuse me, I don't want to be late for my meeting."

With that, I brushed past the crowd of reporters, my bodyguards surrounding me and the other members of our entourage following behind.

We were nearly at the door to the building when an outburst from the crowd caught my attention.

"You're lying, Koch!"

"You Jews have always been money-hungry—that's what this is about!"

"Jews are attempting to extort money from our homeland—is this the thanks we get for trying to help you during the war?"

I glanced over my shoulder in the direction the comments had come from, and saw several police officers clustered around an angry group that appeared to consist of several skinheads dressed in fatigues.

My bodyguards hustled me inside the building then. As we rode silently upstairs in the elevator, I remembered what David and Anson had said about the recent wave of anti-Semitism here in Switzerland, and how Seth Mandel had attributed it to our committee's forthright handling of the investigation. I would be meeting with Mandel tomorrow. For now, I put the matter out of my head and focused on the meeting at hand.

Georg Hadwin was a surprisingly slightly built man with icy blue eyes and a handshake to match. I estimated him to be about my age; perhaps a few years younger. He greeted me respectfully, as I did him, yet I detected an undercurrent of resentment in his tone. I started out speaking German, as it is always good practice, when conducting business negotiations, to use the host's native tongue.

Hadwin replied—and I sensed it was deliberate—in rapid-fire, almost unintelligible Schwyzertutsch. Then, with a belated apology and a hint of condescension, he asked me if I would prefer conducting the meeting in English.

"Of course I would," I said bluntly, knowing full well that most transcontinental business in Switzerland is handled in English.

He obliged, introducing his associates; then I introduced mine. We were seated at a long table in a brightly lit, windowless conference room, Hadwin and several bank association officers along one side, me and the members of my committee along the other, with Bonnie at the far end, prepared to take down a transcript of the meeting.

I outlined our objectives in my usual straightforward way, as Hadwin and his associates seemed to listen intently. When I had finished, I waited for a response.

"As you know, Herr Koch, we have made every effort to oblige your requests," Hadwin said at last, after taking a long sip of water and pausing for several moments in apparent contemplation. "We have released the names of non-Swiss wartime account holders, and lists of dormant accounts dating back to the late 1930s and early 1940s."

"I realize that. And that information has been very helpful so far. But it doesn't address the fact that there were thousands of Jews who were known to have opened accounts here in Switzerland before and during the war, and there is simply no record of that information."

"Which means . . . ?" Hadwin prompted, steepling his fingertips in front of him on the conference table.

"Which means that countless Swiss citizens were used as intermediaries, opening accounts for Jews in order to protect their assets from the Nazis." I deliberately refrained from adding that they also feared detection by Nazi sympathizers in the Swiss banking community. Instead, I continued, with the utmost diplomacy, "Most of those Swiss citizens were undoubtedly acting in the best interests of the Jews who trusted them. Others, apparently, were not."

"Mmm. And it is unfortunate that we will probably never know exactly what happened, isn't it, Herr Koch?" Hadwin flashed me a look that was obviously meant to convey sympathetic sincerity.

It didn't fool me in the least.

I continued, undaunted, "In order to track down those missing accounts, we will need to see lists of nondormant wartime accounts held by Swiss citizens, Herr Hadwin, under the assumption that some of those people would undoubtedly have been acting as agents for foreign Jews."

"And how would that information—if it were made available—allow you to pinpoint which of these Swiss middlemen had acted unscrupulously?"

"I suspect that some of these accounts were illegally cleaned out after the war. A complete investigation of the records might show us which ones, and we might, through painstaking research, be able to trace their origins."

"I'm certain you understand that we would truly love to help you resolve this distressing matter in whatever way we can," Hadwin replied. "But the truth is, our clients rely on our banks to preserve their privacy. We must maintain that reputation, and we have every intention of doing so."

"To the detriment of justice?"

His lip curled. "Of course not, Herr Koch. We have, as I pointed out, willingly cooperated with those requests of your committee that we were able to meet."

"So you have no intention of providing us with additional records?"

"I don't believe that there *are* additional records that will aid in your investigation."

"Isn't it up to our investigators to decide which records are relevant?"

"Not when the privacy of our trusting depositors is at stake."

"What about the reputation of the Association of Swiss Banks in the eyes of the world? Isn't that at stake?" I asked. "You must be aware that a lack of total cooperation on the part of your association suggests an ongoing conspiracy to conceal assets deposited by Holocaust victims."

He shrugged. "I don't agree. We cannot be held responsible for what happened decades ago, when there is no evidence."

"But you can be held responsible for allowing us to search for that evidence," I replied. "And there is every reason for our committee to believe that such evidence exists in files you are withholding, or perhaps have destroyed."

"We have destroyed nothing relevant to your investigation," Hadwin said, anger rising in his voice.

"There seems to be some dispute about that," I pointed out. "As the Senator told you last week, we have been informed by a reliable source that documents pertaining to the accounts in question may have been shredded recently."

"And as I told the Senator, I have no knowledge of any such paper shredding incident."

"That may be true. But I have every intention of looking further into these allegations," I replied. "And I intend to see that the files in question, if they do exist, are made available to us."

"You might be asking for the impossible."

"Maybe. Maybe not. If your banking association continues to resist compliance, Herr Hadwin, I'm afraid that I will have to take drastic measures."

"Such as . . . ?"

"You might find that New York, and even the U.S. Federal Reserve, won't be as willing to cooperate with your financial institutions as we have been in the past."

"Is that a threat, Herr Koch?" he asked, his originally pale complexion having been transformed into an irate flush.

"This is a negotiation process, Herr Hadwin," I replied calmly. "I'm merely discussing our intended reciprocation to your position."

We continued to discuss the situation, and that involving the missing gold believed to be stashed in Swiss vaults, but had made little progress by the time the meeting adjourned several hours later. It was clear to me that Hadwin wasn't going to willingly come up with the records of Swiss wartime account holders for our perusal.

While I had no trouble believing that he had illegally shredded documents to avoid a public scandal, I wasn't entirely convinced that he would be willing to actually commit a murder in order to put a halt to the investigation. But I instinctively didn't like or trust the man, and the scenario certainly wasn't implausible.

We would be meeting again in a few days for further discussion, with Swiss government officials joining our group. I fervently hoped that some progress could be made by then—both in the investigation process, and in the mystery of who had attacked, and nearly killed, Anson Hubbard.

In the meantime, I was joining Gisele for dinner this evening, and was most anxious to see what I could find out about her past, if she was at all willing to talk.

As we made our way to the elevator banks after leaving the conference room, I saw Bonnie accidentally bump into one of my bodyguards. Flustered, she dropped a sheaf of papers all over the floor.

I stooped to help her pick them up, and noticed that her hands seemed to be shaking. "Are you feeling all right, Bonnie?" I asked, concerned.

"I'm just a little tired," she said, not meeting my gaze. I thought her voice seemed more high-pitched than usual. "It must be jet lag catching up to me, or something."

I nodded, handing her the last sheet of paper and watching as she tried to assemble them in the binder she was carrying. She seemed distinctly skittish, as though something had happened to rattle her since we had last spoken this morning.

But what could have happened? She had been in my company all day, seated right down the table, taking notes throughout the meeting.

An elevator arrived and I stepped into it with my bodyguards, leaving her to wait with the rest of the group for the next one. But as we headed down to the lobby, I couldn't help wondering what was going on with Bonnie—and whether her sudden, strangely anxious state was relevant to the case.

Something told me that it was.

* * *

"Is this your first trip to Switzerland?" Gisele asked me over her menu.

We had just been seated at a small, round candlelit table in a cozy corner of the charming restaurant in the heart of the historic Old Town district. She had been recognized when we arrived, much to her apparent delight. She chattered and mingled with other diners before we were seated, obviously in her element and basking in the adoring attention. Meanwhile, I had not been recognized—much to *my* delight. After this afternoon's unsettling outbursts from the neo-Nazi protestors in the crowd, I was more than happy to keep a low profile for the time being.

"Actually, I've been to Switzerland—including Zurich—a few times before," I told Gisele.

"Then you must have tasted our national specialty?"

"Roesti?"

She nodded and smiled, obviously impressed that I knew she was referring to the delicious Swiss-style hash brown potato dish.

"I was going to suggest that you try it if you hadn't," she told me. "I crave it when I'm back in the States. I've had versions in New York that have come close, but nothing quite matches the dish that's served over here."

"Just as there's no place in the world where you can get a bagel like the ones in New York," I said.

"So I've heard, although I'm not very big on bagels. It's something about the water used in preparing them, isn't it? New York water makes them better?"

"I have no idea. But I make it a point never to order a bagel when I'm travelling. I know I'll only end up disappointed."

"You truly love your hometown, don't you, Ed?" she asked. She set her chin in her hand and looked thoughtful.

"Of course I do."

"That's how I always felt about Zurich. I grew up here. It was home. As much as I love my life in the United States with Anson, I've never quite gotten used to being away from Switzerland. Coming back always makes me feel good . . . as if I belong here."

"People certainly treat you as though you do," I pointed out. "Everyplace you go, they recognize you."

She looked pleased that I had noticed—not that I could have helped it. She was bombarded with attention at every turn.

In fact, as I was in my room getting dressed for dinner a short time ago, I had turned on the television. A local news station had shown footage that had been shot of Gisele that afternoon while she was shopping in the posh stores along Bahnhofstrasse, which is Zurich's version of Fifth Avenue. She looked glamorous and beautiful, dressed fashionably in a short wool coat and dark glasses.

There had also been a relatively brief, in comparison, segment devoted to my meeting with Georg Hadwin. The cameras had captured the question-answer session I'd had with the press beforehand, but not the ugly anti-Semitic comments from the crowd as I made my way inside.

"I do get my share of attention here," Gisele was saying now, with seeming modesty. "But it isn't necessarily because of anything *I* ever did to deserve it. My father was a renowned Swiss scientist, as you probably know."

"He discovered the vaccine for Dobry's Syndrome," I said.

"That's right. From that moment on, he was a national hero. An international hero, to be more accurate. His discovery saved the lives of thousands and thousands of children."

"You must be very proud of him."

"I am. I always was. My father was a wonderful man. All his life, he worked hard to help people. In that way, Anson reminds me of Papa. He's a good, noble man, too—a man who cares about helping people."

"How *is* Anson? Have you had any word about a change in his condition?"

"Nothing has changed," she said with a sigh. "David says the doctors are optimistic that he'll come out of the coma, but that there's no telling when. I just hope that when he does, he'll agree to retire. It's time to put all of this behind him. He needs to start enjoying life."

"Anson has always seemed to enjoy life," I couldn't help pointing out.

"He has, but he's never relaxed. I would love to travel . . . to perhaps even spend part of every year here in Switzerland. He would enjoy that as much as I would—although, for different reasons."

"Oh?"

She nodded. "Anson has never been the outdoorsy type. I love to ski, and hike, and ride horses—anything sporting. But Anson is happy to curl up by a fire with a glass of wine and a book and classical music on the stereo."

"I like to be active, too, but there's nothing wrong with unwinding once in awhile," I said, wondering when was the last time I had been able to spend time that way. How well I knew that the rigorous life of a high-profile politician doesn't allow time for much relaxation.

"Do you think you can talk to Anson about retiring, Ed?" Gisele wanted to know.

"Gisele, I would never try to talk someone into doing something he might not choose to do. I will say that I suspect Anson might not be opposed to the idea."

"Not after what he's been through," she said decisively; then, shifting gears, asked, "How was your meeting today? Did it go well?"

Before I could answer, the waiter arrived to take our order. I had considered going with one of the lean, vegetarian dishes, but at the last minute opted for the house specialty at Gisele's urging. I could imagine what my doctor would say about my ordering a meat and cheese fondue. I vowed to get back onto my usual healthy eating plan first thing tomorrow, but it seemed a shame not to partake of the local cuisine just this once.

Besides, tomorrow, after my meeting with Seth Mandel, we would be embarking on a goodwill sight-seeing trip to the Alps. I figured I might be able to get some exercise in, and perhaps even some skiing or hiking. I had missed my usual morning routine on the treadmill these last few days, and was looking forward to being active again.

After the waiter had taken our order and brought us the spice-laced Swiss wine Gisele requested, she once again asked me about my meeting.

"It went about as I expected," I told her, not certain how much she knew about the situation.

"In other words, Georg Hadwin isn't going to allow you full access to wartime financial documents."

"He's claiming he's allowed us full access to everything that matters." I took a sip of the wine the waiter had poured into my glass. It had an unusual flavor.

I must have made a face, because Gisele said, "You don't like it?"

"It's not my favorite," I admited.

"I suppose that like anything else, you have to develop a taste for it," she said with a smile, sipping from her own glass. Then she asked, "Don't you believe that Hadwin is telling the truth?"

"I won't take his word for it. I intend to persist in this matter. If the documents really are missing, then there's not much I can do."

"Anson said there were rumors about paper shredding."

"That's right. But there's no proof that it actually occurred. I can hardly make formal accusations without evidence."

"Maybe it's best just to leave it alone," Gisele commented.

Startled, I looked up at her. "What do you mean?"

"If they say they've shown us everything, maybe we should assume that they have."

I was conscious of her use of "us" and "we." It seemed deliberate, as though she intended to remind me that she and I were on the same team. Yet I got the distinct impression that it might not be entirely true.

"Are you suggesting that we drop the investigation?" I asked her.

"No, no, of course not! Nothing like that."

"Then . . ."

"I just think," she paused to sip her wine, "that maybe it's best not to press for the banking association to come up with documents that might not even exist. It's just as I told Anson, who tends to be outspoken—perhaps too much so—when it comes to causes he believes in. What do we have to gain by antagonizing Georg Hadwin and his associates . . . not to mention the Swiss government?"

"We didn't set out to antagonize them," I pointed out. "It's a matter of whether they're willing to do the right thing here. Perhaps as a former Swiss citizen you're feeling a bit defensive, and that's understandable."

She seemed to balk at my suggestion, but only momentarily. "Perhaps you're right," she said, with a shrug. "I don't want to believe that my homeland could have been anything less than noble in its dealings with the Holocaust victims during and after the war. My father was always sympathetic toward the Jews, and I felt the same way, growing up here at the time."

"Do you remember much about the war years?"

"I was young—at the age when a girl is far more wrapped up in herself than in what's going on in the world around her. I didn't pay much attention to the details. All I knew was that the Nazis were bad and that terrible things were happening to innocent people. And Papa would say that it was important that we try to help them in whatever way we could."

"What about your mother?" I asked cautiously.

Gisele flinched, slightly, but noticeably. "My mother . . . I don't remember her saying much about the war," she said. "She was always on the quiet side."

"Were you close to her?"

"Not really. Not as close as I was to Papa. I was a real Daddy's girl," she said with a faraway look in her eyes. "When I was very young and we were living in a cramped little house in a run-down neighborhood with no room to run and play, I used to sit for hours in the basement with him, watching while he worked with beakers and test tubes."

"Doesn't seem very interesting for a young child."

"No, but I thought it was. I adored him, and everything he did fascinated me. Papa would try to explain what he was working on, but it didn't make much sense to me then. Not until I was older. By then we had moved to a much bigger house and I had more space of my own. And Papa had built his own laboratory, a far more elaborate place than that small basement workshop. I would still pop in to see him from time to time, and I knew he was working on something important. But it wasn't until the breakthrough came that I was able to grasp the sheer enormity of what he had accomplished. Papa was a brilliant man."

"You must miss him."

"I do." She seemed to snap back to the present, tilting her head and looking me in the eye once again. "But he's been gone for years. I've had time to get used to the loss."

"What about your mother?"

"She died before Papa did."

"She must have been young. What happened to her?"

A shadow crossed over her blue eyes. "She had a freak accident one summer while she was at our estate in France. She . . . fell. In the barn. And broke her neck."

"How tragic."

"It was. Terribly tragic," Gisele agreed, then sighed. "But again, it happened so long ago. Anson and I had just gotten married. He helped me through the grief." She hesitated, then said, "I think I'll go call David and check to make sure Anson is all right. I keep thinking about him, and it's just . . . it's so difficult being this far away from him."

"Maybe you should go back to the States early," I suggested.

"Oh, I couldn't do that," she said quickly. "It would be letting him down. I had promised Anson I would come on this trip so that my presence would help to pave the way for the committee's investigation. That's what I'm here to do."

"Well, I wish your presence had had a more positive effect on Georg Hadwin," I told her. "We really need his cooperation right now."

"I realize that. But you have to understand, Ed, that the Swiss financial institutions have always prided themselves on a code of secrecy. To a man like Hadwin, any threat to that code must be taken very seriously. And this investigation is a threat."

"That doesn't give him the right to shred important documents."

"No, it doesn't. If you'll excuse me, I'm going to go make that call now, before our meals come."

She rose and walked away from the table. I watched her go, and saw her stop to chat with a group of people at a nearby table. They clearly recognized and revered her, and she was gracious and effusive with them. It was easy to see why people were drawn to her. She was obviously comfortable in the spotlight, and thrived on attention—yet she didn't come across as being self-absorbed or arrogant.

Anson would be proud, I found myself thinking as I watched his wife entertaining the small group of admirers.

I knew that he loved her, and it pained me to think that she could possibly be a part of something that would hurt him. But our conversation just now had done little to put my fears to rest.

Gisele might not be the most obvious suspect in the case, but I couldn't rule her out.

Not yet.

TEN

The meeting with Seth Mandel was scheduled first thing the following morning, and was to take place right at the hotel. Mandel and his group had pushed for us to get together at their storefront headquarters not far from where I was staying, but my security detail had flatly vetoed that idea.

As it was, they were noticeably wary as we waited for Mandel to show up in the small hotel suite that had been set aside for the meeting. Their ultravigilant demeanor only reminded me that I was in danger here in Zurich, and that Seth Mandel might be the reason for that.

Bonnie showed up ten minutes before Mandel was scheduled to arrive, looking as though she hadn't gotten much sleep the night before. She greeted me rather cagily, I thought, prompting me to ask her whether she was feeling all right.

"I'm fine, sir," she said, not quite meeting my gaze. "Why do you ask?"

"You look a bit pale," I said, although that wasn't quite it. She always looked pale, and her makeup free face wasn't any more ghostly than usual. But there was something about her that told me she was anxious, and that, given the opportunity and some privacy, I might be able to get some information out of her.

As it was, my bodyguards were surrounding us, and I had several documents I wanted to look over before the meeting with

Mandel. There were a few reports Anson had drawn up chronicling the movement of radical Swiss Jews and Mandel's rise to leadership, as well as information about the recent rise of vocal and occasionally violent anti-Semitism in Switzerland, particularly in Zurich.

Mandel arrived—alone, to my surprise—fifteen minutes late. That was surprising given the importance of punctuality in Switzerland—and yet, not surprising at all, once I glimpsed the sullen expression on his face.

He was older than I had expected, with longish curly brown hair that was graying around the temples, and dark eyes that bore an antagonistic expression behind wire-rimmed glasses. He wore jeans, sandals, and a striped, hooded wool pullover that gave him a bohemian-intellectual aura. He spoke English with only a slight accent, and didn't address me as Mr. Koch, or even Mr. Mayor, or anything at all. It was clear that he wasn't here on friendly business, which was fine with me.

I'm used to dealing with belligerence, and it takes a lot to throw me.

"Why don't we get down to business?" I suggested, after we had shaken hands—stiffly—and been seated at the small table.

My bodyguards stood alert around us, and Bonnie sat beside me, tapping away on her keyboard.

"Why *don't* we get down to business?" he echoed with more than a hint of sarcasm. "I would like to request that your committee drop its inquiry into the missing funds."

"And why is that?" I asked promptly. "Our inquiry is being made on behalf of all Jews. And as a representative for a Jewish organization, you, more than anybody else, should be interested in seeing justice served after so many years."

"I didn't say that I wanted the investigation dropped. I simply don't believe that your committee should be handling it."

"Why not?"

"Because it should be handled by an insider—somebody who is aware of the dynamics at work within the Swiss government, financial institutions, and society."

"Somebody like yourself?"

"Absolutely."

"I have the backing of the United States government. You don't have the resources or the clout to undertake such an investigation," I pointed out bluntly.

"And you don't have as much at stake as I do," he fired back. "Do you have any idea what has been going on here since that big-mouthed Senator started firing off accusations at Georg Hadwin and the Swiss government?"

"I understand there have been a few incidents of anti-Semitism."

"Is that so?" He leaned forward, his eyes burning into mine. "Did you hear about the ten-year-old Jewish boy who was beaten by his classmates after their teacher discussed Hubbard's comments in class, and told the children that the Jews were trying to blackmail the Swiss government? That little boy suffered serious brain damage. The doctors say he'll never be the same again."

"Of course that's unfortunate. But—"

"Did you hear about the neo-Nazi rally last week to protest the investigation? It took place outside a synogogue. The place was torched. Burned to the ground."

"I know. I read about it. But—"

"You don't know what havoc people like you and Hubbard are wreaking on the Jews of Switzerland, all in the name of justice." Mandel narrowed his eyes at me. "You're concerned about votes. Getting reelected. Using a worthy cause to boost your standings in the polls. That's what it's about for you."

"That's not what it's about for me," I said truthfully.

I wanted to add that Anson's intentions were also sincere—that I knew he wasn't just doing it for the exposure. But why was it necessary for me to defend Anson's motives, or my own?

Seth Mandel just looked at me, hostility burning in his eyes. "You're putting too many people in danger with the way you're going about the investigation. You're giving the Swiss people an excuse to hate Jews. You can't go on doing this."

"I have every intention of going on—for the good of Jews," I said firmly, unwilling to let him intimidate me. Still, I was aware of Ambrose and Tony bristling on either side of me, and of the furious gleam in Mandel's eyes, and I couldn't help thinking about what had happened to Anson.

Was Seth Mandel behind it?

As I faced his potent anger, it wasn't hard to believe that he was.

"If you don't stop the investigation, you're playing with fire," he said in a low voice. "You're taking an enormous risk. Don't say that I didn't warn you."

"What is it, exactly, that you're warning me about?" I shot back. "Are you threatening me?"

"Threatening you? Why would I do that?" He shrugged and stood, glancing from me to my security team, all of whom looked ready to pounce. "If you'll excuse me now, gentlemen, I have another engagement."

With that, he turned and sauntered out of the room, letting the door slam loudly behind him.

There was a moment of silence.

Then Bonnie looked up at me, clearly taken aback. "He's one frightening character, Mr. Mayor. I don't like the sound of what he had to say. You'd better be careful."

"I'm always careful," I assured her. "And he's not going to convince me to back down any more than Hadwin convinced me."

"But somebody tried to stop Anson, and look what happened to him. Aren't you worried, Mr. Mayor?"

I shrugged. "I don't give in to threats or terrorism. Never have."

Inside, though, I felt a nagging twinge of doubt.

Was I being a fool to keep going full speed ahead with the investigation? I knew that my cause was morally right. Still, I didn't necessarily relish the idea of losing my life in the name of justice.

"Are you enjoying the trip, sir?" Byron Klein asked.

I looked up from the open report on my lap to see him standing over me in the aisle of the rented minibus we were travelling in. Our entourage was trailed by several vehicles containing the press, an official government escort, a representative from the American consulate in Zurich, and additional security.

I nodded in response to Byron's query, although "enjoying" was probably somewhat inaccurate.

We had been riding for several hours through breathtaking scenery—along country roads and highways that wound past quaint farmhouses and grazing cows and climbed amidst towering evergreen forests and across rolling alpine meadows.

But rather than gazing out the window to enjoy the view, I had been wrapped up in some very necessary city financial reports that had been faxed to me from New York before our departure. Although huddling over paperwork wasn't a particularly fun way to spend a road trip, I supposed I needed the mental distraction from the various other complications of the past few days.

Besides, I wasn't the only one who didn't seem to be captivated by the breathtaking panorama outside the windows. Gisele had slept for the duration of the trip, and Bonnie had sat brooding, staring out at the passing scenery as though she wasn't really seeing it.

"I'm about to e-mail an account back to my editor. Do you have any official comment on your meeting this morning with Seth Mandel?" Byron wanted to know.

"No—other than that I respect his concerns, but have no intention of backing down where this cause is concerned."

"Was that what he wanted you to do?"

"Mr. Mandel feels that it would be in the best interests of all Jews if his group were allowed to take over the investigation."

"And you don't agree?"

"Of course not. His group is a radical organization with a reputation for using militant tactics to achieve their goals. I don't think that's in anyone's best interests, do you?"

Byron shrugged. "So you're going to continue to pursue the investigation as you had intended, then, sir?"

"By all means."

He smiled. "It's good to know you haven't lost the reliable Koch spirit."

"I never will," I replied. "Why would I? I know that what I'm doing is right and fair. Nobody's going to bully me into backing down."

"I'm sure that the Senator would be proud to have you on his side, making sure his cause doesn't die in his absence."

We chatted on, then, about mundane things—the weather and the scenery and the plans for our group to go hiking first thing tomorrow. Klein told me that he wasn't much of an outdoorsman, and wasn't particularly looking forward to it.

I told him that I felt the opposite way. I've always prided myself on staying in good shape, and I looked forward to the challenge of hiking in these rugged mountains.

What I didn't mention to him, or even wish to acknowledge to myself, was that the feeling of foreboding had followed me from Zurich. There was no apparent reason for it, at least nothing I could put my finger on. But I felt a distinct, nagging sense that I was no safer now than I had been back in the city.

I also knew that there was nothing I could do about it. I was no closer to solving the case than I had been when we arrived in Switzerland. If anything, the field of suspects had expanded, making the possibilities more complex than before.

I was, of course, certain that whoever had rented that car back at JFK airport using the name Zedekiah Gold had used the name deliberately. I was also fairly certain that he'd been a hired thug. Nobody directly involved with Anson or with the Swiss bank investigation at a high level would risk recognition.

The question was, who had hired the hit man?

Seth Mandel?

Georg Hadwin?

David Berkman?

Bonnie Tyson?

Gisele Hubbard?

Everyone had a possible motive. No one had convinced me that he or she was beyond suspicion. All I could do was hope that soon, the culprit would unwittingly slip up and reveal his or her identity.

But I knew that might only happen when the would-be assassin decided to strike again . . .

And that I was the most likely victim.

The snow-dusted cluster of resort chalets where our group would be staying was nestled amidst vast, rugged white mountain peaks sharply outlined against the dark blue late-afternoon sky. The air was noticably thinner here, and I found myself huffing a bit as I headed from the bus toward my quarters, intent on making a few phone calls back to New York before joining the others in the main lodge for dinner.

"Are you all right, Mr. Mayor?" Lou Sabatino asked, walking alongside me and breathing more heavily than I was.

"I'm fine. Are *you* all right, Lou?" Each word I spoke released a puff of frost into the cold, thin mountain air.

"I guess so. Just have to get used to the altitude."

I glanced at my other guards and was reassured to see that they seemed to be faring better than the relatively heavy-set Lou. This was one time when I couldn't afford to have their faculties impaired in any way.

Jack Moreland, the consulate representative, fell into step beside me. The middle-aged American, who had introduced himself to me before we left Zurich, had an easy smile and a low-key demeanor that seemed to contrast sharply with Jerrold Gifford, the government official who had also accompanied us on the trip. He had been friends with Gisele's father years ago, and it was because of her that he had been assigned to this particular duty. I expected a jovial type; or at least someone who could perhaps bridge the vast gap between our committee and the banking association.

But Gifford, who appeared to be in his mid-seventies, was a formal European, somewhat stodgy, and not entirely sociable. I wondered if the slightly stand-offish attitude was just his personal style, or could be attributed to the conflict between our committee and the Association of Swiss Banks. This two-day jaunt to the mountains was officially meant to be a goodwill tour, but if Gifford's less-than-affable mood was any indication, he didn't see it quite that way.

"Is there anything I can do for you, Mr. Koch?" Jack Moreland asked. "Do you have any questions? Any concerns?"

"Just one," I said, in a low voice. I turned and indicated, with a tilt of my head, Jerrold Gifford, who was trudging grimly along several yards away. "Is Gifford always this charming?"

Moreland grinned. "He's not the warmest guy I've ever met. But he's really not so bad once you get to know him."

"I just figured he might have an attitude problem because of the status of our investigation."

"That, too." Moreland's grin faded. "You have to understand, Mr. Koch, that the Swiss government isn't entirely thrilled with your committee's implications of Nazi compliance, whether or not it can be substantiated. This country prides itself on its long history of neutrality—and on its banks, with their strict code of privacy."

"I'm fully aware of that," I told Jack Moreland. "And I'm certainly not making any direct accusations. All I ask is that we be allowed to look into the matter to our satisfaction, so that, whatever happened fifty-odd years ago, retribution—if it turns out to be necessary—can be made to the victims of the Holocaust and to their rightful heirs."

"Believe me, I stand behind you on that objective. And of course I'll be glad to help smooth the way. I just wanted to make sure you understand where Jerrold Gifford is coming from. He's under tremendous pressure from Georg Hadwin and his associates."

I shrugged. "The sooner they realize that it's in their best interests to stop opposing the investigation, the better. We have no intention of backing down, and, as I warned Hadwin yesterday, I'm fully prepared to see that they face severe consequences if they choose not to comply with our investigation."

"Between the two of us, I don't think that will happen," Moreland said in a confidential tone. "They have too much at stake. They can't afford having their banks lose their operating licenses in New York State."

"Of course they can't. And we can't afford their withholding documents that might explain what could have happened to the millions of dollars that foreign Jews entrusted into their hands."

We had reached the door to my chalet, and Moreland said he would see me at dinner in the lodge later, before trudging away through the snow.

I stepped inside and looked around. The decor was simple and rustic—white walls, boxy pine furniture, a large red and green area rug centered on the hardwood floor in the main room, and a big stone fireplace with a fire blazing on the open hearth. There were floor-to-ceiling windows that allowed breathtaking views of the mountains. The walls sloped overhead, and the A-line of the ceiling was intersected with wooden rafters.

I found the master bedroom after opening two other doors—one leading to a closet, the other to an outside deck. After unpacking my small bag, I settled in at the desk in the living room to make some calls back to New York.

First, I touched base with Helen, who briefed me on various matters, then informed me that there had been a subway car derailment that afternoon in the Bronx. Fortunately, it happened at an off-peak hour just past the first stop on the line, and the train had been nearly empty. No one had been injured. But the motorman was under investigation for possibly being alcohol-impaired. I asked Helen to keep me posted on any developments. She said she would, then told me to watch my step in Switzerland.

"We're counting on you to come back safely, Ed," she said. "We really need you around here."

Next, I called my Finance Commissioner and spent almost an hour going over the report I had studied on the way up here on the bus. He agreed to fax an amended version first thing in the morning, then said, in parting, "Don't take any chances over there, Ed."

I promised him, a bit wearily, that I wouldn't.

With my official business taken care of, I dialed Charley Deacon at the precinct, not really expecting to get ahold of him. To my surprise, he was there.

"Mr. Mayor!" he exclaimed. "Is everything all right? I thought you went over to Switzerland."

"I am in Switzerland, Charley. I just wanted to touch base and see what was going on with the Kinsella case."

"We've picked up a suspect in the shooting, thanks to that tip from the customer behind him in line."

"You're kidding!" Finally, some good news. "How did you track him down?"

"Through the video rental place in Manhattan. The clerk there thought she recognized him from the composite police sketch. She's going to try and ID him in a lineup, and so is the lady from the rental place."

"When is this going to happen?"

"First thing tomorrow, with any luck."

"So who is this guy?"

"His name's Bruno Green. Lives on the lower east side."

"Is he Jewish?"

"Nope."

"Any political or personal motive for being opposed to the Senator's committee?"

"Not from what I can tell. If you ask me, he's your average thug. Has an arrest record for burglary, assault, passing bad checks—relatively minor stuff. And he refuses to talk to us or admit to anything."

"Have you been able to establish a link with the Hubbard shooting?"

"Between you and me, I'm fairly certain there is one. But there's no concrete evidence. I've been in contact with the Westchester detectives on that case, and they're going to question him. I'll keep you posted and I'll let you know if anything changes, Mayor. In the meantime, please be careful over there."

"I will, Charley," I promised, stifling a sigh.

It was getting to be a tiresome refrain. It seemed that everyone I talked to these days warned me to be careful. I knew they all meant well, but I didn't particularly appreciate the constant reminders that my life might be in danger. As if I could possibly forget.

I hung up, thinking about the suspect they had apprehended. As I had theorized, it sounded as though he was a hired hit man. Hired by whom?

I pondered my list of suspects again, and decided it could have been any one of them. There was no way of narrowing the field until I had more information from Charley.

Finally, I put in a call to the Westchester hospital and asked to be connected to Anson Hubbard's room.

David Berkman answered the phone, as I had anticipated.

"Mr. Mayor!" His weary voice perked up. He sounded surprised and even pleased to hear from me. "How's everything going over there?"

"About as we anticipated." I filled him in on the latest developments with Georg Hadwin and Seth Mandel, but didn't mention the Bruno Green angle.

"I'm not surprised that neither Mandel or Hadwin met you

with open arms, Mr. Mayor," Berkman said. "And frankly, I hope you'll watch your step while you're over there."

"Then you believe that one or the other of them was behind the attempt to assassinate the senator?"

There was a pause. "I honestly don't know, Mr. Mayor. I'd hate to think so, but . . . Well, what do *you* think?"

"I'm with you. I don't want to believe it. But somebody tried to kill Anson—twice—and if it wasn't somebody who had good reason to stop our investigation, then who was it? You're close to him, David. Can you think of anybody else in his life who might have a motive for wanting him out of the way?"

"Not a soul," Berkman replied. "Anson is a good man. This just isn't fair."

His voice broke then. He sounded utterly sincere in his despair. Still, I wished that I could see his face to be sure.

"How is he, David?" I asked. "Any change in his condition?"

"None at all. He's still unconscious. It's terrible seeing him this way. I'm glad that Gisele isn't here. How is she holding up?"

"She seems to be doing well," I told him. "She's worried, of course. But she seems to be keeping her fears to herself."

"Just so you know, Mr. Mayor . . ." Berkman began, then trailed off and hesitated.

"Just so I know what?"

"Gisele has a history of emotional . . . issues."

I sensed that he had been about to say "problems," but decided to tone it down.

"Oh? What kind of issues?" I asked cautiously, not wanting to seem overly curious about Anson's wife.

"She doesn't handle stress very well. She gets easily depressed and anxious under the best of circumstances. And she and Anson are very attached to each other. He's her entire world. If anything happened to him . . . well, I don't know what she would do. So please try to be there for her if she needs someone to lean on. She may not reach out to you—but then again, you never know."

"I'll keep an eye on her," I promised . . . as if I wasn't already doing just that. "And I can ask Bonnie to do the same."

"Bonnie?" Berkman cleared his throat. "She and Gisele aren't exactly on the best of terms, Mr. Mayor. It isn't that they don't like each other, but . . ."

"What is it, then?" I prodded, intrigued.

"I think they're jealous of each other's roles in Anson's life, to be honest. But please don't mention to either of them that I said that."

"Of course I won't."

We chatted on for a few moments before I told Berkman I had to hang up and get ready to go to dinner.

"What are you still doing at the hospital at this hour?" I asked, realizing it was well past midnight back home.

"I hate to leave his bedside. I promised Gisele I would stay with him—"

"But I'm sure she didn't mean around the clock, David. You should go home and get some rest."

"Actually, I have been going back to the house in Bedford for a catnap every once in a while," he said. "I have a room there, and anyway, I like to check on things and make sure there's nothing suspicious going on."

"Has there been any word from the police about their progress in tracking down the sniper who shot Anson?"

"None at all. I keep checking. They have no leads. Apparently, he got away without being seen by anyone."

"Except Gisele," I pointed out.

"Except Gisele. And in her frame of mind, she hardly got a good look at him. Remember, she wasn't even positive that it was a man."

"But she was fairly convinced that it was," I reminded him. "Wasn't that what you told me?"

"Yes, it was. And that's what she said. But given her emotional . . ."

"Problems?" I supplied deliberately.

"Yes. No! Not problems. It's not as though she's mentally ill . . ."

"Emotional issues, then."

"Given her emotional issues, Gisele isn't the most reliable eyewitness. What wife would be, after realizing her husband has just been shot?"

I wondered if he always was so defensive where Gisele was concerned, or if he knew I was suspicious of her. I had thought he picked up on that when we were discussing the shooting at the hospital. But did he know I also had my reasons to suspect him?

"You're right about Gisele," I told Berkman. "She had every reason to be anxious at the time, and has every reason to be emotionally vulnerable now. I promise I'll stay close to her whenever I can."

"I appreciate it, Mr. Mayor. And I know Anson would, too. Enjoy your hike tomorrow. And watch your step . . . you're in some rough terrain."

"I will," I said, uncertain whether he was speaking literally or figuratively. Not that it made a difference. Either way, he was accurate.

Dinner was a casual affair, served buffet-style in the large, private lodge building a short walk from the chalets.

I was seated with Jerrold Gifford and Gisele, and found that the two of them, at least, seemed to be on good terms with each other. Gifford was, if not effusive, at least somewhat more talkative than he had been earlier. I actually saw him smile and heard him chuckle once or twice. He and Gisele tried to include me in their conversation about various topics, all involving Switzerland—and mostly revolving around people I had never heard of and places I had never been. Some of it was interesting. Her family used to vacation at this resort and at nearby Davos when she was young, and she had some amusing stories about meeting up occasionally with the British royals on the slopes. But both she and Gifford kept lapsing into Schwyzertutsch, almost without realizing it, and I had difficulty following much of the conversation.

Instead, I focused on the food.

We had been served an authentic Swiss meal that included Geschnetzeltes Kalbfleisch nach Zurcherart, which is chopped veal in a rich cream and mushroom sauce; sausages; cheese fondue; Roesti; and Raclette, a melted Valais cheese dish served with potatoes, gherkins, and pickled onions. There was plenty of beer and bottles of red Swiss wine, and the mood around me was festive.

As I nibbled the savory, unusual fare, I kept noticing that Bonnie

Tyson, seated at a different table with Byron Klein and Jack Moreland, still seemed vaguely distracted despite the jovial atmosphere. She picked at her food, looked off into space, and didn't appear to be involved in the conversation around her. Once, she glanced up and caught my eye, but quickly glanced away.

I made a mental note to find some time alone with her as soon as possible, so that I could try to uncover whatever it was that was bothering her. There was, of course, the possibility that her shift in disposition had nothing to do with the case . . .

But I suspected that it did.

Gisele's voice interrupted my train of thought. "I'm afraid we're boring you, Ed. I'm so sorry."

"Boring me?" I held my veal-laden fork poised in front of my mouth. "You're not boring me, Gisele. I find Switzerland fascinating."

"Yes, but how rude of me to go on and on about it with Herr Gifford. It's just that I miss everything about Switzerland, and particularly Zurich. It will always be home to me, no matter where I live." She seemed to be speaking partly to me, and partly to Jerrold Gifford, who looked pleased.

"I can understand that. As I said, it's how I feel about New York," I told her. "Have you ever been to New York, Herr Gifford?"

"A few times," he said, wearing a slightly distasteful expression that told me what he thought of my city. Still, he said diplomatically, "I found it to be a very exciting and interesting place."

Sure you did, I thought.

The conversation turned to a discussion of travel in general, and I discovered that both Gisele and Gifford were seasoned travelers, as I am. Things were more congenial as we discussed our trips to various places, and we were all laughing by the time we were served coffee, accompanied by elaborate Swiss chocolates, amazing white truffles, and delectable meringue pastries filled with cream.

It was as though Jerrold Gifford had forgotten that he was supposed to see me as the enemy . . .

Until a newspaper photographer approached to snap our picture, accompanied by a reporter who asked, "Mr. Koch, have you and Mr. Gifford reached an agreement regarding access to bank documents?"

"That decision doesn't rest with Mr. Gifford or with the Swiss government," I told him, conscious that Jerrold Gifford had stiffened beside me and the smile had faded from his face. "It will be made by Georg Hadwin of the Association of Swiss Banks, and I'm optimistic that he will agree that full disclosure of all relevant documents must be made if our investigation is to be carried out in the most efficient manner."

"Do you have any comment, Mr. Gifford?"

"No comment," he said tersely.

"But what about—"

"No comment!" he repeated, glaring.

"And you, Mrs. Hubbard?" The reporter turned to Gisele, unfazed. "As a former Swiss citizen and the wife of Sen. Anson Hubbard, who is chairman of the committee, you must be feeling considerably torn in your loyalties."

Gisele, who had always seemed at home in the spotlight, appeared flustered. "I have no comment," she finally said, and waved the camera away.

Jerrold Gifford stood and asked to be excused.

As he left the table, I looked at Gisele. She had dipped a spoon into her black coffee and was stirring it around and around, clearly agitated.

"Are you all right?"

She shrugged. "I just wish you would drop this whole thing!"

Surprised at her candid outburst, I said, "You can't really mean that, Gisele. You know how much this matters to Anson. He wouldn't want me to drop it."

"You can't be sure about that. And look what it's doing to me!" Her voice was rising slightly, a telltale shrill note creeping in. "That reporter was right. I'm caught in between."

"You don't believe that it's right for the Association to withhold documents that might shed light on what happened to millions of dollars that may have been stolen, do you?"

"I don't know what I believe!" she said, sloshing some coffee over the edge of the cup. The dark liquid splashed the sleeve of her rose-colored silk jacket, but she didn't seem to notice or care.

"I just think that the committee's actions should be up to Anson, and since he can't make any decisions right now, we should let things drop until he can. He might decide that it isn't worth the strain we're creating in this country."

I contemplated that.

"Won't you please just drop it, Ed?" she asked, her tone more modulated now, as though she'd managed to get control of her emotions.

"I wish I could, Gisele. If only for your sake. But I need to do the right thing. I have promises to keep, and so does Anson. We promised the Holocaust survivors and their descendents that we would get their money back, or at least find out what happened to it. And that's what I intend to do, if it's at all possible."

She looked at me for a long time, as though expecting me to change my mind.

When I said nothing, she pushed back her chair and stood.

"If you'll excuse me, Ed, I'm going to go back to my room. I'm suddenly just completely exhausted."

"Get some rest, Gisele," I said, patting her arm.

She nodded and walked away without another word.

I watched her exit the lodge after briefly saying good night to the few people who waylaid her. Then I turned my attention to the table where Bonnie had been sitting. I realized that her chair was vacant, and looked around the dining room. She was nowhere to be seen.

With a sigh, I realized that my curiosity about Bonnie wouldn't be satisfied until tomorrow—*if* I managed to corner her alone, and *if* she was willing to open up to me when I did.

ELEVEN

The next morning dawned gray and blustery. I could feel the wind slamming against the walls of the chalet as I dressed, and I wore several layers in anticipation of the biting cold outdoors. I prepared a cup of coffee in the chalet's kitchenette, and fixed a simple breakfast from ingredients I found in the cupboards—a bowl of muesli, toast, and some fruit. It was more than I usually ate in the morning, but I figured I would need my energy for the hike ahead.

I called Charley Deacon to see if the suspect had been positively identified in the lineup, but I couldn't get through to him. I left a message that I'd call back later, knowing I would be out of reach for most of the day.

I met up with the rest of the group in the lodge. The mood was considerably more subdued today, most likely due to the early hour and the liquor that had flowed so liberally the night before.

Gisele was there, deep in conversation with Jerrold Gifford, and looking like a Nordic fashion plate in coordinated hiking gear. She smiled and waved at me, and I assumed she harbored no ill feelings from the night before. Gifford, too, nodded in my direction, although he looked less than thrilled to see me.

I spotted Bonnie sitting alone on a bench in one corner, and hastily made my way over to her to take advantage of the situation.

"Bonnie, are you all right?" I asked, dispensing with any pleasantries.

She looked up, startled, and I saw in her troubled gray eyes that she wasn't the least bit all right. Still, she nodded—just as I expected her to.

"No, you aren't all right," I said sternly, sitting beside her on the bench. "What's the matter? You've been brooding about something ever since the meeting with Hadwin the other day."

"No, I haven't."

"Of course you have. What happened?"

"Nothing happened." She frowned. "I'm just tired, like I told you. It's jet lag."

I studied her face, noticing that she was reluctant to meet my gaze.

Still, it was clear that there was no dragging anything out of her right now. Whatever was bothering her, she obviously didn't want to share.

I fought back a touch of uneasiness as I got up and walked away from her.

Fritz and Ludwik, the two Swiss guides who would be leading our hike, stood up and commanded our attention. They were rugged, blond young men wearing similar snowflake- patterned wool sweaters, and I wondered absently if they were brothers. Unfortunately they spoke English with such thick accents that it was difficult to make out what they were saying.

I did hear a warning to stick with the group, and something about frostbite and avalanches.

"Did he say avalanches?" Lou Sabatino asked in a whisper, leaning toward me.

"I think so."

"Great," he said flatly.

"How's the altitude problem coming along?"

"I've adjusted to it. But I'm still a little short of breath. And it's pretty damn cold out there."

"You aren't cut out for the outdoorsy life, Lou," I told him.

"I won't argue with you there, sir. This place is beautiful and all, but I'll take Manhattan any day."

"So will I," I said, struck by a sudden, acute wave of homesickness.

What I wouldn't give to be back in New York, strolling down the street in the Village near my apartment or sitting at my desk beneath the painting of Fiorello La Guardia. I wouldn't even mind having Mom and Pop hovering over me and infiltrating Gracie Mansion with homemade gefilte fish and "Murder She Wrote" reruns at this point, so anxious was I to just get back home, where I belonged. I missed the sounds of the traffic, the smell of roasted nuts and hot dogs wafting from sidewalk vendors' carts . . .

A sudden scraping of chairs and chattering wrenched me from my daydream and alerted me that the guides had finished their spiel. We were ready to set out on our alpine hike. I pulled on my gloves and walked outside with the rest of the group.

The sky seemed to hang low overhead, and was a murky dark gray color that seemed to promise snow.

"Lovely day for a hike," Lou muttered beside me.

"Oh, don't get all grouchy. The fresh air will do you good," Ambrose told him. "Just think . . . you might even lose a pound or two."

"I need to lose more than that, after all that cheese and sausage I ate last night."

The two of them bantered good-naturedly as we headed toward a trail that disappeared between the trees that covered the rocky, snow-dusted terrain.

I was shivering, and I couldn't help wondering if it was simply due to the chilly mountain air. The feeling of uneasiness that had haunted me for days seemed to have grown stronger today. Though I struggled to push my misgivings aside and concentrate on what the guides were telling us about splitting into two groups, I couldn't quite relax.

Several hours later, I found myself standing at the edge of a vast precipice, gazing at the most dazzling vista I had ever seen. The sun had come out, and the snowy slopes sparkled beneath a clear blue sky with just a few high white wisps of clouds.

"Don't you just feel like Maria in *The Sound of Music*?" Jack

Moreland asked me, flashing his wry grin, as we stood gazing out over the land.

I laughed. "I'm not about to burst into song, if that's what you mean. But it is gorgeous up here."

"And the hard part was coming up. Now all we have to do is eat lunch and head back down."

I nodded, thinking that maybe I had been wrong to be so apprehensive earlier. The open air and exercise had made considerable difference in my attitude.

Both Gisele and Gifford had split off with the other group, which consisted of more skilled hikers. Their absence might also have something to do with my mood shift. I didn't have to face the constant reminder that virtually no progress had been made in the standoff between our committee and the banking association. No, I could almost forget that I was here on business, and that my life might be in danger to boot.

Fritz, who was guiding our group, summoned us over to the tree-rimmed clearing where he was spreading a delectable-looking feast on a picnic cloth draped over a flat rock. As I sat nibbling bread, rich Swiss Gruyere, and Bundner Fleish—air-dried beef, a Swiss specialty—and sipping steaming hot chocolate from a thermos, I found myself almost letting go of my reservations and relaxing.

My bodyguards, while still appropriately vigilant, were joking among themselves as Fritz gave lighthearted yodeling lessons to a couple of reporters.

Even Bonnie, who sat nearby, seemed to have brightened a little. She actually smiled when our eyes met, and I wondered if I had been wrong to think that whatever was bothering her had to do with the meeting with Hadwin. I told myself that she might simply have been tired, as she had claimed, or that maybe she was just one of those people whose moods are unpredictable. After all, I didn't know her well enough to jump to conclusions.

Fritz announced that it was just about time to head back down the mountain.

"Anyone who wants to take a last look at the view should do it now," he said, and I actually managed to understand him despite the accent.

I decided to head back through the trees to get another glimpse of the view that had inspired this sudden feel-good spirit.

Lou accompanied me, since my bodyguards weren't about to let me out of their sight, even in this remote location.

We made our way along the steep rise to the point where the trees opened up to the impressive panorama.

"It's really something, isn't it?" Lou asked, gazing out over the terrain. "Maybe I should take back what I said about belonging in the city."

"Nah," I told him. "It's a nice place, but you wouldn't want to live here. I bet it's impossible to get decent Chinese takeout at this altitude."

He laughed at that, and we turned to head back.

As we did, something captured my attention.

I couldn't decide, later, if it had been a sound coming from the rocky overhang above us—perhaps a footstep—or just a sudden awareness that somebody was lurking up there.

I only knew that for whatever reason, I glanced up in time to see something enormous looming, and then tumbling over the edge.

I yelled out, shoving Lou in one direction and leaping out of the way in the other as a gigantic boulder thundered to the ground, landing precisely where we had been standing.

Hunks of dirt and snow and rocks rained down in its aftermath, and we instinctively flattened ourselves against the stone ledge, covering our heads with our arms.

Finally, all was still.

"What the hell was that?" Lou asked. "An avalanche?"

"That was no avalanche," I said, feeling strangely calm despite my still-racing heart. "Somebody was up there. Somebody pushed that boulder over the edge. Somebody had every intention of hurting us badly, maybe even killing us . . ."

And somehow, that somebody had gotten away once again.

"I just think we should go home, Ed," Gisele said for what seemed like the hundredth time, burying her head in her trembling hands. Her voice was high-pitched, and I had noticed that her eyes seemed to grow more and more wild with fear ever since we had arrived back at the lodge a short time ago.

"I can't leave just yet, Gisele," I repeated patiently. "I have to meet with the Association again back in Zurich tomorrow. But you can fly back to the States first thing in the morning if you want to."

She didn't reply, only sat silently, rocking slightly as she seemed to be trying to retain control of her emotions.

She had been terribly upset ever since Lou and I had rejoined the rest of the hikers back on the mountain and he had reported what had happened. Ludwik's group had already met up with ours, so everyone was there. Gisele, upon hearing that we had been attacked, had burst into tears.

"Who would have done such a thing?" Ludwik had asked, as the press members present started clamoring for the details.

"I have no idea." I glanced around at the assembled hikers, studying everyone.

I had noticed that Bonnie appeared terribly agitated, and that Jerrold Gifford's face was an inscrutible mask as he kept an arm around a weeping Gisele, supporting her.

Along with Fritz and several of my bodyguards, I had walked the short distance up a nearly vertical trail. There was a makeshift wooden barrier midway along the way, flanked by several ominous posted signs in German, French, and English.

DANGER! DO NOT PROCEED BEYOND THIS POINT!

Fritz told us that there had been a landslide up ahead not long ago, leaving the scenic overhang—long a favorite spot for photographs—unsafe for hikers. After warning us to tread carefully, he led the way past the barriers along the steep incline toward the spot where the culprit must have stood.

"Could it have been an accident?" Fritz asked as we ascended through the thicket of pine trees.

I exchanged a glance with Lou. I wondered how much the two guides knew about the purpose for my trip to Switzerland, and decided not to go into any detail about the attempts that had already been made on Anson's life.

I told Fritz, "I don't think an enormous boulder could have rolled off a cliff by itself, so an accident doesn't seem likely."

"But who would want to do such a thing?"

"That's what I'd like to know," I muttered.

It could have been any one of our fellow hikers—or someone else, who had been watching us. It wouldn't have taken long for someone to realize I was in a vulnerable position, and thus take advantage of that to scramble up the incline, push the boulder over, and either disappear, or rejoin the group.

We arrived at the overhang.

I expected to see footprints, at the very least, in the snow covering the ground there, but there were none. Instead, there were distinct brush-like marks where somebody had clearly disturbed the snow, but deliberately covered up their footprints—probably by dragging a pine bough along behind them until they reached the heavily-travelled trail again.

We could see where the boulder must have been positioned. There was a cluster of enormous rocks perched precariously at the very edge of the precipice. Fritz explained that before the landslide, the boulders had been several feet from the edge, and thus posed little danger to those below. Now, however, it wouldn't have taken much effort for someone to give a giant push and send one hurling over the edge.

"That's why this part of the trail has been temporarily closed," he had announced. "So that there wouldn't be an accident like this one."

"Well, it was no accident," I reiterated grimly.

Now, as I sat in the lodge with Gisele, who seemed to be on the verge of falling apart, I wondered whether she could have done it. Physically, I decided she was capable. She was in good shape, and the rock was already strategically positioned.

Was her distress simply a cover-up?

And what about Bonnie? She had been silent during the hike back down to the lodge, seeming to be lost in her own thoughts.

Jerrold Gifford had hiked alongside Jack Moreland, the two of them engaged in subdued conversation—about what, I had no idea.

Byron Klein hadn't even tried to question me about the incident. For that, I respected him—and perhaps was a bit suspicious.

Suddenly, I felt paranoid, and understandably so. It was easy to view everyone as a possible suspect.

What about the members of the press?

What about Fritz and Ludwik?

Could one of them have been planted here by Mandel or Hadwin? There was no way of knowing.

Gisele finally lifted her head from her hands and looked up at me. She was clearly disturbed, and I knew that she wasn't faking her chagrin. That could mean that she was innocent—and it could mean that she was guilty, and was traumatized by what she had done.

"I'll stay here until your business is wrapped up," she told me, and her tone was calmer than it had been. She seemed to have reached some kind of inner reconciliation—at least, for the time being.

"You don't have to do that, Gisele. You can go back if you're frightened."

"I know I can. But I made a promise to Anson, and to myself, that I would see this through. How can I go running away just because of something that might even have been an accident?"

"Do you think it was an accident?" I asked her.

"No," she said quietly, looking me in the eye. "I think that somebody wants you to drop the investigation—or at least settle for access you have already been given. I think that whoever did this also tried to kill Anson." There was a tremor in her voice as she spoke those last words, and I reached out to pat her hand.

"I think you're right about that, Gisele."

"Then how can you go forward, Ed? How can you put yourself in danger this way?"

"I can't let somebody succeed in scaring me off, Gisele. I owe it to the people who are counting on our committee to see that justice is served. I owe it to the thousands of Jews who have been cheated out of their money—and the millions of Jews who died at the hands of the Nazis."

"But being a hero could get you killed, Ed."

"I have no intention of getting myself killed, Gisele," I said truthfully.

Because I'm going to find out who's behind this before they have the chance to strike again.

But I didn't say it aloud. Not to her.

I still wasn't certain of her innocence, and I knew that until the would-be killer was caught, I could trust no one. Doing so might prove deadly.

TWELVE

After trying again unsuccessfully to reach Charley Deacon, I crawled into bed. But I didn't sleep well at all, and abruptly came fully awake at dawn to the sound of voices arguing. They were faint, and seemed to be coming from outside the chalet, mingling with the ever-present whistling of the wind down the mountain.

I hurriedly climbed out of bed, pulled on a robe, and stepped out into the main room. Tony was standing just outside of my door, looking grim.

"What's going on?" I asked him.

"We just caught someone prowling around outside. Ambrose and Lou are out there with her now."

"With *her*?" I strode to the door. The outside lights were on, and I could see snow swirling against a charcoal-colored sky.

"Wait, Mr. Mayor," Tony protested, right on my heels. "You can't go out there?"

"Why not?" I sat on a chair and pulled my boots on.

"It could be dangerous. We don't know what she was up to."

"I'm going out," I informed him, stopping to grab my parka from the hook by the door and pull it on. "Nothing's going to happen to me with you and the others right there."

With that, I opened the door and stepped out into the frigid morning. Snow was coming down fairly heavily, driven by an icy wind, and I shivered as I walked down the steps and around the corner of the chalet, heading in the direction of the snatches of voices that carried along on the wind.

Tony was right with me, his hand on the revolver concealed at his waist, beneath his jacket.

I saw, through the whirling snow, three figures several yards away. I immediately recognized two of them as Ambrose and Lou. The third was smaller, and bundled from head to toe against the weather. She had her back to me and it was impossible to see who it was.

"What's going on?" I called, trudging through the drifts.

At the sound of my voice, the woman turned.

I gaped, realizing who it was.

"Bonnie!" I exclaimed. "What are you doing here?"

"I needed to talk to you, Mr. Koch."

"So you came prowling around my cabin in the middle of the night?" I asked skeptically.

"It's just about morning. And I've been up all night, knowing I should have come to you before now."

"Come to me about what?" I wasn't certain whether to believe her, though I wanted to. I was reluctant to think that Anson's loyal aide could possibly have harmed him—or me.

"Mr. Mayor—"

I interrupted Ambrose, holding up a hand to quiet him. "Let her talk," I said. "I want to hear what she has to say."

As I spoke, the wind howled and the snow began to come down even harder.

"Can we go inside?" Bonnie asked, stomping her boots and hugging herself. "It's complicated, and I don't want to tell you while we freeze out here."

"Sure we can," I said amiably, ignoring the expressions on my bodyguards' faces. I wasn't about to alienate Bonnie on the chance that she really did have something relevant to tell me. And if she had crept over here in the darkness intending to hurt me, she wouldn't dare try anything now.

"But Mr. Mayor—"

"It's all right, Lou," I cut in, and said to Bonnie, "Let's go."

The five of us waded through the deepening snow back to the

chalet. I closed the door, shutting out the howling storm, and looked at Bonnie.

"Well?" I asked, unzipping my parka and tossing it over a hook.

She hedged, and glanced at my security team. "Can we please talk alone?"

"Are you crazy?" I shot back. "These guys aren't going to let you out of their sight until we all know exactly what you're doing here."

"I told you. I only wanted to talk to you. I have something important to say."

"So say it."

Again, she looked at my bodyguards. "It's really a sensitive matter, Mr. Koch. If anyone ever found out—"

"My security detail is used to being privy to sensitive information, Bonnie. They won't let anything go farther than this room. Nor will they let me go farther than this room with you. So you might as well start talking. Let me take your coat."

She hesitated, then shrugged her arms out of the sleeves of her down jacket. She pulled off her ski cap and didn't bother to fuss with her flyaway, disheveled hair.

"Let's sit down, shall we?" I asked, as though I were entertaining her for coffee and cookies in the den at Gracie Mansion.

We made our way to the couch, and sat.

I waited.

She fidgeted.

I said, "Talk, Bonnie."

She faltered. "I'm afraid . . ."

"Of what?"

"I don't want to put myself in any danger." Her hands played with her gloves in her lap. "You would have to promise me, Mr. Koch, that you won't tell a soul what I'm going to tell you."

"Come on, Bonnie. You know I can't make that kind of promise until I know what it is. But I can promise that I won't compromise your personal safety in any way. You have to trust me."

She looked up, her worried eyes searching mine.

I nodded reassuringly. "Go ahead," I said gently. "Tell me."

After glancing once more at my bodyguards, she took a deep breath and said, "The other day, during the meeting with Georg

Hadwin, you said that you needed access to certain bank files. Files the Association of Swiss Banks isn't willing to show you."

"That's right. I need a list of all of the wartime accounts held by Swiss citizens, not just those that are dormant or belonged to foreigners."

"I saw that list."

"What do you mean?"

"I mean . . ." She exhaled heavily. "I saw that list. It was faxed to Anson's home office sometime last month, while he was in Washington."

Startled, I asked, "Are you certain?"

"I'm positive. I wasn't supposed to be there that day, but I had stopped in to pick up something he needed to have FedExed to Washington. While I was there, the fax came in."

"Did you notice where it came from?"

"Just that it was someplace in Switzerland. I didn't pay much attention. He's been getting a lot of stuff from here ever since he started working on the committee, so it didn't really faze me. But I did notice that it said, at the top of the list, that the account holders were Swiss. It struck me as unusual, because at the time, I didn't see why that would be relevant. I didn't realize it until you brought it up in the meeting the other day."

"So you're saying that Anson had, in his hands, the very information we're now seeking? The information that Georg Hadwin is determined to withhold?"

"I'm not saying it was in his hands. I decided to put it into the FedEx package I was putting together so that I could send it right to him. But first, I made a photocopy of it. He likes me to keep copies of anything that I send out, in case the package gets lost en route."

"What did you do with the photocopy?"

"I filed it in his office."

"His New York office?"

"No, I brought it with me to his Washington office. That's where we keep most of his important papers."

"And you FedExed the original fax to him in Washington?"

"I was about to. But Gisele came in as I was preparing the

package. She was angry to find me there. She doesn't like me much, in case you haven't noticed."

"Why doesn't she?"

Bonnie shrugged. "David says it's because she's jealous. I don't know why she would be. There's never been anything more than a professional relationship between Anson and me. But she seems to resent the fact that I work so closely with him, and he entrusts me with so much responsibility. Anyway, when she found me in his office, she demanded to know what I was doing there."

"And . . . ?"

"And I explained that I had stopped by to pick up the documents he needed sent to Washington. She said that she and David were flying to D.C. that night to surprise him for his birthday, and that they would bring him the package."

"What did you say?"

"What could I say? I handed it to her and left. I know he got the package, because the next day he called me to discuss one of the documents that was in it."

"And you never asked Anson about that list?"

"I never thought much about it again. As I told you, I didn't realize it had any significance until that meeting the other day."

"Why didn't you say something to me about it then? I asked you what was bothering you, Bonnie."

"I know you did. But . . ." She inhaled, then let her breath out slowly, shaking her head. "You have to understand, Mr. Koch. I've been working for Anson for years. My loyalty has always been with him, and my job has made me privy to quite a bit of secret information. I've always known enough to keep my mouth shut."

I nodded. I could understand that. I had several longtime aides and employees whom I knew would never reveal to anyone, for any reason, any private information that is sensitive or potentially damaging.

Bonnie went on, "Once I realized that Anson might have had access to something that relevant to the committee's investigation and not revealed it, I knew there had to be a reason. I had to trust him. I couldn't betray what I knew. Not without being able to check with him first. But that's impossible."

"What made you change your mind?"

Her gray eyes collided with mine. "When somebody tried to hurt you yesterday, Mr. Koch. I realized that you were in terrible danger. And I figured that what I know might be able to help you somehow."

I rubbed my chin thoughtfully, contemplating what she had said. Then I asked, "Did you ever take the copy of that faxed list out of the file in Anson's business office?"

"No."

"Then it might still be there?"

"I suppose it could be."

"Is there anyone you can call who can get it for us and fax it here?"

"I can ask David—"

"No!" I interrupted so vehemently that her eyes widened.

"But why not?"

"Bonnie, I don't want to imply that he's behind this—"

"David? Of course he isn't."

"But we can't be certain. Anyone can be involved. And until we know exactly what's going on, we need to ask a neutral party to intervene."

"There's Anson's secretary . . ."

"Bea?" I thought of the sweet elderly lady who reminds me of somebody's maiden aunt. She's been working for Anson since long before he was elected to office. There was no way she was caught up in anything illegal.

"Should I ask her to get the list?"

"Yes. Only don't tell her why. I don't want anyone to know what we suspect."

"What *do* we suspect?"

I paused. "I'm not sure. I don't want to believe that Anson was up to anything unscrupulous."

"I can't believe he could have been."

"But we don't know, Bonnie. And both our lives are at risk if anyone finds out what we're doing."

She nodded somberly. "I won't tell anybody besides Bea. And I won't give her the details. She won't think there's anything strange about it. I'm always needing to ask her to fax things from Anson's files."

"Good. How soon can you get ahold of her?"

She thought about it. "She won't be in the office today, but I can try to reach her at home."

"You do that."

She nodded and stood. "I have her number back in my room." She glanced at my bodyguards, who had relaxed somewhat, but still weren't about to give her the benefit of the doubt.

"Can I go now?" Bonnie asked.

I nodded, shooting a look at Lou and Ambrose and Tony that warned them not to interfere. I was convinced Bonnie was telling the truth.

She got bundled up again and opened the door. The furiously blowing snow created a wall of white beyond.

"Do you think we're going to get out of here this morning, Mr. Koch?" she asked, hesitating and turning back to me.

We were scheduled to head back to Zurich right after breakfast.

I looked dubiously out at the storm. "I don't know, Bonnie," I said, realizing for the first time that we might be stuck here for a while.

The thought was hardly pleasant—especially knowing that the culprit was still in our midst. But I couldn't speculate further on his or her identity until I had that list in my hands—and figured out the significance of its being faxed to Anson.

And that meant there was nothing to do but wait . . .

By mid-morning, it was clear that we wouldn't be going anywhere that day. The snow had turned into a full-fledged blizzard, with high winds driving blinding snow, and it wasn't expected to let up until well past nightfall. Our entourage had gathered in the lodge to discuss the situation, and I joined them, not wanting to arouse suspicion.

Only Bonnie was missing. I assumed she was still in her chalet, trying to reach Bea.

Several members of the press were playing cards and computer games. Jack Moreland wore a Walkman and his head was bouncing slightly in time to the music coming over his headphones. Gisele and Jerrold Gifford were seated together, as usual, chatting.

When she saw me, though, she beckoned me over.

"Isn't this awful, Ed?" she asked.

"Being stranded here? I suppose there are worse things that could happen."

"What about your meeting with Hadwin?"

"We'll have to reschedule."

"That might not be so easy," Gifford spoke up. "He's a busy man."

"And so am I."

He shrugged.

"Did you get much sleep last night?" Gisele asked me. "After what happened, you must have been a nervous wreck."

"Actually, I was fine," I told her. "How about you?"

"I'm happy to say that I had good news from David just before I went to bed," she announced with a smile. "He said that Anson's eyelids fluttered a few times last night. The doctors say he could be close to regaining consciousness, although there's really no way to tell for sure."

"That's wonderful," I said, heartened by the news. I wanted nothing more than to see my old friend pull through and make a full recovery. And the sooner the better . . .

If Anson regained consciousness, I would be able to ask him directly about the list.

Provided I still trusted him. Yet as much as I wanted to believe in him wholeheartedly, I knew logic demanded that I be objective.

What Bonnie had told me just didn't add up.

I couldn't believe that Anson could have obtained exactly the information our committee needed, and then kept it a secret.

Just how had he gotten his hands on that list in the first place? Knowing that Hadwin had so far resisted our attempts to locate such documents, I realized that the two most likely possibilities seemed to be bribery or blackmail. After all, how else would one get access to highly confidential information?

The thing was, it wasn't easy for me to accept that the Senator could have stooped so low . . .

Even for a noble cause like ours.

Even if he was desperate to boost his standing in the polls.

But what if Anson *hadn't* been the one who tracked down the list?

What if somebody else had asked that it be faxed to his office?

The only two likely candidates for that seemed to be Gisele and David.

Had one of them obtained it using illegal means, thinking they were doing Anson a favor? I could imagine how he would have reacted to that, once he found out. If he was as honorable as I'd always believed him to be, he would have been horrified. The Anson I knew—or thought I knew—wasn't likely to use it to further our cause, no matter what the consequences.

I had to reconsider the possible motives for his near-assassination.

Had he been caught with the list by someone who had then ruthlessly tried to kill him?

Did that person assume that I, too, had access to the off-limits information?

I had to get my hands on it. I had to see it for myself. I was certain that the key to the case lay in that document.

"Gisele," I said abruptly, standing. "Please tell me if you hear anything else about Anson's condition."

"I will. I'm going to try to reach David again in a little while. I tried a little while ago, but there was no answer." She looked disturbed, as though struck by a frightening thought. "You . . . you don't think that means something terrible happened, do you?"

"Of course not," Gifford told her in a calming voice, though she had been speaking to me. "David might just have stepped out to get something to eat."

Gisele looked to me for reassurance.

"I'm certain everything is fine, Gisele," I told her. "Maybe Anson has already regained consciousness and they've moved him to another part of the hospital."

"But I should have been notified. I should be there with him," she said, her gaze traveling to the snow-obscured view outside the window. "I should be there when he wakes up. We have to get out of here."

"We can't go anywhere with the weather like this," Gifford pointed out. "Don't get all worked up."

"He's right, Gisele," I put in, noticing that her eyes had started to take on that now-familiar, frenzied expression. I realized that she was about to have another of her unsettling panic attacks.

"Just stay calm," Gifford advised, as though he, too, knew what was coming.

"How can I stay calm? My husband needs me!"

"We'll be on our way back to Zurich as soon as we can," I told her. "And you can catch the first plane home."

"But . . . I feel trapped!"

"Don't think about it. Why don't you try to enjoy your last day in Switzerland," I suggested. "Remember how homesick you are when you're back in New York? How you wish you could be here? It might be a while before you can get back to Zurich again, especially if Anson has a long rehabilitation period."

"I don't care about Zurich. I need him," she said plaintively, sounding like a little girl. "I need Anson. I can't stand being so far from him. He needs me. If he's awake, he's wondering where I am. What will he think when I'm not there?"

"David will explain," I told her. "You know that David will tell him that you came here for his sake."

"No!" She clasped her hand to her mouth, tears welling in her eyes. "I didn't. That's not the only reason. I . . . I came because I was afraid . . . I couldn't stand seeing him lying there so helplessly . . . Oh, God . . ."

"Gisele," Gifford said, "that isn't entirely true. You did what you thought was best."

"I did?"

"You did. And no one can blame you for that."

"No one can blame me for that," she echoed his words, even as mascara-streaked tears streamed down her cheeks. "No one can blame me."

I found myself feeling sorry for her, as much as I wanted to remain detached. She really was a mess.

Uncomfortable with the emotional display and with my own suspicions of Anson's wife, I excused myself and headed back to my chalet to await word from Bonnie, leaving Gisele in Jerrold Gifford's hands.

* * *

The afternoon dragged on, and so did the storm.

I reached Charley at last, and was informed that Bruno Green had been identified by the woman from the car rental place as the man posing as Zedekiah Gold. Detectives had been questioning him relentlessly, but he refused to give up any information.

"He's tough, Mayor," Charley told me. "If we only had something we could throw at him—something that would scare him into telling us who hired him. We've tried everything, but he won't crack."

"Keep trying, Charley. And if I come up with something, I'll be in touch right away. What about a link with the Hubbard shooting in Bedford? Did the Westchester police manage to tie him to that?"

"Actually, no. He's got an alibi for that one, Mr. Mayor. And it's airtight. He was at work. He does building maintenance at a bunch of places on the Upper East Side. His boss and two coworkers have already confirmed that he was with them that night."

"Interesting," I said, rubbing my chin. "But it doesn't prove that he didn't kill Kinsella."

"Nope. Sooner or later, we'll manage to get him on that, Mr. Mayor. We won't let him get away with it."

After hanging up, I sat at the desk in my chalet, working my way through the stacks of papers I had brought with me in my briefcase, and waiting to hear from Bonnie. I also tried in vain to reschedule the appointment with Georg Hadwin. It seemed he would be unavailable to meet with me for the next several days, which was a serious problem. I couldn't afford to stay away from New York any longer. It looked like I would have to fly back tomorrow, and try to schedule a return trip as soon as I could get away again—or entrust matters to someone else on the committee in Anson's absence.

I tried to keep my mind on my work, but I kept wondering what was keeping Bonnie, and whether she would be successful in obtaining the list. And if she did, would it mean anything to the investigation? Or would it be just another dead end?

Finally, as long shadows began to fall across the red and green carpet, there was a knock on the door of my chalet.

My bodyguards were instantly alert, and Lou went over to open it.

"Who's there?" he called, his hand on the knob.

There was no reply.

"They probably can't hear you over the wind," I said. "Just open it, Lou."

He did, slowly, keeping a hand on his weapon.

Bonnie stood there in the swirling snow. In her hand was a sheaf of papers. I stood and hurried over as she stepped inside.

"I finally reached Bea," she said breathlessly. Her usually pale cheeks were bright red from the chill. "I had tried her all day, but she wasn't in."

"Did she get the list and fax it to you?"

"That's what this is," she said, handing over the document in her hand. "It took forever for it to be transmitted, it's so long."

I took it and glanced at the first page. She had been right about the content. It was a list of nondormant accounts held by Swiss citizens during the war years, and detailed deposits and withdrawals made during that time.

"Bonnie, you didn't tell anyone about this, did you?" I asked, carrying it over to my desk and putting it into my briefcase, which I then locked securely.

"Are you kidding? I'm scared, Mr. Koch. If the wrong person found out I had it, who knows what could happen?"

"I'm going to look into this," I told her, "just as soon as we get back to New York."

"How are you going to do that?"

I hesitated. "I'm not sure," I finally admitted. I had no idea who, if anyone, to trust. I didn't dare ask Gisele or David about it. The only person I really needed to talk to, the only one I would risk telling, was Anson—and that was impossible until he had regained consciousness. Even then, he might not be capable of such a discussion for quite some time, until he had recuperated considerably.

For the time being, things had come to a standstill.

"Thank you for telling me what you knew, Bonnie," I said. "It was the right thing to do. And try not to worry."

"I'll try . . ." But she didn't look convinced. "I can't wait until this whole thing is over and things are back to normal. I miss home, and I miss Anson."

I passed along what Gisele had told me about him fluttering his eyelids, and Bonnie's face brightened. "Maybe he's coming around, then," she said optimistically. "Do you think he'll pull out of this, Mr. Koch?"

"I think he will," I told her.

I just didn't want to think about what he might face when he did.

I went to bed early, after a night spent alone at my desk, going over the rest of the work I had brought with me and making several phone calls back to New York regarding city business. Things had been relatively quiet in my absence, although the motorman of that subway train that had derailed had been found to be intoxicated.

As I lay in the dark listening to the storm and thinking about the case, I wondered again where that list had come from, and why it had been suppressed, and who had known of its existence.

And as I did, I was struck by a sudden thought.

It was a hunch, really, one that came out of nowhere, yet it made so much sense that I didn't see why I hadn't come up with it sooner.

With the winds still slamming the chalet and snow still coming down furiously outside, I turned on the lamp, got out of bed, and walked over to the bureau. Opening the top drawer, I pulled out my briefcase and removed the faxed copy of the list.

I returned to the bed, sat on the edge of the mattress, and looked again at the first page. As I had suspected, the list was alphabetical. That would make it infinitely easier to find the information I sought.

With trembling fingers, I flipped through the pages, searching for the name that would unlock the mystery at last.

If it wasn't here, I would have to take my chances and wait to talk to Anson.

But if it was here, I would know who had tried to kill him, hoping to stop the investigation—and why.

I realized that I was holding my breath as I turned one more page, and then another, scanning the list of names.

Was it here . . . ?

Was it . . . ?

"My God," I murmured, seeing, in bold black and white, precisely the evidence I had hoped—and yet dreaded—to find there.

After a long moment, I reached for the phone and grimly dialed Charley Deacon in New York.

THIRTEEN

We boarded the flight to New York an hour late the next afternoon, due to a mechanical difficulty.

As we waited in the Zurich airport lounge, I found myself fighting the urge to pace the room. I didn't want anyone to know of the anxiety that had been churning inside me since I had made my chilling discovery the night before. I had managed to act nonchalant during the bus trip back to Zurich from the mountains, pretending to be completely absorbed in a stack of city budget reports. Nobody had seemed to notice that anything was amiss.

But by now, my agitation must have been relatively transparent, because I could feel Byron Klein watching me with a shrewd gaze as our group waited for the boarding announcement.

Finally, he came over and asked, "Is everything all right, Mr. Mayor? You seem disturbed about something."

"Of course I'm disturbed. This delay is frustrating. I have a considerable amount of business waiting for my attention in New York."

"That's it?"

"What's it?" I asked, irritated.

"That's all that's bothering you?"

"Of course it is. I'm the mayor of New York. I don't have time to sit around airports twiddling my thumbs."

"Huh," he said, still watching me in a way that told me he wasn't convinced.

I shifted my gaze away from his, looking around the lounge. Gisele sat alone on a couch, her cellular phone clutched to her ear. I wondered who she was speaking to. She appeared to be chatting in an animated manner, looking almost like her old self in a fashionable burgundy pants suit, her hair impeccably swept up on top of her head, and dark glasses lending an added touch of glamor. I hadn't yet spoken to her today; she had slept throughout the trip back to Zurich.

But I had learned, through Charley Deacon, that Anson had been stirring and was expected to regain consciousness any time now. I found myself torn upon hearing that news, and dreading what lay ahead.

Out of the corner of my eye, I saw Bonnie lift her head from the magazine she was supposedly reading, though she hadn't turned a page in twenty minutes. She darted a glance in my direction, then buried her head in the article once again.

"She seems awfully skittish," Byron commented, and I saw that his reporter's eye hadn't missed a thing.

"Who seems skittish?"

"Bonnie Tyson. I've noticed that she's been acting strangely for days now," he mused, almost to himself.

"Really? I hadn't noticed. I haven't really spoken to her recently."

That was the truth. The last contact I'd had with her was yesterday afternoon in my chalet, when she turned over the list. I had been half-expecting her to confront me this morning before we left the resort, to ask whether I'd made any progress on the case. She hadn't, and for that, I was grateful. I couldn't risk giving anything away. Not now. Not when I was so close to seeing the mystery resolved . . .

If we could just get on the damn plane!

It was another ten minutes before there was a telltale click over the PA system. The boarding announcement for our flight was finally made—first in German, then in French, and finally in English.

Flanked by my bodyguards, I walked briskly toward the jetway at last.

On the plane, I found myself seated next to Gisele, with my bodyguards located in front of and behind us, as well as across the aisle.

Gisele looked pleased to see me. "Ed, how have you been? We haven't had a chance to talk yet today."

"I've been busy, actually. I've been taking advantage of these delays to catch up on all kinds of paperwork."

"What about your meeting with Georg Hadwin? Jerrold mentioned that you hadn't been able to reschedule it, and that's why you're flying home now."

"That's true," I said, knowing Gifford must have heard that news through Hadwin himself. I hadn't spoken to the government official since yesterday, except for a brief, civil farewell this morning.

"It's too bad you've had another setback with the investigation. But I can't say I'm sorry that it's going to be put on hold for the time being. I've been so worried about you, Ed. About all of us . . . Oh, Miss?"

She had flagged a passing flight attendant, who turned and asked, "Can I help you?"

"I'd like a glass of water, please, so that I can take some medication before we take off," Gisele said.

When the flight attendant hurried away to get the water, I asked casually, "What kind of medication are you taking, Gisele?"

"Oh, just a mild sedative. I've always been a nervous flier." She removed a small orange prescription bottle from her purse.

When the flight attendant brought the water, I managed to catch a glimpse of the label on the bottle of pills. I realized that it wasn't a mild sedative at all, but extremely powerful anti-anxiety medication.

Gisele swallowed two capsules, then leaned back, and said to me, "Wake me when we get to New York. I'll probably be out this whole trip. I'm exhausted."

"What about Anson?" I asked her. "How is he?"

"Things are looking up," she said, and I saw that her smile

seemed genuine. "I'm hoping that by the time we land, he'll be conscious. I can't wait to see him. You have no idea how much I've missed him."

"I can just imagine," I murmured, and picked up the airline's magazine from the pouch in front of me.

I settled back to flip through it absently as beside me, Gisele drifted off to sleep.

Gisele woke up only when the Fasten Seatbelts bell rang as we began our descent into JFK airport in New York. Outside the windows was nothing but dense white clouds.

Looking utterly refreshed, Gisele stretched and looked around, then at me. "What's going on?" she asked languidly.

"We're going to be landing soon," I told her. I reached into the pocket of my trench coat, which I had put on halfway through the flight. I fumbled around and took out a pack of gum.

"We're landing already?" she asked.

I had to smirk at that. For me, the flight had been endless.

"Why are you wearing your coat? Anxious to get off the plane?"

"You better believe it. Would you like a stick of gum?" I offered her the pack.

"No, thanks. I have to watch my sugar intake. Too much makes me crazy."

The flight attendant came through the cabin, checking to see that everything was in order for landing. It wouldn't be long now.

"I'll bet you're glad to be back," Gisele commented to me as she snapped open a compact and studied her reflection. "I know how much you've missed New York this week."

"I'm always glad to get back. Are you feeling bad about leaving Switzerland behind?"

"It's never easy." She brushed some pink rouge onto her high cheekbones, and added, "But of course I'm anxious to see Anson."

"I'm sure you are. And I know that as soon as he's feeling better, he and I are going to be able to get to the bottom of this investigation."

The plane bumped as it dropped lower.

"I don't mean to ruin your plans, Ed," Gisele said, "but I doubt that Anson will be able to work on anything but his rehabilitation in the near future. And as I said, I'm going to urge him to retire."

I shrugged. "Then I'll have to pursue this thing on my own."

"Ladies and gentlemen," came a voice over the public address system. "We're on our final approach to John F. Kennedy International Airport. In preparation for landing, please see that your seatbelts are securely fastened and your tray tables are locked. We should be on the ground in a few minutes."

Lou, seated across the aisle, caught my eye, and we exchanged a meaningful look.

"But Ed," Gisele was saying, "if Georg Hadwin won't agree to give you the information you need, or even meet with you, how are you going to pursue anything?"

"There are other ways to get information," I told her, tugging on my seatbelt to make sure it was snug.

"Other ways?"

"I'm sure you know what I mean, Gisele," I said pleasantly. "After all, you were the one who got the list in the first place. What did you do? Have your old friend Jerrold Gifford pull some strings for you?"

'What are you talking about?"

I saw that she had gone pale beneath the rouge she had just applied.

"I'm talking about the list of Swiss citizens who had non-dormant accounts during the war years."

"But . . . that's the list Hadwin wouldn't give you."

"That's right. And he didn't."

I paused.

The plane bumped again, dipping lower.

"I don't understand," Gisele said, her voice high and frantic. "I don't see what this list has to do with me . . . or Jerrold."

"You obtained the list from him, Gisele. You were hoping to help Anson's cause—you knew it was something he needed for his investigation into the missing funds."

She was wild-eyed. "What are you—"

"You didn't even tell him what you had done, did you, Gisele? Because you knew your husband wouldn't approve of the method you had used to get your hands on it. He's an honest man. He would never stoop to illegal snooping into sealed records. But then, Anson never saw the list or even knew you had it, did he?"

She faltered. "What list?" she asked feebly.

"He didn't know because it turned out that there was something on it that you didn't want him to see. A name that you never expected to find there."

"I don't know what you're—"

"Hans Jurgen," I said succinctly. "Your father's name, Gisele."

She stared at me. Then she seemed to recover a bit, and sputtered, "So what if my father had an account in a Swiss bank? That doesn't mean anything."

"What about the fact that he was almost penniless in the years leading up to the war, Gisele? And then, right around the time that you mention him as being sympathetic to the Jewish cause, he started making deposits. Large deposits."

There was a whirring sound as the wheels lowered beneath the belly of the plane.

"He wanted to help the Jews," Gisele said, her voice high-pitched again, but quiet, as though she feared being overheard. "Papa was just like a lot of other people. He was trying to help them hide their money from the Nazis. I told you. He was sympathetic to their cause."

"Is that why he systematically emptied the account as the war years wound to a close, Gisele? The timing coincides with your family's change of fortune. You moved to a bigger house in a nicer neighborhood. Your father built a state-of-the-art lab. And he did it with money he stole from victims of the Holocaust."

The wing flaps hummed as they were positioned for landing.

"My father wasn't a thief!" Gisele informed me, her blue eyes icier than the Alps. "He was a hero! He saved the lives of thousands of children!"

"I'm not arguing with that, Gisele."

The plane banked to the right.

"But in order to come up with that vaccine," I continued, "your father needed a fancy lab. He needed new equipment. Research assistants. And all of that took money he didn't have . . . until he cleaned out the life savings of people he had written off as dead. And most of them probably were."

She was staring at me in horror, shaking her head slowly, mutely.

"I can imagine how upset you were when you realized that your beloved Papa wasn't a hero after all, Gisele," I said. "You were distraught. So distraught that you snapped. You were desperate not to let anyone find out what you had learned. You knew that Anson's committee would eventually uncover the truth, and you had to stop them. You had to stop him. Your own husband."

She buried her face in her hands.

"So you hired a hit man to kill him," I concluded.

"No!" Her head snapped up. "I never wanted to kill him. I told that oaf to shoot *at* him—scare him!"

"Bruno Green?" I asked casually, wondering if she was telling the truth.

If she hadn't intended for Anson to be killed, I could release that last nagging doubt that had been in the back of my mind all day.

You see, I always trust my instincts. And my instincts had told me all along that Gisele Hubbard truly loved and needed her husband. That was why I couldn't imagine her wanting to kill him, no matter how emotionally unbalanced she was.

"Yes, Bruno Green," she answered, narrowing her eyes. "That idiot! I only wanted to shake Anson up a little so that he would be afraid. So that he'd back off the investigation. Instead, the idiot went and killed a bodyguard!"

"And what about Anson's car being nearly forced off the road?"

"I had nothing to do with that!" she said, so promptly and so vehemently that I believed her. "That was a coincidence, Ed! I swear!"

"But the shooting at your home? Did Bruno Green botch that, too?"

"No." She shook her head, and I saw that tears were spilling from her eyes. "No, I did. I shot him. I never meant to do it!"

She was sobbing, her arms wrapped around herself as she rocked back and forth. She seemed to have forgotten I was here, or where we were.

Outside the windows, the thick clouds gave way to wisps, and the cityscape came into view as we raced toward the ground.

"So you only meant to scare Anson off the investigation, is that right, Gisele?"

"Yes. Yes! I've always been an expert markswoman. Papa taught me to shoot at our estate in France. I only wanted to break the window of Anson's office. But I was so damn nervous that night . . . I couldn't hold the gun straight enough to aim carefully. I panicked . . ."

"And you shot him."

"It was . . . it was an accident. I swear! I never wanted to hurt him. I never wanted to lose him. That's why I did it in the first place. If he had ever found out about Papa . . . if word ever got out, his career would have been ruined. And we would have been penniless. We would have lost everything. How could he ever forgive me for that? And what about David?"

"What about David?"

"Come on, Ed, he's Jewish. Do you know how many of his ancestors were wiped out in the Holocaust? Do you know how poor David was growing up? His family had lost everything. How could he ever forgive me if he knew what my father had done?"

There was a rushing sound as the wheels touched down, then the plane bounced and the wheels touched down again, hurtling us along the runway.

Gisele let out a low, soft moan. "I never meant to hurt Anson, Ed . . . you've got to believe me."

"And what about me? Did you mean to hurt me when you pushed that boulder over the cliff?"

"Of course not! I only wanted to scare you off. And I did . . ."

"No, Gisele," I said quietly. "You didn't."

The plane roared along the ground, then slowed to a stop.

Gisele was looking at me, and her eyes grew wide. She clasped a trembling hand over her mouth as though she had suddenly realized what she had done.

"No . . ." she whispered and shook her head. "No . . . I—I didn't do it. I didn't do any of it."

The plane turned and began to taxi to the gate.

"You just told me that you did."

"I'm on medication . . . I can't even think clearly."

"Well, you spoke clearly. I heard you very clearly."

"You don't have proof of anything!"

I shrugged. "You just confessed to me, Gisele."

"I didn't confess to anything!" she denied, sounding desperate.

"It sounded to me as though you did."

The plane came to a halt at the gate and the bell dinged, signaling that we were free to go.

Gisele jumped to her feet and grabbed her purse, turning abruptly toward the marked exit door a few feet away.

"Just a moment, Ms. Hubbard." Lou Sabatino had risen from his seat and stood in the aisle, blocking her way. "I'm going to be escorting you into the terminal."

"Move out of my way! What are you—?"

"There are some gentlemen waiting there who would like to ask you some questions," I interrupted Gisele, who was attempting to push her way past Lou. "And if you don't make a big fuss, none of the other passengers will realize what's going on. There won't be an embarrassing scene. Byron Klein and the other reporters won't even have to know."

Gisele stared at me as it dawned on her what was happening.

"You can't prove anything!" she said again. "Anson will stand by me. He'll never let you pin this on me."

I shrugged and stood, shoving my hands into the pockets of my trench coat.

With Lou grasping her arm firmly, Gisele was steered toward the exit. I followed behind, my other bodyguards surrounding me.

Inside my pocket, I clicked the Stop button of the tape recorder my mother had insisted that I bring along, to record my impressions of Switzerland.

"Everyone should keep a travel journal," she had said when she pressed it on me as I left Gracie Mansion that last morning. "I know you'll be glad I told you to bring this along."

For once, I thought incredulously, my mother had been right.

Chuckling to myself, I stepped out into the terminal just as Charley Deacon and several other detectives surrounded Gisele.

"Hey, look, it's the mayor!" That had come from a passenger in the waiting area.

"Ed! Welcome back!" someone else called.

"How'm I doin'?" I asked.

"You tell us," suggested the first passenger. "How *are* you doin'?"

"Couldn't be better," I said contentedly, "Now that I'm back home."

EPILOGUE

"And now, ladies and gentlemen," I boomed into the microphone, standing before the packed ballroom of the Waldorf-Astoria, "it brings me great pleasure to introduce Senator Anson Hubbard!"

The applause was thunderous.

It lasted the whole time it took Anson to shuffle to the podium from his seat nearby. He was moving gingerly, wincing slightly, still not fully recovered from the bullet that had shattered his body. The doctors had said that physically, he wouldn't be back to normal for quite some time.

I knew that emotionally, he never would be.

How could he ever get over what his wife had done?

How could he forget that the woman he had loved for forty years had hired a hit man to shoot at him, and then, when that plan had backfired, had shot at him herself?

Anson believed, as I did, that she hadn't meant to hurt him, though the authorities were dubious about that. But Bruno Green had backed up Gisele's claim, admitting that she had asked him only to fire at our group that night as we exited the building on Wall Street. Hitting Kinsella had been an accident. It would never have happened, Green had said, if the bodyguard hadn't thrown himself in the path of the bullets upon hearing the shots.

He hadn't counted on the freckle-faced kid from Maryland behaving like a hero.

As soon as he was able to make arrangements for them, Anson had seen to it that Kinsella's wife and daughter would never have to worry about their future, or money for college. He had set up a trust fund for the little girl, and had taken to visiting her quite often. If you ask me, those visits were as beneficial for him as his monetary help was for Kinsella's widow and daughter. Spending time with them was helping him to heal his wounded spirit, and to reconcile what had happened. And the baby brought joy into his shattered, lonely world.

"Seeing that little girl is almost like having a grandchild," he had confided to me.

He went on to say that he had always wanted children, but he had known that Gisele's emotional problems would never allow her to handle the responsibility. He had resigned himself to remaining childless for her sake.

"And I didn't mind, Ed," he had said sadly. "I was so in love with her that it didn't matter. I still am. No matter what she did, she's my wife."

The applause continued to reverberate through the crowded ballroom even after Anson had reached the microphone. He stood, gazing out over the crowd, and I could see tears in his eyes. I wondered what he was thinking.

I figured I knew.

He was thinking about Gisele.

My poor, sweet Gisele, as he called her. He visited her almost every day in the private mental hospital David had found for her not far from their Bedford estate. Anson was holding out hope that someday, Gisele would be able to come back home and they could put the past behind them.

David had confided to me, privately, that it didn't look very likely. She had suffered a complete breakdown after her arrest. It turned out that after I tipped off Charley Deacon about her involvement, the detectives had used the information to prod Green into confessing that she had hired him. They had met when she hired him to do some maintenance work at the Hubbards' east side townhouse, and she had known about his criminal record.

She had paid him very well, and he had figured that since she wasn't asking him to actually harm anyone, it couldn't hurt to cooperate.

Now Bruno Green was being tried for the murder of Bill Kinsella.

Gisele's doctors had deemed it unlikely that she would ever be mentally fit to stand trial for what she had done. But her punishment had already been dealt. She would spend the rest of her days locked away from the world, out of the spotlight she had once adored, never again able to visit the beloved homeland she had left behind.

Justice had been served.

I had asked Gisele, right after her arrest, about the name Zedekiah Gold. Bruno Green had confessed to the authorities that she asked him to use that particular alias, though he had no idea why.

Gisele revealed that she had always known that Zedekiah meant "God's Justice" in Hebrew. It had been the name of a close friend of her father's back in Switzerland; a friend who had disappeared during the war, never to be seen again.

In her mind, her father hadn't done anything wrong, no matter what the rest of the world thought. He was a hero; he had saved the lives of countless children through the discovery of that vaccine. Besides, the people who had entrusted him with their money and their gold weren't coming back. If nobody claimed them, the Swiss government would most likely turn the funds over to charity, as was a common practice in that country. Why shouldn't Hans use it for his own noble cause?

To Gisele, then, keeping her father's name clean—no matter what she had to do in order to achieve that—would ensure "God's Justice."

I sighed at her misguided efforts to do the right thing, and turned my attention back to the far more pleasant matter at hand.

"Thank you," Anson was saying into the microphone, over the applause, and his voice cracked with emotion as he looked out over the room. "Thank you very much."

I scanned the crowd and saw familiar faces amidst the strangers. There was David Berkman, flanked by his elderly parents. There was my Chairman of City Planning, Monica Hoffman, with her wheelchair-bound husband Sheldon and their grown children.

They, along with scores of other Holocaust survivors and descendants of victims, were here today to honor Anson Hubbard, whose dedication had resulted in the restoration of their lost fortunes.

As the Senator began to speak, I looked out over the sea of beaming faces, and I, too, smiled.

God's Justice had indeed been served.

ONE

Chestnuts roasting in the open air . . . lavishly decorated department store windows . . . bell-ringing Santas on bustling street corners . . .

Nowhere in the world are the holidays more festive than they are right here in New York City.

And don't tell me I'm biased. I may be mayor of the Big Apple, but if you ask anyone, anywhere, which city they'd most like to visit in December, I'd be willing to bet it's my own hometown.

And this year promised to be as merry as any other—until the glorious season was interrupted by a shocking murder. . . .

I'm not foolish enough to think that you catch a cold simply by being exposed to cold weather, no matter what my grandmother used to say.

But when I woke the morning after Thanksgiving to find my nose streaming and my head hot and pounding, I couldn't help but wonder if it had anything to do with my participation in yesterday's parade.

Don't get me wrong. I didn't regret marching for hours behind the Rockettes, waving at throngs of adorable children that lined the route. But I had been feeling run-down ever since getting over the stomach virus I'd caught during my post–Election Day visit to Washington.

And I had realized, when I saw the weather Thanksgiving morning, that it wouldn't do me any good to be out in driving rain with temperatures hovering around freezing. I had already done that once this week, at a funeral for a police officer who had been killed by a sniper in Brooklyn.

Anyone who knows me can vouch for the fact that I'd be as likely to back out of marching in New York City's annual Thanksgiving Day Parade as I would be to pack my bags and retire in Sandusky.

So, there I was on Thursday, smiling and waving all the way from the Upper West Side to Herald Square.

And here I was on Friday morning, telling my driver to pull over in midtown, en route to City Hall, so that I could hop out of the car and dash into Duane Reade to pick up some of my favorite honey and lemon lozenges.

Though it was just past nine, and a light snow had been falling since dawn, I noticed that the sidewalk was crowded with business people, tourists, and early bird shoppers.

My bodyguard, Ambrose Kaloyeropoulos, insisted on coming along, of course. When you're mayor of New York City, there are very few places where you're allowed to venture unescorted—and none of them are out in public.

I found the lozenges in a hurry, and Ambrose and I made our way to the line at the front of the store.

"Hey, Ed," someone said, coming up behind me. "How's it going?"

I looked around. Most of the time when someone says, *"Hey, Ed,"* it's a total stranger. That, too, comes with the territory when you're mayor of New York.

This time, however, I actually recognized the speaker. It was the middle-aged niece of my longtime secretary, Rosemary Larkin, who had retired over a year ago.

"Louellen," I said, transferring the bag of throat drops into my left hand and shaking her hand with my right. "It's good to see you. What has your aunt been up to?"

"She's spending the winter down in Miami Beach again," Louellen informed me, adjusting her thick bifocals on her long nose. "Right about now, Aunt Ro's probably lying in the sun, drinking freshly squeezed orange juice, reading the *Times,* and chuckling about the weather we've been getting here."

"She always did hate the cold and snow." Personally, I'm not overly fond of either, but I have no intention of spending my retirement years anyplace other than right here in New York. Not that I'm opposed to winter vacations in warmer climates.

In fact, I was looking forward to my upcoming trip to Barbados, which I had been planning for months now.

Louellen was nodding her dyed blond head. "But as much as Aunt Rosemary loves the weather in Florida, she's pretty homesick. You know how she loves New York."

"Who doesn't?"

She smiled and nodded.

I covered my mouth as a cough slipped out.

"Are you coming down with something, Ed?"

"Just a little cold."

"What are you taking for it?"

"Nothing yet," I said, holding up the cellophane bag of lozenges. "But I'm going to pop one of these in just as soon as I pay for them."

"Nah," she said with a brusque shake of her head that was sharply reminiscent of her aunt. "You don't want those. They're candy."

"They're not candy," I protested. "They always work just fine."

"Think what you want," Louellen said with a shrug. "What you need is the old Larkin family remedy. Didn't Aunt Ro ever tell you about it?"

"Not that I can recall."

"What you need is a pan of hot salt water, whiskey, honey, and some oil of peppermint—do you keep oil of peppermint in the kitchen at Gracie Mansion? Why am I asking? You must," she said, as if no kitchen would be complete without the stuff.

"I'd have to check with my chef," I told her, knowing Lucien wouldn't take to my concocting a potion of hot salt water, whiskey, and honey, oil of peppermint or no oil of peppermint.

He had very definite ideas about what one did and did not do in a kitchen, as he had let me know on more than one occasion.

I knew better than to wander in and start whipping up a snack or anything else when he was on duty.

"So anyway, Ed, as I was saying, you put it all together, and you sip it. I'm telling you, you'll be good as new by tonight," Louellen promised.

"Sounds interesting," I said politely, aware that Ambrose was shifting his weight from one foot to the other and trying not to look amused.

I glanced at the head of the line, where the cashier was calling, "Void! Void! I need a manager."

"And if by chance *that* remedy doesn't work," Louellen started to say, "you need to find a rushing brook and stick your head—"

"Where are you headed this morning?" I asked her, to change the subject.

"Shopping. I wanted to buy some film for my camera." She motioned at the black nylon pouch dangling around her neck.

"Your camera?"

"I promised my grandson up in Albany that I'd take pictures of the roller coaster. It's supposed to be the largest in the Northeast."

I blinked. Had I missed something, or had she just told me she was going shopping?

"What roller coaster, Louellen?"

"The one at Highview Meadows."

"Oh."

That roller coaster.

"And I wanted to see the reindeer at the petting zoo. It's the biggest petting zoo in the Northeast."

"I see. So that's why you're going on this little expedition?"

"Of course that's not *why*. The main reason is that I have a lot of Christmas shopping to do."

"Why are you going all the way to New Jersey to shop, Louellen? Don't you live right over on Thirty-third, just off Fifth?"

She nodded, looking vaguely uncomfortable. "I *will* do some shopping here in the city, of course, Ed. But I couldn't help wondering about that gigantic new mall. It's the biggest enclosed mall in—"

"Yeah, I know, I know," I cut in. "In the Northeast."

"No," she said a little smugly. "In the world."

"It can't be."

"Oh, it is."

"Well, what's so wonderful about a huge suburban mall, when you can shop for anything you want right here on Fifth Avenue? Or Madison?" I couldn't help asking.

"It's *cold* on Fifth Avenue. And Madison. In the mall, I don't even have to wear a coat."

I couldn't argue with that. But . . .

"And anyway," she continued, pulling out a compact and checking her pink lipstick in the mirror, "it's so easy to get to Highview Meadows now that they're running that shuttle service from the corner."

"What corner?"

"That corner," she said, snapping her compact closed and pointing just outside the store.

Sure enough, there, on the opposite corner of East Thirty-fourth Street, was a cluster of people—mostly eager-looking women and teenage girls, none of them seeming to mind the fact that they were forced to wait in subzero temperatures as snowflakes drifted relentlessly from the gray sky.

I had noticed the crowd earlier as I stepped out of my car, and had assumed they were waiting to see the famed windows of Ramsey's Department Store.

But now I realized that the store was a few yards away from the throng. Even more intriguing, there was no one standing between the velvet ropes that traditionally funneled shoppers and tourists past Ramsey's windows.

Strange.

This year's display was supposed to be more spectacular than ever, with animated scenes depicting American Christmases through the ages. My good friend Sybil Baker had told me all about it. She was all jazzed about the fact that her pal Muriel, one of Ramsey's window designers, had borrowed her enormous vintage radio for the Depression-era scene.

"How much are they charging for this shuttle service?" I asked Louellen, rubbing my chin and staring at the traitorous crowd.

"It's free. And I heard that the drivers are going to be handing out vouchers for free sleigh rides at the winter carnival they've set up behind the mall."

"Is that so?"

"And someone even said they're serving free hot chocolate in the international food court."

"The *international* food court? What nationality came up with hot chocolate?" I asked wryly.

"I don't know . . . maybe the Swiss?"

I sighed and looked again at the register, really starting to get impatient. I had a ten o'clock meeting with my deputy mayor and a press conference right after that.

Luckily, the store manager had fixed the void in question and the cashier had taken the next customer in line, who was standing in front of me. Thank goodness I was almost out of there.

"You're still going to buy those things?" Louellen asked, motioning at the bag in my hand.

"You better believe it. You're still going all the way to Jersey to go shopping?"

She grinned. "You better believe it."

"Mr. Mayor,what do you think of Highview Meadows?"

The question came at the tail end of the press conference, from a twenty-something reporter whose trendy faux fur jacket and matching headband suggested she knew a thing or two about shopping.

"What do *you* think of Highview Meadows?" I shot right back at her.

"Me?" She looked a little taken aback. "To be perfectly honest, I think it's an amazing place. I can see why everyone in New York is so hot to do their Christmas shopping there instead of in Manhattan, which brings me back to my original point—"

"Highview Meadows has nothing to offer that we don't have right here in New York's many fine shopping districts. In fact, anything we offer here in New York is bigger and better—the best bargains money can buy. Does that answer whatever question you were about to ask?"

"But Highview Meadows has a skating rink and—"

"Did something happen to Rockefeller Center while I wasn't looking? Or to the Wollman Rink? Or to—"

"What about the petting zoo at the mall in Jersey?" someone called out.

I cleared my aching throat before firing back, "Have you been to the Children's Zoo in Central Park since it's been renovated? The place is incredible."

"They're offering free sleigh rides."

"And hot chocolate," another reporter, a pretty, young brunette, put in.

I guffawed as loudly as the rest of the crowd did at that.

"You need to go all the way to Jersey for free hot chocolate?" I asked the woman, who was now blushing furiously. "Honey, didn't anyone ever tell you that you weren't going to make any money in journalism?"

"But, Mr. Mayor," someone else objected, "there's no clothing tax in New Jersey. That alone has been luring shoppers out of New York until now. How can Manhattan stores compete with the added attraction of the hugest indoor mall in the world?"

"How," I retorted, "can New Jersey compete with the tree at Rockefeller Center, and Radio City Music Hall, and carriage rides in Central Park? How can one measly mall compete with the excitement of the holidays here in New York? Malls are a dime a dozen across the country, but there's only one Big Apple."

"Mr. Mayor," another reporter began, but I held up a hand and shook my head.

"I'm finished," I announced. "I've got a lousy cold and a full schedule, and the last thing I want to do is feed some ridiculous rumors about how this sprawling suburban Grinch is stealing Christmas from the Big Apple."

Perfect, I thought as I sailed from the podium and out of the press room.

Too late, I realized I'd made an enormous mistake.

Why, oh, why, had I trumpeted to every major media source in Greater New York that I had a cold?

That meant it was only a matter of time before . . .

⋆ ⋆ ⋆

My mother called five minutes after I arrived at Gracie Mansion Friday evening, having canceled my evening engagement because I felt so rotten. I often spend weekends at my apartment in the Village, but I was having the whole thing painted over the next few weeks.

"How are you feeling, Eddie?"

"I'm fine, Ma." Thanks to my stuffy nose, I couldn't keep it from coming out *I'b fide, Ba.*

"You don't sound fine. They said on the six o'clock news that you were very sick."

"Oh, for the love of . . ."

"I'm coming right over," Joyce Koch informed me. "With some homemade chicken soup."

When it comes to medical breakthroughs, my mother rates her homemade chicken soup right up there with the Salk vaccine. For some reason, she actually thinks I like the stuff and insists on making it for me in sickness *and* in health.

"Ma," I said patiently, "I don't need chicken soup. Especially at this hour." It was well past nine o'clock.

"Have you eaten dinner yet?"

"I was just about to."

"What were you going to have?"

I hesitated. Lucien was off tonight, since I was supposed to be dining at the new Le Cirque with friends.

"You need chicken soup," my mother repeated when I paused too long.

"All I need is to stay home tonight and rest. I'll be—"

"You need chicken soup," she said for the third time. "You also need a Glugol Muggle."

In case you were wondering, a Glugol Muggle is a wonderful concoction handed down from generation to generation on my mother's side of the family.

To make it, you squeeze the juice of a grapefruit, an orange, and a lemon into a saucepan. Add one tablespoon of honey and then one or two jiggers of your favorite liquor. I prefer scotch. Bring the ingredients to a boil and drink it immediately.

My mother did have a point.

I probably did need a Glugol Muggle. Maybe even two Glugol Muggles.

Still . . .

"You don't have to come out in the snow just to—"

"I should let my son suffer alone? No," my mother said firmly. "I'm coming. I'll be in a cab, so tell the security at the gate that your mother's on her way and not to monkey around when I get there."

I started to protest, then realized it would be useless. She probably already had the matzo balls waiting in a Tupperware container by the apartment door.

"Where's Pop?" I asked instead, reaching for a Kleenex and blowing my nose. "Tell him to drive you. It's safer than a cab in this weather."

"Lately, I don't know," she said, and I could picture her shaking her head sadly. She's been convinced my father's eyesight has been failing for years, and drags him off to an optometrist every chance she gets.

"What's wrong?" I asked absently.

"He's driving me crazy. Every time we get into the car, it's an argument. Just yesterday we were heading out to Commack to visit your cousin Sylvia, and he got into one of those EZ-Pass lanes."

Uh-oh, I thought. I knew he hadn't applied for an EZ-Pass electronic toll tag for his car, even though I had tried to explain to him that it is an incredibly efficient means of toll paying and would, in just a year, save him hours of waiting in traffic.

Pop simply couldn't grasp the notion of paying into an account and placing an electronic tag on his car so that the toll would automatically be deducted every time it passed through a toll booth. He doesn't even like to use tokens at New York's many bridges and tunnels.

To him, the only dependable means of paying tolls is the old-fashioned way, involving cash and human beings.

"So anyway," my mother went on, "I said, 'Lou, get out of the lane, you're in the wrong lane,' and he kept saying, 'What? What are you talking about?' He wouldn't budge, Eddie. Kept telling me to look how short the line was, and why would he want to get into a longer line?"

I shook my head, picturing the scene all too clearly.

"Then we got up to the booth, and he stopped and was looking for the toll collector. I said, 'Lou, that's not how it works,' and he said, 'What are you talking about?' again. And so I said to him—"

"Ma," I cut in, "I hate to interrupt, but all I asked was where is Pop tonight?"

"He's not here."

"Where is he?"

"It's Friday."

"So? It's Friday."

"So? Your father's out playing pinochle, Eddie, remember? He's been playing pinochle every Friday night for months."

"Good for him. What about you?"

"What about me?"

"Don't you have a folk dancing class to go to tonight, or something?"

"I gave that up. The girls at the center"—that would be the neighborhood senior citizens' center, around which Mom's social life revolves these days—"decided folk dancing was too strenuous after Hattie Baumgartner had an episode during one of the classes."

"What kind of episode?"

"Oh, it was nothing. That one, she's always huffing and puffing like her heart is going to give out on her any minute. She just likes the attention. So we're starting a watercolor class, but not until April."

"Why not?" I said absently, flipping through a stack of personal mail on my desk.

I stopped to open my latest statement from Ramsey's Department Store. I had recently returned the sweater I'd bought for Pop on his last birthday—he said the argyle pattern was too "busy"—and wanted to make sure the credit appeared on my account.

"Because most of us go to Florida at this time of year, Eddie. We won't start until everyone's back."

"Mmm-hmm." The Ramsey's envelope contained an announcement that the store's world-famous Santa's Winter Wonderland would be opening the Friday after Thanksgiving—which meant today.

"That reminds me, Eddie, Aunt Honey asked me if I could get her menorah back from you, so if you can—"

"What?" I looked up from the billing statement I had just unfolded. There are times when you really have to pay attention when you're talking to my mother. "Why would I have Aunt Honey's menorah?"

"Pat"—that would be my sister—"told her you borrowed it the last time you visited her in Scarsdale."

That would be this past summer.

"Why," I asked my mother, "would I borrow a menorah in July? Why would I borrow a menorah at all? I happen to have a lovely menorah of my very own that I brought back from my trip to Israel several years ago, thank you very much."

"I'm just telling you what Pat said, Eddie. Why don't you call Aunt Honey and—"

"Ma, I don't have *time* to call Aunt Honey. I don't even have time to call *you.*"

"Such a son. How did I end up with a son who can't make time for his own mother?"

Exasperated, I said, "Ma, I'm a terrific son. I always make time for—"

"I know. Can't you take a joke?" She heaved an exaggerated sigh. "I'm leaving now, Eddie. The soup is piping hot. Make sure you have a bowl and spoon waiting. And a mug for the Glugol Muggle."

I don't know how the woman does it.

Twenty minutes after hanging up the telephone, I was presented with a mug of steaming Glugol Muggle, a bowl of homemade soup, freshly squeezed orange juice, a dazzling array of over-the-counter cold remedies, and a pair of fuzzy slippers.

"I don't wear slippers," I reminded her, eyeing them dubiously.

"That's why you have a cold," Ma informed me, shoving one on my foot. "How does it fit? Too big? Too tight?"

"Where did you find slippers on the spur of the moment?"

"They were going to be one of your Hanukkah presents. I unwrapped them." She squeezed my toes through the end of the slipper and pronounced them a perfect fit. "Now eat your soup."

"But—"

"Eat."

I ate.

And as I ate, I watched the Fox ten o'clock news, rolling my eyes when they aired footage of this morning's press conference, including the discussion of Highview Meadows.

They followed that up with an interview taped earlier this evening with Barnaby Tischler, general manager of Ramsey's Department Store. Barnaby's an old friend of mine, and I wasn't pleased to see him looking drawn and worried as he spoke to the reporter about whether the new mall in New Jersey was hurting his business, which, incidentally, was already rumored to be in trouble.

"We at Ramsey's are as dedicated as we always have been to providing every shopper with personal attention and quality merchandise at competitive prices," Barnaby said—woodenly, if you ask me. And he seemed to be on edge as he adjusted his glasses on the end of his long, narrow nose.

"Do you call thirty dollars for a lipstick a bargain price?" my mother wanted to know, waving her hand at the television screen. "Melissa told Pat she paid thirty dollars for a lipstick at Ramsey's."

Melissa would be Pat's grown daughter, who lives with her husband and child on the Upper West Side.

"I'm sure," Barnaby went on, running a nervous hand through his thinning salt-and-pepper hair, "that New Yorkers are able to recognize the benefits of staying here in town to do their shopping. . . ."

"What are you putting in your lipstick that you think you can charge thirty dollars for it?" Mom demanded of the televised Barnaby Tischler. "Is it made of gold?"

"Shh," I said, trying to hear what he was saying.

" . . . and we are an old-fashioned department store that believes in old-fashioned service. Every member of our staff is committed to showing consumers that they have every reason to shop locally this holiday season. And, kids, don't forget that the one and only Santa Claus is waiting here at Ramsey's to visit with you during our first-ever extended hours in our famous fifth floor Winter Wonderland!"

I had to smile at that. The Ramsey's Santa is as integral to the fabric of this great city as I am.

The publicity surrounding the Ramsey's Santa was inspired way back in the thirties, when a skeptical little boy visited the department store, sat on his lap, and demanded proof that he was the "real" Santa.

Legend has it that Santa glanced up at the child's mother, who had been in a wheelchair after a bout with polio. In that moment when their gazes locked, she suddenly felt a tingling sensation in her legs. Moments later she was standing and taking tentative steps for the first time in a year.

A handful of people witnessed what happened that day. One of them was a newspaper reporter waiting in line to see Santa with his toddler, and he wrote the story as a Christmas Eve feature. It was picked up by wire services everywhere, and sales at Ramsey's skyrocketed.

Nobody seemed bothered by the fact that no one had thought to get the names of the child or his mother so that the story could be verified. And a subsequent revelation that the reporter happened to be a distant cousin of Cornelius Ramsey, the store's founder, did nothing to diminish the magical aura that would surround the Ramsey's Santa for decades. The giant store on Thirty-fourth Street has been a cornerstone of the Manhattan retail scene ever since.

Until now, that is. As I mentioned, the word is that Ramsey's has been in trouble for some time now.

Apparently, I wasn't the only one who'd heard that particular rumor.

". . . and I would like to ask you, Mr. Tischler," the television reporter was saying, "is it true that Ramsey's sales have plummeted drastically over the past year, while sales at Weatherly Brothers, your Thirty-fourth Street neighbor, have improved tremendously?"

"I can't speak for Weatherly Brothers," Barnaby said stiffly, "but I wouldn't say our sales have 'plummeted drastically.' Ramsey's, like many other retailers, has simply been feeling the effects of a rather cautious economic climate."

"Well, I'll take Ramsey's over Weatherly Brothers any day," said Mom, always one to put her two cents in. "I'll never forget the time I bought that expensive dress from them for Pat's wedding—do you remember that, Eddie?—and the sequins started dropping off while I was doing the hora. Remember? Shiny turquoise sequins were rolling all over the dance floor."

"How could I forget? One dropped into Uncle Reuben's cognac."

"Oh, that one and his liquor. He couldn't put his drink down for a few minutes to dance at his niece's wedding? But, you know, he almost choked on that sequin. He could have died and ruined Pat's wedding, all because of that crazy dress."

"Well, I don't know about *that* . . ."

Mom ignored me, on a roll. "When I took it back to Weatherly Brothers and showed the department manager what happened, he said I must have been dancing too hard. I said, 'Who do you think I am? Ginger Rogers?' Dancing too hard . . . Did you ever hear of such a thing?"

"No," I told her honestly, "I never did."

"You know, Eddie," she went on, bouncing off the subject in her usual way, "it's a shame that everyone's leaving New York to do their holiday shopping across the river. I finished mine in June—you know how I like to get things done ahead of time—but if I hadn't, you can bet I wouldn't be on that shuttle to Jersey like the other girls at the center."

So even the "girls" at the center were making the trip to Highview Meadows? That was remarkable, considering that some of them complain about having to cross an avenue to catch a bus.

I know this because several of my mother's friends lobbied me last year to set up bus stops directly opposite each other on both the east and west sides of Lexington Avenue in front of their building. They informed me that the buses traveling downtown could then stop on alternate sides.

"But that would mean you would have to wait twice as long for a bus to stop," I pointed out patiently.

"Well," came the reply, "that would be easy to fix if you just use your brain. All you have to do is put twice as many buses on the route."

There's no arguing with the girls at the center, so I wisely kept my mouth shut. And these days, whenever I run into one of them while I'm visiting my parents, I assure her that I'm still working on the bus problem.

"What are you going to do about this problem, Eddie?" Mom asked, and it took me a moment to realize she was talking about the Jersey shopping center.

"I don't know," I told her, rubbing my chin thoughtfully. "Short of blowing the whole place up, I'm not sure what I can do."

"Eddie!"

"I'm kidding, Ma."

"I knew that," she said defensively, patting me on the arm. "You'll come up with something, Eddie. That's why you're the mayor."

"But you're the mayor, Ed," Barnaby Tischler protested on Monday night in his office, leaning forward in his chair and placing his oversized palms facedown on his desk. "There has to be *something* you can do. That's why I called you here to meet with me."

I shrugged and took a handkerchief out of my suit pocket, blowing my nose. I was on the tail end of what had turned out to be a nasty cold, and would have liked nothing better, after a long Monday at the office and a charity banquet on Staten Island, than to have gone back to Gracie Mansion to collapse.

But Barnaby had phoned this morning and practically begged me for this private late-night meeting in his office, tucked into the cavernous depths of the old store's top floor.

It was a large and drafty office reminiscent of some downtown loft space, with tall windows overlooking Thirty-fourth Street. It contained your standard business furniture as well as a stationary bike and a treadmill. Odd, I thought, considering that Barnaby Tishler is a tall, gaunt Abe Lincoln of a guy who looks as though he's never exercised a single moment in his fifty-odd years.

I told him, "I can't *force* people to stay in town to buy their holiday gifts, Barnaby. This Jersey thing is a problem we've been wrestling with for decades, all year round. We've always lost shoppers who want to go across the state border to Jersey and Connecticut and beat the clothing tax."

"Believe me, I know that. But this is different, Ed. That mall has shuttle stops all over Manhattan, and a lot of them are right in front of our big department stores. They're snatching customers right out from under our noses. People who were headed into my store have been changing their minds at the last minute when they see the shuttles, and they're going to Jersey instead. Can't you do something?"

"I wish I could. But nobody has been breaking any laws, Barnaby. Can't *you* do something?"

"Believe me, I'm trying. I'm doing everything I can do. I'm advertising like crazy, offering coupons and other incentives. I'm even extending our hours. We're going to be open twenty-four hours around the clock on every weekend from now until Christmas to accommodate people who can't find time to shop because of work schedules."

"That's a great idea."

"It's not going to be enough, Ed. Ramsey's is as much a part of Manhattan as Bloomingdale's and Macy's, but I don't know how much longer we're going to stay open. If things don't pick up this season, I'm going to have to file Chapter Eleven."

"I'm sorry to hear that. It would be a terrible shame."

"Yes, it would. And that's not all."

Something in his tone caused me to lean forward in my worn visitor's chair. "What's going on, Barnaby?"

He glanced at the closed office door as though expecting to see the silhouette of an eavesdropper against the frosted glass window. There was no one there.

Still, his voice was nearly a whisper as he said, "Someone has been making bomb threats."

"I heard about the one that happened during your Columbus Day sale," I said, remembering that they had evacuated the store, brought in the police department's special bomb squad, and found nothing.

"There was one during our Election Day sale too."

I had been traveling the following day, I remembered—I was

in Washington the rest of that week. I hadn't heard about it, or any others.

"Was that all?"

He shook his head. "There was one on Saturday too. That one I managed to keep out of the papers, but, Ed, this can't go on. People are going to be *afraid* to shop at Ramsey's."

"Who do you suspect of making the threats."

"Simon Weatherly," he said promptly. "Who else could it be?"

I was vaguely acquainted with the young manager of Weatherly Brothers, a descendant of the store's wealthy founding family. Simon had recently taken over the business from his ailing uncle, Mortimer. I had heard several longtime employees had quit soon afterward. Apparently, Simon's people-management skills left much to be desired.

Which wasn't surprising. On the few occasions when our paths had crossed, he had struck me as a spoiled, imperious character.

Still, that didn't mean he was behind the bomb threats to Ramsey's, and I pointed that out to Barnaby, who shook his head.

"It's him," he said. "He's determined to put me out of business. He wants to buy our building and move Weatherly Brothers in. Our store is far bigger, and it's located on the corner."

"But, Barnaby, do you actually think he would stoop so low as to phone in bomb threats?"

"I don't think there's any limit as to how low Simon Weatherly would stoop to eliminate the competition, Ed."

"Do you have any proof that he's behind this?"

"Not a shred. But my gut instinct—"

He was cut off in mid-sentence by a sudden commotion from somewhere outside the office.

"What the heck is that?" I asked. "It sounds like dogs barking."

"It *is* dogs barking." Barnaby shoved his chair back and strode to the door, throwing it open. "It's part of our store security system. We release several Dobermans into the store after closing, to make sure no would-be thief is hiding on the premises."

"Dobermans?" I frowned. "Isn't that sort of . . . outdated, when it comes to security?"

"Oh, we implement quite a few modern security measures as well, Ed. But we have found in this area, as in many others, that you can't beat certain old-fashioned techniques. And, as you know, we pride ourselves on being an old-fashioned kind of store." Barnaby peered out into the hall, where the barking sound coming from one of the floors below seemed to be growing more frantic.

I glimpsed my bodyguard for the evening, Mohammed Johnson, who was stationed just outside Barnaby's office. He appeared more cagey and alert than ever, his thick brows narrowed over his dark eyes as he gazed down the hall in the direction of the barking. Either he isn't crazy about dogs, or he sensed that something wasn't quite right.

"Hmmm," Barnaby said, looking troubled.

"What is it?"

"The dogs sound more frenzied than they usually do. They might have found something."

"You mean someone?"

"It could be nothing." Barnaby turned away from the door. "A couple of years back, they sniffed out a terrified computer repairman who was here after hours, fixing a glitch in the system in our payroll department."

"Interesting," I commented, unable to help feeling vaguely unsettled.

Maybe it was just the prospect of being hounded by those dogs myself as I headed out of the store later. I could see the headlines tomorrow: "MAYOR ATTACKED BY PACK OF ANGRY DOGS."

Or maybe, in retrospect, the sense of trepidation that stole over me was due to some sixth sense that told me something was about to happen.

Something huge and horrible.

"As I was saying," Barnaby continued, returning to his desk and speaking loudly over the racket the Dobermans were making, "I don't have evidence that specifically points to Simon Weatherly, and he's denying any involvement."

"How do you know that?"

"Because I called him here for a meeting to confront him with the situation. You know, man-to-man."

"When was this?"

"Just this evening. He stormed out of here an hour ago. He

was furious when I asked him if he knew anything about the bomb threats. As I said, he denied everything."

"Well then, maybe he's not responsible."

"Of course he is. Who else would—"

The ringing of the telephone on his desk caused yet another interruption.

"Excuse me, Ed," he said, picking it up. "Tischler here . . . what? What happened? Why don't you just tell me—" He broke off and listened briefly, then said, sounding resigned, "All right, I'll be down there in a second."

He hung up the phone, already on his feet, reaching for the suit coat he had draped over the back of his chair. "That was my security chief. Something's going on downstairs."

"Did the dogs find someone hiding in the store?"

"I have no idea. It's probably nothing." He paused, and I knew he was thinking of Simon Weatherly and the bomb threats. "I *hope* it's nothing. I'll be back in a few minutes."

Oh, no, you don't, I thought, jumping up and following him to the door. "I'm coming with you."

No way was I going to sit there like a potential late-night snack for that bunch of Dobermans on the loose, even with Mohammed stationed nearby.

Barnaby, perhaps reading my mind, didn't argue. He led the way back down the dimly lit hallway lined with offices, past the elevators to a door marked EXIT, saying, "Let's take the stairs. It's only one floor below, and these old elevators take too long."

Mohammed and I followed him down the dank stairwell to the fifth floor, and through another door, where we found ourselves in another hallway. The place was a maze, I thought as we made several turns, approaching the sound of dogs and voices.

Whatever was going on had the dogs in a frenzy, I decided, and said as much to Barnaby.

"I hope it's just another computer repairman," he told me, looking distracted as we pushed through a set of double doors.

"Something tells me it isn't, Barnaby," I said, reading the sign over the door. "Unless you keep computers in the employees' locker rooms."

"I just hope it isn't anything disastrous," Barnaby returned, moments before we rounded a corner, opened another door, marked RESTRICTED, and saw a cluster of security guards and barking, jumping black Dobermans several yards down a long hall. They were gathered around an open door. Several of the guards held the dogs' leashes, and appeared to be struggling to quiet them.

It wasn't clear at first what had them in such an uproar.

But as we approached, I realized that the open door led to a storage closet, and whatever it was must be lying on the floor just inside.

"Mr. Tischler, I'm afraid—" The security guard who had glanced up and started to speak stopped short when he saw me. "Good evening, Mr. Mayor."

I nodded politely, and Barnaby stepped forward.

"What is it, Collins?" he asked. "What's going on?"

"You'd better take a look," he said, stepping aside and motioning at whatever lay waiting inside the closet.

I was right behind Barnaby, peering over his shoulder.

The expletive that spilled from his lips was echoed by one of my own.

There, on the floor, lying in a pool of blood, was a crumpled figure clad in a familiar crimson velour suit with white fleece trim.

Someone had murdered the Ramsey's Santa Claus.

TWO

"Drink this, Barnaby," I said firmly, placing a glass of cold water, fetched from a nearby cooler by Mohammed, in his badly trembling hands.

He obeyed blindly, seated stiffly on a bench beside a row of employee lockers.

Down the hall, a team of detectives from the New York Police Department was examining the body and the grisly scene.

"I can't believe this could happen," Barnaby said, handing the glass back to me and burying his head in his hands. "What could anyone have done to deserve such a death?"

I thought back to the gala event just before Thanksgiving, when this year's Ramsey's Santa had made his first public appearance. His true identity, in keeping with tradition, had been withheld as part of the store's Santa gimmick.

"What was his name?" I asked Barnaby.

"The Santa?" He sounded hesitant. "I have no idea which one it was."

I frowned. "I thought you use only one."

That, too, was a part of the Ramsey's legend.

Unlike other big department stores, which have an entire staff of Santas, many on duty simultaneously in carefully contrived, mazelike settings, Ramsey's boasts of an old-fashioned single-Santa policy in keeping with their old-fashioned tradition of service.

Each year the store's search for the perfect Santa begins in the summer months, amid considerable publicity. There are always hundreds of applicants, some from as far away as California and Florida. Everyone, it seems, is eager for the chance to carry on the Ramsey's legend.

Now Barnaby looked distinctly cagey as he informed me, "Until this year, we *have* used only one Santa. But I'm afraid that just wasn't working out for us anymore, Ed. We had to go to a multi-Santa situation like the other stores. It was the only way we could compete."

"What do you mean?"

"When you have only one Santa, you're limited to relatively short shifts. After all, the guy has to take breaks. He has to go home eventually. And when he's not there, the kids can't see him. They're unhappy. They leave the store. And that means, obviously, that their parents leave with them. When the parents leave, they obviously stop spending—"

"Obviously," I cut in. "But that means you're lying to the public, Barnaby. You deliberately created a media circus around the Santa-selection process this year, just as you have in the past."

"But I never—"

"Let me finish. You led the public to believe that there's only one lucky candidate—make that *unlucky,*" I amended, glancing at the activity around the body down the hall, "who gets to be the Ramsey's Santa."

"I know."

"That's all you have to say?"

He bristled. "What do you want me to say? This is progress, Ed. We can't keep doing *everything* the old-fashioned way. We're losing money here. And anyway, very few people know about the new setup. We've had very tight security behind the Winter Wonderland enterprise, and only those directly involved have access to the area. That spot where the body was found was in the restricted area. No one not involved with the Santa setup is allowed past the door opening to that hallway—it leads down to the Wonderland display."

"It doesn't seem possible that you can keep such an enormous secret, Barnaby."

"Everyone—the security people, our few employees who have knowledge of the situation, and, of course, all the elves and Santas—has been required to sign statements that he or she will reveal to no one—including the press, of course—that there is more than one Ramsey's Santa."

"I see."

I have to admit, the whole idea of such clandestine action revolving around a mere Santa Claus display seemed vaguely ridiculous to me.

Yet, a man connected with the operation had just been murdered.

The behind-the-scenes details concerning the Winter Wonderland had taken on serious implications.

Footsteps approaching from down a nearby hall caused both of us to look up.

A police detective was walking quickly toward us. He was a tall, handsome, dark-haired Latino who appeared to be in his early forties, if that.

"Mr. Mayor, Mr. Tischler, I'm Detective Lazaro," he said, his black eyes somber. "I'm with the homicide squad. We've secured the crime scene. The police forensic unit has arrived, and so have pathologists from the medical examiner's office. We need your cooperation with the investigation, as witnesses."

"Of course," I responded promptly.

Barnaby protested, "We didn't witness anything. We were in my office—"

"We're going to need to ask both of you a few questions," the detective interrupted.

"Certainly," I said, standing.

I had become familiar with the specifics of crime-scene investigations, having recently been present at homicide scenes both at City Hall and at the Regal Theater over on West Forty-sixth Street. Of course, I went on to solve both those cases, as you may have heard.

"Mr. Tischler, we'll speak with you first—that is, if you don't mind, Mr. Mayor."

"Not at all."

I watched as he led the badly rattled Barnaby down a hall to a small office that had been turned into a makeshift interrogation room.

As soon as they were out of sight, I made my way—preceded by a wary Mohammed, of course—back toward the closet where the body had been found. The area had been cordoned off by the police. Before trying to get closer to the body, I took note of the surroundings.

Rows of employee lockers ran along either side of the closet, with benches scattered about the large room. There were several vending machines along one wall, and one of those coolers that held a large, upside-down blue plastic bottle of spring water.

In addition to the closet, there were doorways leading to men's and women's rest rooms, and another that was marked PRIVATE. AUTHORIZED PERSONNEL ONLY.

I noticed a display of framed photos running the entire length of the wall opposite the lockers and stepped over to investigate. Each frame bore a brass plate containing the year in which the photo was taken, and they dated back to the early nineteen twenties.

They appeared to be group shots of the store employees taken at the annual Ramsey's Christmas party. I spent a few minutes idly glancing over them.

Then I moved back toward the closet, noting that the Dobermans were nowhere to be seen, and most of the store's security force had dispersed. Uniformed officers stood by as police photographers snapped pictures of the scene and detectives bustled around, dusting for fingerprints and examining the body.

"I'm afraid we're going to have to ask you to step back, Mr. Mayor."

I turned and nodded at a chubby young cop who had spotted me hovering on the fringes. He had an open snack-sized bag of Fritos in his hand and was munching as he spoke.

"I just wanted to see what was going on over here," I told him, incredulous that anyone could think to buy a snack from the vending machines in the midst of this horror.

"Just a routine homicide investigation." His eyes shifted from mine, and I glanced in the direction they had taken.

He appeared to be ogling a uniformed female police officer.

She was trim and attractive, with a long blond braid poking from beneath her cap.

She looked vaguely familiar. I figured I must have seen her at the policeman's funeral last week, which had been mobbed with not just uniformed officers, but hundreds of friends and family members. New York City cops are the finest citizens around.

Well, most of them, I thought, glancing back at the detective, whose lecherous eyes were trained on the attractive female cop across the room.

"Have you identified the victim yet?" I asked him.

He reluctantly returned his attention to me, popped another chip into his mouth, and rubbed his balding head, looking hesitant.

"As you know, Officer . . ."

"Holt," he supplied when I paused for his name. "Doug Holt."

"Officer Holt, I'm the mayor of this city, and a potential witness to the crime," I pointed out. "What reason could you possibly have for withholding information about the victim's identity? I'll find out soon enough."

"I guess everyone will." He shrugged, finished crunching the chip, and swallowed. Then he revealed, "According to the wallet they found in his pocket, his name is Angelo Calvino. He's seventy-two. Lives down in Little Italy."

"Any motive?"

He lowered his voice and rattled his cellophane bag as he reached inside for another handful of chips. "If you ask me, it was probably a mob hit."

"And you're basing this information on . . . ?"

"You saw him. Shot in the back of the head, execution style. And as I said, he lives down in Little Italy."

"A lot of people live down in Little Italy," I said brusquely. "The vast majority of them are not involved with the mob."

"Some are."

"If I were you, Officer Holt, I would resist the urge to jump to conclusions. I would also wipe my mouth," I said, noticing the pronounced film of orange seasoning the chips had left around his lips.

I turned and walked away, sidling closer to the body. The Fritoeating officer was either too humiliated to stop me, or had returned his attention to the pretty female cop nearby.

In any case, I managed to position myself close enough to take in some specific details of the murder scene.

Lest you conclude that I'm some kind of ghoul, allow me to point out that I was driven closer not by mere morbid curiosity, but by a genuine desire to help with the investigation.

Given my past successes in cracking high-profile murder cases, I had been forced to acknowledge, privately and publicly, that I happen to be gifted with extraordinary powers of instinct and reasoning. As any professional detective will attest, both those traits are crucial to the process of crime solving.

With politics firmly and fondly standing as my primary vocation, I had no intention of pursuing a career with the NYPD.

By the same token, I shoulder an enormous responsibility to the citizens of this city, and I had no intention of allowing the dangerous and despicable murderer of one of their most beloved icons to roam free, not to mention destroy the world-renowned ambience of New York at Christmastime.

And so I did what any mayor would do under the circumstances. I vowed to do whatever I could to help New York's Finest solve this case. That meant taking advantage of both my proximity to the crime scene and my God-given talents.

The man on the floor was lying on his stomach, his limbs twisted in a grotesque position. He wore a familiar red velour suit with white trim, a matching cap, and black boots. From beneath the hat and his prone face, I could see tufts of white from his hair and whiskers.

They were spattered with scarlet splotches.

And the upper portion of the suit was so soaked with blood from the gaping head wound that it was difficult to tell where the velour left off and the fuzzy white trim began. But as I edged closer, I saw that the blood was a darker shade of red—that indicated it was beginning to dry.

My sharp ears heard a familiar voice announce from somewhere in the vicinity of the body, "Warm to the touch. No evidence of rigor mortis."

I didn't have to position myself any closer to know who was

speaking. Even if I hadn't instantly recognized the figure crouched by the corpse, I would have realized the distinctly gravelly voice belonged to Darius Jones, a friend of mine who happens to be a forensic pathologist. He had obviously been sent by the medical examiner's office to investigate.

"My preliminary conclusion is that death most likely occurred within the past three hours," Jones announced, straightening and addressing his assistant and one of the detectives standing by. "However, that is, as you understand, a tentative conclusion. Go ahead and bag the hands."

I strained to hear what else they were saying, but couldn't quite make it out.

Then somebody called the detective away, and I seized the opportunity to zero in on Darius.

"Mr. Mayor!" he exclaimed, his large mocha-colored eyes glad, as always, to see me, yet understandably puzzled. "What are you doing here?"

"I just happened to be meeting with Barnaby Tischler in his office upstairs when the body was discovered."

He let out a low whistle. "Talk about a coincidence. For a minute there I thought maybe the homicide squad had made you an official detective."

I chuckled and shook my head.

"They should. If it weren't for you, they would have two unsolved cases on their hands."

"I'm sure they would eventually have solved both the Kreig murder and the Matthews case. But I like to do what I can," I acknowledged. "For the good of the city."

"Well, it looks to me like you've got your hands full with this case." He glanced over at the body, which was still being photographed. "When it hits the papers that the Ramsey's Santa has been murdered . . ." He trailed off, shaking his head. "Think of all the children who will be devastated."

"I am thinking of them. That's why I'm going to work with the detectives, if I can, to find out who did this. Is there anything you can tell me about the condition of the body?"

He looked around as if to ensure that no one was eavesdropping, then said in a low voice, "I'm not supposed to give out information to anyone other than the authorities."

"The mayor *is* an authority, Darius."

"True . . ." Still, he hesitated.

I was about to bribe him with the promise of that green peppercorn pâté he adores, when he finally shrugged and started talking.

"The victim was killed within the last three hours. Single gunshot wound to the head, fired at close range. No sign of a struggle."

"Where was he killed?"

"It doesn't look like the body has been moved. I would guess that he was shoved from behind into the closet and immediately killed right where he fell."

"Did they find the weapon?"

"Not yet. The investigators are searching the vicinity though."

"Anything else you can tell me?"

"At this point? No. The autopsy will—"

"There you are, Mr. Mayor."

I turned to see Detective Lazaro standing behind us. He didn't appear pleased to find me chatting with a pathologist.

"If you'll come with me, please," he said crisply. "We're ready to question you."

"Absolutely," I agreed amiably, and, trailed by Mohammed, followed him down the hall.

"Would you please state your name and address for the record?"

I blinked. "Edward I. Koch. Gracie Mansion. New York, New York."

The detective smiled faintly and made a note on the pad in his hand. "Just following procedure, Mr. Mayor."

"Of course."

"What was your purpose for being on the premises this evening?"

"I was meeting with Barnaby Tischler. He's an old acquaintance of mine."

"Acquaintance or friend?"

"Friend," I amended.

"That's what he said. What was the purpose of the meeting?"

"He asked me to discuss the problem Ramsey's Department

Store is having with the new Highview Meadows mall over in Jersey."

"The problem being . . . ?"

"Ramsey's is losing business to them. They're running shuttles for shoppers from the corner of Thirty-fourth Street right outside his store. He wanted to know what I could do about that."

"And what can you do?"

"Nothing," I told him bluntly. "They're not breaking any laws."

"Did he mention any other problems the store is facing?"

"Besides financial ones?"

The detective nodded.

"He did say that there have been several bomb threats in the past few months."

"Did he mention suspecting anyone in particular?"

"Yes, he did."

"And that would be . . . ?"

"Simon Weatherly."

"What did he say about Weatherly specifically?"

I recounted my conversation with Barnaby to the best of my ability, then asked whether the detective thought the bomb threats were linked to the murder.

"If you don't mind, Mr. Mayor, I'm asking the questions here," he said politely. "Did you notice anything unusual at any time during your visit to Mr. Tischler?"

"Aside from the Dobermans suddenly going wild downstairs—I'm assuming that occurred at the point when they discovered the body in the closet—no, I didn't."

"How did Mr. Tischler react to the disturbance?"

"He seemed mildly concerned. He went to the door and listened."

"Did he comment as to what might have caused the dogs to bark?"

"He said it was probably nothing. He mentioned that the dogs had found a computer repairman on the premises late one night. That was all he said about it, until the telephone call came from security."

"How did he react to the call?"

"He seemed concerned, but he wasn't aware until we got down here that someone had been murdered."

"How do you know that?"

"How do I—Because he didn't say anyone had been murdered. And he was visibly shaken when we saw the body. Barnaby isn't a suspect in this case, is he, Detective?"

"As I said earlier, Mr. Mayor, I'm the one who's asking the questions here." He sounded considerably less polite than he had before. "Is there any additional information you can add to aid in our investigation?"

"I'm afraid there isn't at this point. I didn't see or hear anything unusual, as I said."

"I would appreciate, Mr. Mayor, if you would keep all the details of this case to yourself."

"Of course I will. You didn't think I'd go blabbing inside information to the press, now, did you?"

He offered a tight smile. "No, I didn't. And I apologize for taking up so much of your valuable time, Mr. Mayor. I realize you are a busy man."

"Never too busy to lend a hand when it comes to something like this, Detective. In fact, I fully intend to assist the police department with this investigation, as I have in the past."

He pursed his lips. "That won't be necessary, Mr. Mayor. The homicide squad is quite capable—"

"I didn't say it wasn't capable, Detective. Only that I intend to provide whatever insight I can into this murder."

"As I said, if there is any additional information you can provide—"

"And as I said, I have nothing to add at this point. When I do have information, I will be glad to share it with you."

He hesitated, then threw up his hands in a helpless gesture. "You go ahead and do whatever it is that you feel is necessary, Mr. Mayor."

"I always do," I said with a curt nod.

When we emerged from the makeshift interview room, Detective Lazaro told Mohammed that he would find a police officer to escort us downstairs to my car.

"That isn't necessary," I said. "We know the way."

"It *is* necessary. This is a crime scene. Officer Varinski?" The detective beckoned to a nearby cop.

It turned out to be the attractive blonde I had seen earlier.

"Yes?" She smiled pleasantly, but it didn't reach her pale blue eyes. She looked distinctly rattled. I wondered if she was new on the force. Maybe this was her first murder.

Then again, maybe not.

Maybe some cops never get used to the sight and smell of blood and gore. I know I wouldn't.

"Would you mind escorting the mayor and his bodyguard to the main entrance on Thirty-fourth Street?" the detective asked her.

"Not at all."

Mohammed radioed into his walkie-talkie for my driver to bring the car around, then told the female cop he remembered her from when he worked in the same precinct a few years back.

"Katrina, isn't it?" he asked her.

She smiled faintly and nodded.

"I'm Mohammed Johnson."

"You kind of look familiar," she said in a hesitant way that told me she didn't recall him.

"I do?"

"But I can't quite remember . . ."

"That's not surprising," Mohammed said. "I worked in the precinct for only a few months, and you were busy planning your wedding at the time. I remember some of the guys teasing you about having a stash of those bridal magazines in your locker."

"Yeah, well, they still like to tease me," she said a little grimly.

I didn't doubt that a young, exceptionally attractive female police officer inspired some measure of attention from her fellow officers, and not all of it pleasant.

"Thank you again for your help, Mr. Mayor," Lazaro said, shaking my hand.

"No problem. I'll be in touch," I told him before following the female officer down the hall.

She turned left where I expected her to turn right, and right where I thought we should turn left.

"This place really is a maze," I commented as we stepped into a narrow stairwell marked EMPLOYEES ONLY.

"It does seem like one, doesn't it," the officer agreed, holding the banister with one hand and fiddling with the tip of her braid with the other as we descended several flights to the first floor.

I found myself scanning the shadows, perhaps half expecting to see a blood-covered killer lurking there.

For some reason, I suddenly became aware of the unsettling notion that danger was hovering nearby. My heart started pounding and my hands clenched into nervous fists.

Feeling ridiculous, I told myself the killer had to be long gone. If he had concealed himself anywhere in the store, that pack of panting Dobermans would undoubtedly have sniffed him out long before now.

And anyway, I was perfectly safe, in the company of not only my own armed bodyguard, but an armed police officer. I decided my mind must be playing tricks on me.

Still, I was relieved when we emerged into the dimly lit cosmetics department. The officer swiftly led the way to the main entrance, where two more uniformed cops were stationed, along with a Ramsey's security guard, who quickly unlocked one set of doors for us.

I saw him blatantly looking the blond officer up and down the way the detective upstairs had done, but he stopped when he saw that I had noticed what he was doing.

I turned to her and thanked her for the escort.

"Are you all right?" I asked her, noticing that she still seemed vaguely upset.

"I'm fine," she assured me with a faint smile. "It's just upsetting to work on cases like this."

I noticed one of the uniformed cops nudging the other, a burly oaf who nodded and muttered, "That's why female officers should be assigned to desk jobs. They can't hack the rough stuff."

That sexist comment deserved a retort.

Before I could open my mouth to offer one, the woman, Officer Varinski, turned to him.

But instead of blasting the chauvinist, she merely said, "Maybe you're right, Jake. I can't speak for all women, but when it comes to violence, I can't help feeling like a real wimp. It bothers me to see someone gunned down in cold blood like that poor man upstairs."

With that, she turned, nodded politely at me, and went back into the store.

I shook my head, bemused. Most of the female cops I've met would have jumped down a guy's throat for even hinting that they're weaker—physically or emotionally—than male officers. But this one had somehow managed to put him into his place without even raising her voice.

Mohammed and I were halfway down the icy sidewalk, heading toward the familiar black sedan parked at the curb, when a photographer jumped out at me, causing me to gasp and jump.

"Mr. Mayor," a reporter I hadn't noticed before called out. "Is it true that someone has been murdered inside Ramsey's?"

"No comment," I said gruffly, still blinking from the camera's flash, and pushed my way past the nosy media hound to the car.

Only when I was safely in the backseat and my driver was pulling away from the curb, turning the corner and heading uptown, did I allow myself to heave a big sigh of relief.

It's not often that I manage to spook myself like that.

Then again, it's not often that I'm thrust into the middle of a murder scene.

"Are you all right, Mr. Mayor?" Mohammed asked, looking concerned.

"I'm fine, thanks, Mohammed." I turned to look out the window at the twinkling white Christmas lights that sparkled in the trees dotting the island in the middle of Park Avenue.

So festive, I thought, noticing that a light snow was falling. On a nearby sidewalk, a uniformed doorman was standing on a ladder to hang an enormous boxwood wreath over the door of an apartment building.

With another sigh, I vowed once again to do everything I could to catch the murderer and protect New York's reputation as the merriest city in the world.